Praise

"A spellbind[ing] [story that] unfolds in the first installment of Jennifer J. Chow's Magical Fortune Cookie series."
—*Woman's World*

"The story itself is light, sweet, and delectable. The ensemble of interesting characters adds a crispy texture to the narrative, and true to the cozy mystery genre, a central mystery—the ill-fated fortune—keeps readers engaged from start to finish."
—*The Big Thrill* on *Ill-Fated Fortune*

"This first in a new series featuring a likable Chinese American heroine will appeal to fans of Jenn McKinlay, Eve Calder, or Joanne Fluke."
—*Booklist* on *Ill-Fated Fortune*

"Nobody writes cozy mysteries quite like Jennifer J. Chow. No matter what is going wrong in my life, I know that all I need to do for some comfort is turn to one of Chow's books. Chow has done it again with *Ill-Fated Fortune*. I did not want to leave Felicity's side even for a moment, and you won't want to either."
—Jesse Q. Sutanto, Edgar Award–winning author of *Vera Wong's Unsolicited Advice for Murderers*

"A magical new culinary cozy mystery series filled with family, friendship, and heart—and a pinch of real magic."
—Gigi Pandian, *USA Today* bestselling author of the Secret Staircase mysteries, on *Ill-Fated Fortune*

"Who doesn't love a magical bakery? Readers will enjoy following Felicity Jin, her friends, and her mother in

Ill-Fated Fortune. Check your fortune: I believe it will tell you to read this book."
—Emmeline Duncan, author of the Ground Rules mysteries

"*Ill-Fated Fortune* expertly combines magic and murder. This story is an absolute treat that you'll want to binge read."
—Olivia Matthews, author of the Spice Isle Bakery mysteries

"Combine one magical baker with a ruthless baking rival. Add a custom-made fortune that seemingly predicts death and mix well. Toss in a skeptical police officer and a well-crafted cast of characters with plenty of delightful cultural touches and you have a well-baked culinary cozy mystery. *Ill-Fated Fortune* is a deliciously magical culinary cozy that will leave you hungry for the next delectable installment in this new series by Jennifer J. Chow."
—Valerie Burns, Agatha, Anthony, Edgar, and Next Generation Award finalist

"Charming isn't adequate to describe Jennifer J. Chow's series debut, *Ill-Fated Fortune*. I was immediately pulled into the story by the powerful first line and an instant, deep connection to the narrator. There is real magic in this story—and not just from the baking skills of Felicity and her mom. Along with the terrific writing, I was treated (and it was nearly as good as those fortune cookies sound) to a glimpse into a culture and place that I didn't know. This book contains so many elements readers will love. Plus a fun mystery. A new series is about to be born."
—Carolyn Haines, *USA Today* bestselling author of the Sarah Booth Delaney series

St. Martin's Paperbacks Titles
by Jennifer J. Chow

Ill-Fated Fortune
Star-Crossed Egg Tarts

STAR-CROSSED
EGG TARTS

Jennifer J. Chow

St. Martin's Paperbacks

First published in the United States by St. Martin's Paperbacks, an imprint of St. Martin's Publishing Group.

STAR-CROSSED EGG TARTS

For information, address St. Martin's Publishing Group, 120 Broadway, New York, NY 10271.

www.stmartins.com

ISBN: 978-1-250-32325-5

Our books may be purchased in bulk for promotional, educational, or business use. Please contact your local bookseller or the Macmillan Corporate and Premium Sales Department at 1-800-221-7945, ext. 5442, or by email at MacmillanSpecialMarkets@macmillan.com.

St. Martin's Paperbacks edition / February 2025

Printed in the United States of America

10 9 8 7 6 5 4 3 2 1

For Ellie: Wishing you enchanting adventures within these pages and beyond!

ACKNOWLEDGMENTS

Since I wrote about a wedding, I can't help but acknowledge my own wonderful bridesmaids: Barb, Liz, and Samantha. Thank you for being with me back then and now—so glad for our deep friendship across the years.

I'm indebted to readers and writers who boosted *Ill-Fated Fortune* when this new series launched. Shout-out to the many supporters, including *A Bookish Moment*, the_beachbum_bookworm, ben.cooker.3, bonniereads777, bookscoffeebrews, bookswithamymarie, chelsmarieantoinette, Christina Estes, CJ Connor, cooking_with_my_cozys, cozycraftyreads, The Cozy Mystery Book Club, cspina, days_with_the_doyles, Delia Pitts, Dru Ann Love, dvalerisactual, general.fiction.reviews, jessabellareads, Kim Davis, kyladietz_, literary_escapism, literarylady14, Lori Caswell, madcowmandy, nina_the_bookworm, novelsalive, Paula Charles, rants_n_reads, r.m.kerr, *Sarah Can't Stop Reading*, showyourshelfie, storeybookreviews, thephdivabooks, Vanessa Westermann, and wellreadtraveler. Sorry if I missed anyone, but know that I'm very appreciative! I'm thankful for reviews, recommendations to bookstores and libraries, and sign-ups on my Cozy Connection newsletter at my website, jenniferjchow.com.

Grateful to listeners of my Magical Fortune Cookie

books and the amazing Catherine Ho, who narrates my magical characters.

Many thanks to the Minotaur crew: Lily Cronig, for making my stories sparkle through editing magic, and Sara Eslami-Black and Sara LaCotti, for constantly cheerleading and boosting my book. Heartfelt gratitude goes out to Janna Dokos, Olya Kirilyuk, Kelley Ragland, John Simko (appreciate the wordsmithing!), and Nathan Weaver.

As always, I'm glad Jessica Faust is in my literary corner. Thank you to the entire BookEnds team—and extra doggie treats for Olive.

Community is key in an author's life, and I am beyond grateful for Chicks on the Case, Crime Writers of Color, Mystery Writers of America, Sisters in Crime, and my local writing group.

I find it enchanting when my books get buzz, so thank you to ABC30, *The Big Thrill*, *Book Riot*, *CrimeReads*, *Criminal Element*, *Geek Girl Authority*, *Kings River Life Magazine*, *Murder & Mayhem*, *The Sun-Gazette*, *Visalia Times-Delta*, and *Woman's World*.

Authors who do joint events with me receive special accolades. Huge bouquets of love to Lorie Lewis Ham, Naomi Hirahara, Gigi Pandian, and Iris Yamashita. I'm also thankful for the author panels I've gotten to be part of for Ashland Mystery Fest, ITW, and Murderous March.

Thank you to my relatives for all the support—I love how we crowded out an entire room at one event. Cheers for the Chows, Lims, and Ngs!

I know I'm blessed to have time to write and be an author. That's only possible through the love and encouragement of my closest family. I don't need a Wishes candle because you've already come into my life: ❤s to Steve, Bella, and Ellie.

CHAPTER 1

I put the last egg tart in place on the tiered circular display, stepped back, and admired my handiwork. From a distance, if you squinted and tilted your head just right, you might actually mistake it for a wedding cake made of gold, or Jin. Fitting, since "Jin" was both my surname and the Mandarin word for "gold." I grinned. Guess I'd been fated for this job.

Happily, I even got to rope in loved ones as other vendors. My best friend, Kelvin Love (who has the most fitting name to cater a wedding), handled the elaborate floral displays. And my godmother, Alma Paz, made the candle arrangements, including the votives for the cake table. She'd even handcrafted bowl-shaped lace holders for each votive candle.

Once the late afternoon dissolved into evening, the small candles would be lit, and the cake made of egg tarts would turn into an enchanting display. Quite literally, because my mom had used her magic to bake joy into every last bite. After all, that's what we Jins do—pour joy into our signature recipe treats to flow out to others. Except my own brand of magic came with an extra bonus: I made special fortune cookies that provided happiness *and* accurately predicted future happenings.

I added a stash of business cards to the table. I'd been made official co-owner of Jin Bakery with my mom, and I now had business cards to attest to that exciting fact. Besides, I figured it wouldn't hurt to have my contact info out there. If people were in the area for the wedding, maybe they'd decide to check out our local bakery, too.

Plus, many of the guests were from nearby Fresno, the bride's hometown, though a fair share hailed from up north, where the groom's relatives lived. It wasn't too much of a trek from NorCal to visit Pixie, right? Not for delicious egg tarts, pineapple buns, and fortune cookies, all coated with magic.

"It's beautiful," someone whispered from near my shoulder. I would have startled at the interruption, but the voice was so gentle, it didn't scare me in the least.

A bridesmaid must have snuck into the main tent without my noticing. Maybe the soft grass surrounding the tent had masked her footsteps. Or she'd minced along in those stiletto sandals.

She was a wisp of a young woman, just a few years past twenty. Even though I was twenty-eight, I couldn't imagine having ever been so bright-eyed and hopeful as the girl before me. The twin honey-colored braids wrapped around her head only added to her youthfulness.

"Haley, was it?" I asked.

She nodded, almost bouncing on her heels. "You remembered my name."

"It's distinctive. Very pretty."

She flushed a sweet shade of pink. "I like your name, too. Felicity is lovely."

"Is that a rose tucked behind your ear?" I asked, pointing to the blossom, the full pink petals brushing up against a tiny golden ear cuff lined with diamonds.

She widened her green eyes at me. "Uh, is that okay? I mean, do you mind? Are you and Kelvin together—"

"It's fine," I said, waving away her concern. "Kelvin and I are just friends." Best friends, technically. "I take it he's still working on the flower arch outside?"

"Said he was 'securing the petals.'" Kelvin *was* a stickler for floral quality. Guess that's what made us good entrepreneurs in our little town of Pixie.

I glanced at Haley's T-shirt and jeans. "What time is it? Do you need to change?"

"Four forty-five," she said. "I better get ready."

The wedding guests would show up at six. Right now, only us hired help and the wedding party, plus the parents of the bride and groom, were roaming the surrounding green space.

"Jada's in our tent doing makeup, and she said she'd help me," Haley said.

"I should get going, too." I'd promised the bride, Leanne, that I'd check on the tea ceremony. Not that I'd be super helpful. I'm third-gen Chinese American and had had to google what the traditional tea ritual entailed.

I followed Haley's bouncing steps out of the larger main tent into the lush green of Pixie Park. Our town's biggest park definitely had enough space for the Lum-Wu ceremony. The bride and groom had asked to pitch four tents for the event: a reception tent for food, his and her tents for wedding prep, and a tent for the traditional tea serving ritual.

Pixie Park also boasted a large hill, and it was sure to look magnificent with its aerial view for the actual wedding ceremony and exchanging of vows. Kelvin was on the hill now, fussing over the flowers on the custom arch he'd made.

I waved at him. He bobbed his head at me, his fingers still patting petals into place. Kelvin looked good fancied up, in a dress shirt and pressed slacks. His usual go-to was a casual Henley and jeans.

There was a rainbow of beautiful blossoms decorating the immense arch he'd constructed. I didn't know why Kelvin was so worried. There wasn't a breeze to be found. It was perfect, and the flowers should stay put.

If anything, the temperature was slightly too warm today. Thankfully, it was dry heat, typical of the San Joaquin Valley. Whoever thought tea was a great idea in July had not factored in the weather. Then again, traditions were important. I headed over to the tea tent, and as soon as I put my head through the flap, Leanne squealed.

"You came to help. Thank goodness," she said. The bride-to-be wore a red qipao with a golden phoenix trailing down the front. Her hair was pinned up, and pearls were scattered across the hairdo as decoration, matching the dangling pearl earrings she wore.

"How can I assist?" I asked.

"With the hot plate. You're good in the kitchen. Er, bakery. Can you get it started?"

"I can try." I mean, I was hired to cater the cake, not the tea. But I'd done the bare minimum online research. Maybe I could fake my way through.

The problem wasn't with the hot plate. Somehow the extension cord had gotten pulled out, so the electricity wasn't running through.

I replugged the cord and turned it on. I needed to get the water hot enough to steep the tea leaves, and then cool it down. The relatives would not be happy if they got burned while drinking the special celebratory tea.

And the beverage was supposed to be sweet, not bitter

to the taste. I added in dried dates and longan for sweetness and to symbolize good fortune for the marriage.

The water burbled before me, and I transferred the liquid over to a red teapot decorated with a golden double happiness symbol. After the tea had steeped for several minutes, I added some cooler water to lower its temperature.

Leanne paced before me. "I'm so nervous. We're supposed to start at five on the dot." It was already ten past.

That's when I glanced around the small tent. The two chairs for the elderly relatives were set out, but no cushions were in sight for the couple to kneel on. And we were alone in the cozy space. "Where is everyone?" I asked. Especially Colton. There'd be no tea serving without the groom.

"Nova is trying to find the silk pillows." I'd met all the wedding attendants briefly, and she was the lead groomsperson, if I remembered correctly.

Leanne continued, "And Colton is getting his parents. I hope they survive being in the tent together. It'll be a big surprise when they realize they were both invited to the wedding."

I arranged four matching red teacups along with the pot on a golden platter. "You didn't tell them beforehand?"

"Colton's idea. They had a nasty divorce, and he thought they'd back out of coming if they knew the other one would be there." A grimace appeared on her pretty heart-shaped face.

Okay, then. We'd see how this would turn out.

Soon enough, Colton entered the tent decked out in a black tuxedo. He had a steady hand placed against the small of the back of an older man and practically shepherded him over to one of the two chairs. There was no mistaking the family resemblance, everything from the square jaw to the puffed-up hair to the air of superiority hovering around them. Classically handsome, some would call them, and they were well aware of it.

"Why didn't you tell me you invited *your mother* to this shindig?" Mr. Wu said as he moved his chair farther away from the other seat.

"Then you wouldn't have come," Colton replied matter-of-factly.

"That's true." The father settled down on the hard-backed chair, straightened out the tails of his jacket, and waited. A frown stretched across his tanned face.

He didn't have long to wait, because Nova came in then, cushions under one arm, holding hands with an older woman I assumed was Colton's mother. Nova had a tall, chiseled figure, topped off with a spiked purple pixie haircut. The mother of the groom, with her four-foot curvy stature, wore a gold-sequined jumpsuit.

The parents managed to sit down next to each other, although the mom also scooted her chair a few more inches away. They glared at each other as Nova bustled at their feet to place the padded cushions before the elders, one pillow in front of each parent.

I tried to thaw the ice between the estranged couple by saying, "This will only take a few minutes of your time, Mr. Wu and Mrs. . . . ." I didn't know what to call Colton's mother.

She gave an almost growl from the back of the throat. "It's Ms. Hung now."

The father of the groom raised his voice. "Can't say I'm surprised you didn't keep my illustrious name. Only on my side can we trace our lineage all the way back to—"

Ms. Hung put her hand up. "I dropped the name because I'm no longer married to your giant ego."

"Mom, Dad, please." Colton hurried to kneel on the floor before them, and Leanne followed suit with a quick drop. I winced, doubting that the silk pillows buffered much of the hard ground.

I moved forward with the tea set, careful not to jostle the pot and cups on the tray. First, Colton served his dad. Leanne repeated the gesture, offering up the beverage with a respectful request for him to drink.

According to my research, the parents were supposed to provide warm wishes—and hongbao money—to the couple. Instead, the dad whispered to Colton, loud enough for everyone around to hear: "It's still not too late. Won't be official until everything's signed and filed, you know."

Colton bristled, Leanne blushed, and Nova arched her eyebrow.

After an awkward pause, Colton served his mother. The tea ceremony continued without anyone acknowledging Mr. Wu's rude comments. At least Ms. Hung didn't spout foolish, unwanted advice. She did give the couple envelopes, but they weren't the typical red ones wishing double happiness. They were, instead, a stark white, the color of death and mourning.

Leanne put the envelopes away with trembling hands. I wasn't superstitious, but even I knew this was an inauspicious way to start a wedding.

CHAPTER 2

Their tea duties done, the groom's parents scrambled out of their chairs and darted for the tent flap. Seemed like Ms. Hung and Mr. Wu could not stand being together in an enclosed space for any longer than necessary. Thank goodness the actual ceremony would take place outdoors.

Ms. Hung reached the exit first and dashed out. Mr. Wu waited a few moments, probably to ensure enough of a gap, before leaving. But as he did so, he clipped a new person coming in. Leanne's man of honor. "I'm here," he trilled.

"Turner. You're a sight for sore eyes," Leanne said, her shoulders relaxing.

"And I've brought presents for you two lovebirds." He did a show-host flourish. I admired the dramatic gesture and wondered what he did for work. Ballroom dance instructor? He had a striking side profile and enough flair for it.

"Living presents," Turner said, as Leanne's parents walked in.

They were one of those couples who looked alike. I wondered if they'd always appeared that way or if they'd morphed over time. They didn't dress alike, but there was something similar about their thin lips that curved into matching reserved smiles (without teeth showing).

Mr. and Mrs. Lum didn't bother to pull the distanced chairs closer together. They took their seats, sipped a bit of tea, and placed their red envelopes in exact parallel lines on the platter to complete the ritual.

"Thanks, Mama and Baba," Leanne said.

Once the bride's mother and father issued polite nods and left, I started to gather the dishware, even as the couple continued kneeling. "Any more relatives?"

"Only Miles," Colton said. He ran a hand through his puffy hair.

"Who's only a cousin," Nova added. Interesting. In my research, I'd read that the tea ceremony was for elder relatives, to show them respect.

"I don't know why I included him." Colton clenched his jaw. "He's clearly unreliable. Should've told me earlier he couldn't get the license—"

Leanne put a hand on her groom's arm. "Aw, don't be too tough. He's still family. And from the Bay Area. Maybe he didn't know this county's rules for officiating."

"Whatever. You've always had a soft spot for him."

Leanne's mouth twitched at his words.

"Okay, then," I said, picking up the teapot to break the tension. Still half-full. "Let's get to it."

We waited for a while, but Miles didn't show.

"We're moving on," Colton said. "You're up, Nova and Turner."

Oh, that was different, but sure. It was his wedding—and hers, of course. Though Colton had usually called the shots on everything that had to do with the ceremony logistics.

"Ready whenever you are," Nova said, flashing the couple a smile.

Not to be outdone, Turner added, "I was born ready." He loped over to a seat. "Dibs," he called out to Nova.

While the couple had used terms of kinship with their relatives, like mù qín for "mother," when serving the tea, Leanne now searched for a proper term to call Turner. Finally, she said, "My fearless leader, please drink this."

A choking noise. But not from Turner, who was chugging the tea. Colton was making the sound. But he seemed assuaged, once Turner had slapped down a bulging red envelope.

They finished with Turner. As he passed me on his way out, he winked at me with one of his hazel eyes, like I was part of an inside joke.

When Nova sat before them, Colton spoke first. "My, er, college chum, have some tea."

"I hope you're not comparing me to fish," Nova said, even as she drank the tea. "Some communications major you are."

"You were always the better student," Colton muttered.

"Truth," she said.

Leanne offered Nova tea, and Nova placed a traditional red envelope on the platter. Things were looking better. Despite the verbal jabs, the wedding attendants seemed to have best wishes for the couple. Maybe that would block out the previous bad vibes that had come from the groom's parents.

Colton tapped his smartwatch and groaned. "Where did the time go?"

Everyone rushed out, in a flurry of renewed activity. Off to do some final primping, I expected.

I unplugged the hot plate and left the tray of the used cups and pot to the side. Leanne hadn't asked me to do any washing up, so I strolled away from the tent, relaxed.

My duties were mostly done. I'd add a few finishing touches to the dessert when it was time to cut the cake. Otherwise, I was free to enjoy the beautiful outdoors.

I noticed two figures walking around at opposite ends of the park—Colton's parents, maybe trying to get as far away from each other as physically possible. Leanne's mother and father were already sitting down in the front row of white chairs, with a great view of the flower arch. I again admired Kelvin's handiwork, even though he was nowhere to be seen. Maybe he was busying himself checking the boutonnieres and corsages of the wedding party.

I couldn't tell from their backs how Leanne's parents felt about the impending nuptials. They sat with stiff postures and I wondered if they felt nervous or excited or lonesome.

This was the first wedding I, or for that fact, Jin Bakery, had ever catered. I'd imagined a joyous event of laughter and great food (delicious pastries supplied by our family bakery, clearly). Weren't weddings always happy occasions? And our magicked treats would only enhance a buoyant atmosphere.

Why hadn't we done any weddings before? Was it because Mom disliked the limelight? She never clamored for attention, content to remain happily baking for the residents of our small town. Or maybe she just didn't want to deal with weddings.

I mean, her own marriage must not have been happy. Or at least I figured not, since she never talked about my biological father. There were no records of *their* wedding in our home, or even pictures of the guy. His existence had been sucked away from our lives, and maybe that's as it should be. After all, the man had "abandoned us" (Mom's words) when I'd been a baby.

Part of me still wished I'd known him better, but mainly, I recognized that I already had a great family. An intimate circle of my mom, godmother Alma, and bestie Kelvin. We even owned shops on the same quaint cul-de-sac in downtown Pixie: Jin Bakery, Paz Illuminations, and Love Blooms—each store with our last names attached.

Kelvin was running toward me now, almost hopping in an awkward yet charming jogging motion. That reminded me. We'd had a new addition to our family recently. Whiskers, a pet bunny—but a magical one. She'd mysteriously shown up at our home one evening when I'd made a heartfelt wish on a special candle. I'd wanted my very own companion to guide me in understanding my magic. One moment, I'd noticed the Chinese mythological Moon Rabbit in the sky; the next, the image had vanished, and I had a live bunny hopping with glee at my door. But unlike Whiskers, Kelvin wasn't gleefully bounding over. When he reached me, I felt the tension radiating from him. I could read his moods well. We'd been friends for so long, I considered him like a brother. Except taller, darker, and with a bad penchant for dad jokes.

"What's wrong?" I asked.

"He's gone," Kelvin said. "Vanished."

CHAPTER 3

"Who's missing?" I asked Kelvin. "Is it Colton?" A runaway groom.

"No, it's Miles," he said. The unreliable cousin, according to the groom. Sounded like he'd been slated to officiate originally. It's a good thing they'd found an alternate. There'd be no wedding if Miles was still in charge of conducting the ceremony.

"Did you check Colton's tent?" I asked.

"Yeah, that's where I was. Making sure the flowers the groomspeople had on still looked fresh. Or even pinching a new one if needed—I brought my pruners. There are dreamy heirloom rosebushes on the east side of the park I clipped from earlier."

Only Kelvin could fall in love with *the rosebushes* at a wedding. "Speaking of the park, Miles could just be wandering around. You can start at that *dreamy* east side, and I'll take the west end."

"Meet back here in fifteen minutes?"

I gave him a thumbs-up.

Pixie Park wasn't sprawling, but you couldn't see the entire space by glancing around, even from the hilltop. I made a thorough circuit but didn't see Miles.

I remembered he had a vague resemblance to Colton; they had a similar height and the same cheekbones.

Neither Kelvin nor I had had any success by the time we met back up.

"The restrooms," I suggested.

We headed that way, but ran into Easton, another groomsman, coming out of the building.

"Miles in there?" Kelvin asked.

"No, mate," Easton replied. There was a hint of a British accent in his speech.

"Wouldn't it be funny if he went to the tent while we've been hunting for him," Kelvin said.

On our way to the tents for the bridal party and the groomspeople, Easton chatted with Kelvin. "Hope you don't mind my asking, but what's your ethnic background?" Kinda rude, but Kelvin just shrugged. Maybe he was used to it by now. Honestly, we'd both gotten that question all the time, growing up in small-town Pixie.

"Mixed," he answered. "My mom's Japanese, and Dad's Black." Kelvin didn't mention that his mom had been gone for a while now, not that it was any of this stranger's business.

"I'm biracial, too," Easton said. "White and Black." He scooted closer to Kelvin as they walked, and I trailed behind like a third wheel.

There were "his-and-hers" tents crammed close together on the north side of the park. The backs of the two tents almost touched each other. Colton and Leanne didn't believe in the superstition of the bride and groom not seeing each other before the ceremony; after all, they'd just done a tea ritual together. The attendants also often shuttled back and forth between the tents.

On the bride's side, I found Nova, Turner, and Haley.

"Is it showtime?" Turner asked with a shimmy of his shoulders.

"Not without Miles," I said.

"Why is he trying to ruin this wedding?" Nova asked, her hands on her hips. "I'm going to kill him once I find him." She probably could, with her muscular arms.

She rushed past me even as I said, "Kelvin and I already searched the park."

Nova didn't break her stride. I turned toward the other tent; Colton and Leanne came out, along with Jada, a bridesmaid. Kelvin stood nearby, wringing his hands, clearly feeling concerned for the bride and groom.

"So no luck?" Colton asked my best friend.

"Not anywhere Felicity and I checked," Kelvin answered.

Colton examined his smartwatch and tapped the tip of his polished shoe against the ground. "It's already at the hour. We'll give him ten minutes to show his face. But, honestly, I'll probably need a backup to walk with Haley."

"I have a suggestion." Jada resettled her green square-shaped glasses on the bridge of her nose. Happily, they matched the exact shade of her bridesmaid dress, a long chiffon piece with cap sleeves.

"Yeah?" Colton asked.

"What about *this* guy?" Jada pointed at Kelvin.

My best friend backed up as though she'd shocked him across the tiny distance.

Colton studied Kelvin for a few moments. "Yes, you'll do."

"Uh, I don't have a tie," Kelvin said. All the attendants on the groom's side wore dress shirts in shades of blue with red ties to match Leanne's qipao.

"Ties off," Colton growled.

Turner grinned. "A blinding idea." He took his red tie off and even undid a few buttons on his royal blue shirt.

"You've even got the right color scheme," Colton said, studying the midnight blue of my friend's shirt. "You just need a boutonniere."

Kelvin's eyes glimmered with delight. "Let me dash in and get my pruners." He'd be able to clip off one of those heirloom roses he adored.

He went back into the groom's tent but came back out in a flash. "Huh. Must have left it in the other one."

Kelvin darted to the bride's tent, but returned frowning. "The pruners are gone. They're not in either tent."

"Were you using them on the flower arch?" I asked.

"No. I had everything ready to go for the wedding. They were a spare that I brought along."

"Can't you just pluck a rose off?" I asked.

Kelvin looked affronted. "Never. That would damage the bush. You need to make a clean cut, so you don't hinder any future growth."

How was I supposed to know that? I serve food, not flowers.

Haley hovered nearby, exuding serenity. But obviously she'd heard every bit of our conversation because she said, "Do you need a flower?" She reached for the pink rose behind her ear and handed it over to Kelvin. "Here you go."

"Perfect." Kelvin did his floristry magic with tape, baby's breath, and a pearl pin.

Nova had returned by this time, a grimace on her face. No Miles anywhere near her.

All the attendants gathered in a group, and Kelvin really did fit in. The people on the bride's side wore shades of rainbow, while those with the groom donned different hues of blue.

Good thing he matched, because while we'd been searching for the missing groomsman, invited friends and family had shown up. Rows of white chairs were filled with people, and a nervous officiant stood near the flower arch.

Colton checked his watch again. "Ten minutes past. Time's up." Like a coach, he made everyone huddle around him. "Okay, we've got this."

My original intention had been to hang out in the main tent while all the marriage festivities went on, but now I knew I couldn't linger inside there. Watching Kelvin go down the aisle? I wouldn't miss it for the world. Instead, I'd pop in the reception tent, add the finishing touches to the cake, and spring back out.

It was dark in the main tent, although someone had turned on the fairy lights strung around the perimeter of the space. At the opposite end from me, caterers were placing warming trays out for the buffet. I checked my egg tart tiers, which looked impeccable, and shifted the bride and groom figurines to a jaunty angle. I loved how they'd captured a semblance of Leanne and Colton through 3D printing; Colton told me they'd gone to a studio to get full body scans to customize the toppers.

I lit the votive candles around the display to give the cake a more ethereal glow. The lattice of the lace bowl holders let the light dance out in interesting and mesmerizing patterns.

Strains of orchestral music started reaching me from outside. The processional. I'd better book it to watch them.

I sprinted out of the tent and scooted into a seat in the back row right as Kelvin took a step onto the white runner leading to the arch, where an officiant stood. Good thing the music had been a soothing, slow piece. The paired attendants walking down the aisle had to coordinate their steps to the leisurely song, so I'd made it with enough time to admire Kelvin's entry.

Kelvin played his role impressively, even though I heard a few people mutter, "Who's that?" He and Haley marched in unison, arms hooked together. She seemed absolutely delighted, her eyes glistening, and Kelvin appeared pleased as well. He always loved swooping in and saving the day.

The wedding went off without any problems, even though the officiant glanced down at his notes a lot for reference. A photographer bounced up and down the aisle, trying to capture candid shots. And in the end, Leanne and Colton got married without any fuss. (No objections, even from the parents.)

Everyone was soon dismissed to the main tent for the reception. The bridal party headed in first, but I caught up with Kelvin and pulled him to the side. "You did great up there."

He glanced at his arch. "The flowers *were* impressive."

"Ha. You know what I mean. You marching down the aisle to that lovely song."

"Aw, Lissa"—nobody else got away with using that nickname—"you *are* a romantic. And you know what?"

"What?" I said, though I knew I'd be hearing one of his corny jokes.

"You've just made my *daisy*."

"Really? You had to go there?" I shook my head. "Come on, we're assigned to sit at the staff table in the very back."

I tugged him toward the tent, but Haley returned at that moment.

"Kelvin," she said, "are you coming? I saved you a spot at the head table."

He shuffled his size-twelve feet. "I think I'm supposed to be sitting in a different spot."

She tilted her head in puzzlement. "Oh no, you're part of the wedding crew now. We're at a table up front and will be hitting the buffet in a few moments."

I could sense Kelvin's conflict over getting good food first versus sitting last with me. He certainly deserved the VIP treatment. I nodded at Kelvin to give him the go-ahead. We didn't always need to speak out loud to communicate.

He leaned over and whispered in my ear, "My stomach thanks you."

"Go on," I said, waving the two of them off.

I did get last place in the buffet line, which featured trays of different kinds of vegan, vegetarian, and meat dumplings. A dumpling bar. As predicted, I got the dregs. The dumplings that got burned, or ones with the fillings gone. Whatever. It wasn't always about the food. Except for the dessert.

Speaking of which, Leanne and Colton had made their way over to my egg tarts. They did a thank-you speech to the guests and then each lifted up an egg tart—and smooshed it in the other's face.

Egg tarts are not cake-like enough to fully squash on contact. Or pie-like enough to spread on someone's face. So they kind of crumbled to the ground, but it looked fun. I noticed the photographer snapping pics near them—he hadn't even taken a break to get food, so I considered myself lucky.

Once the newly married couple stepped away from the table, I put down my plate and sprang into action.

I secured the serving trays that I'd stashed and brought them over to the cake table. People must have admired my egg tarts while I'd been moping from my seat in the back because my stack of business cards had dwindled. Excellent.

What wasn't excellent was that I'd stepped on a tart. My heel must have gone down on a creamy custard center because my foot felt wet. I reached down, and in the dimness of the tent, noticed a rose petal.

But it wasn't white like those pinned to the grooms-men's shirts. It was scarlet. Strange.

I picked it up. Nope. I'd been wrong. It was *dripping* scarlet—with blood. I screamed.

CHAPTER 4

Kelvin charged toward me after my scream. He held me by the shoulders and examined my entire body for any harm. After determining that I was okay, he raised his eyebrows at me, but I still couldn't speak. I pointed down at the ground, at the bloody flower petal, which I'd dropped in shock.

My best friend moved me aside. He didn't touch the petal, but he lifted the flap of the tablecloth. A strong flinch, and then he pulled out his cell phone to make the call to 911. Wedding goers were whispering and staring at me, but I couldn't stop shivering.

Colton sidled over and once he heard the words coming out of Kelvin's mouth, hurried to the center of the tent to announce that we'd skip cake time and progress to dancing outside. In a daze, I also followed the crowd out for some fresh air.

A stage floor had been set up for people to dance under the glow of the moon and the twinkling stars. Nobody felt like dancing, though, even if they didn't understand the full extent of the situation. Not that Colton didn't try pretending everything was fine. He even cued up the music on the speakers, and a few of the attendants made half-hearted attempts to appease him.

Once the paramedics showed up, though, everyone stopped pretending. Kelvin had stayed close to the tent entrance to block it, but after the officials went in, he shuffled over to me and slung an arm over my shoulder.

"How bad is it?" I asked him.

"Very."

When the paramedics exited the tent within minutes, I knew there was nothing to be done for the poor soul.

Even though I thought I knew the answer, I still asked, "Who was it?"

"Miles." The missing groomsman, now dead. That's why we couldn't find him earlier.

Kelvin hemmed. "There's something else—"

A new figure waltzed toward us on the grass. "Felicity Jin," she said. "Guess I shouldn't be too surprised."

Detective Rylan Sun. She was the cop who'd looked into a murder in the alley at the back of our bakery a few months ago. She'd even suspected me of the ill-fated death—until I cleared things up with some handy sleuthing. I recognized her familiar ponytailed profile. She also had a penchant for brown suits, and today, she wore a tan version.

"What are you doing here?" I asked.

"Bad news travels fast."

"But this isn't a homicide, right?"

Her lips twisted. "Based on the vic's condition . . ."

I glanced at Kelvin. He'd seen the body. "Tell you later," he mouthed.

"I'll have to separate you two for the interviews," the detective said. "Standard procedure."

I counted the crowd around us. Maybe a hundred people in attendance. "You're going to interview everyone? It'll be a long night."

"More officers are coming. But I live the closest."

"You do?" When did that happen?

"Yeah. I'm renting a place a few blocks from here."

Detective Sun, a Pixie resident. Well, maybe more people around here would open up to her then. Sometimes Pixians weren't the most trusting of Fresnans, and she'd lived in Fresno before her recent move.

Red and blue lights flashed, and I noticed the cop cars pulling in. After the officers marched into the park, the activity got intense.

They secured the main tent, and Detective Sun went into the crime scene. She came back out quickly with a pinched look on her face.

The police split everybody into different sections of the park, and we all got questioned. Detective Sun approached Kelvin first. He twiddled his thumbs while talking to her, a sure sign of frayed nerves.

Not long after, the detective approached me. I wasn't much help since I didn't even try to peek under the table, but Detective Sun asked about my movements throughout the afternoon and evening, especially in regard to setting up the cake table. She quickly finished her questioning.

I wondered how the bride and groom were doing. At least they were holding hands. United in trauma. Leanne's parents stood an arm's distance apart. I didn't know where Colton's parents had gone, but I knew they wouldn't be together.

A deep voice blared from behind me. "Felicity? Felicity Jin?"

"That's me."

I turned around to find a man holding up my business card and squinting at me. Wild. Was he really interested in talking about pastries after this tragedy?

"Uh, how can I help you?" I figured I should be polite even as he scrutinized me. Why was he intensely staring like that, as though poring over my features?

In turn, I examined him back. Two could play at this game. Wait a minute, that telltale shape of a nose. It was just like mine. Could it be? "Are you . . ."

"It's been a long time," he said. "Too long."

He waited while I guesstimated his age. The math worked out. "Richard?" I ventured.

The man nodded, and I stumbled backward even though I'd guessed correctly. In spite of the distance between us, his hand shot out, like he wanted to steady me.

I swallowed and tried out the new word on the tip of my tongue. "Are you my d-dad?"

He grinned. A dimple flashed at me.

This man, standing in flesh and blood before me, was my father. I'd imagined him swooping into my life many times over the years, but never had I predicted it'd be at a wedding. Or if so, it would be mine. But this was someone else's wedding—and there was a dead body lying around.

I shivered once more.

"Do you want my jacket?" My father made a motion to take off his sports coat, but I shook my head.

I appreciated the kindness, though. The care. What had I missed out on without having him in my life? I couldn't connect the gentleman before me with someone who had so easily left an infant and never contacted her in all of twenty-eight years. I took my time studying the man before me.

Besides the same nose, we shared the same ears that slightly stuck out. My dad had an open face, one whose eyes crinkled with his smile. He seemed warm and welcoming. So why had he gone away?

As though he'd heard me ask out loud, my dad said, "I'm sure you want some answers. Why don't we have coffee together?"

I couldn't get coffee. The caffeine wreaked havoc on my magic, but chatting with him would answer so many of the questions I'd stored up in my heart for all these years.

Kelvin showed up by my side at that moment. "Everything okay, Lissa?" he whispered as he slung an arm around my shoulder in a casual but protective way.

"Um, Kelvin . . . meet my father."

My best friend's arm twitched, but his voice was steady as he said, "What a mighty big coincidence you're at this wedding."

It *was* strange. How had that happened? That would be one of my first questions to him.

Kelvin continued, "Do you have any proof of your identity?" Smart guy.

"Of course," my father said. He reached into the pocket of his gray slacks, pulled out a worn leather wallet, and slipped out his driver's license.

I grabbed hold of it. He was five-foot-nine inches, weighed 158 pounds, and was in his early fifties. I didn't know any specifics about him. Except for his name, Richard Zhou. Which had yielded too many Google results before for me to sift through to locate his whereabouts. But it matched the license.

Kelvin glanced at me, waiting for confirmation.

"Seems to be right."

"Flowers," Kelvin said, out of the blue. "What kind did you used to send your wife?" My best friend frowned, probably remembering the time he'd given my mom those specific flowers and she'd chucked them in the trash.

"Easy," my dad said. "Stargazer lilies, her favorite." Not anymore. But he'd passed Kelvin's impromptu test.

I handed the license back. "I'll be ready to go in a few minutes. Just let me check on the bride and the groom."

"Of course, of course," my father murmured.

I went over to Leanne and Colton, who still seemed shocked by the turn of events. They assured me they didn't need anything. I figured I'd leave the egg tarts for them to eat—maybe it'd give them a few bites of serenity. Then again, I wondered if they'd dare venture into the tent after it was cleared by the crime scene team.

"Maybe I can bake you some new treats. Or discount my services somehow." They'd already paid, but it seemed wrong to charge them full price for my services, given the situation.

Leanne, her face ashen, waved me away. Colton gave a polite nod of dismissal. "We'll figure it out later," he said.

I returned to Kelvin and my father, who were staring uncomfortably at each other.

"So, where to, Felicity?" my dad said. "Your choice."

I snorted. "Only one place to go at this hour. Pixie's Old-Time Diner." The town didn't get too creative with its shop names, with the exception of our little enclave in downtown Pixie. And everything closed early. The unspoken curfew in Pixie was ten o'clock, and the local diner was the only establishment that served right to the brink of that "late" hour.

My father said, "I parked over th—"

"I'll take her," Kelvin said, with a polite smile on his face, and a tight hold on my arm. "I'm getting hungry anyway, and we carpooled together in the first place."

My dad backed off. "Sure, no problem. I'll find my own way there."

"Don't get lost," Kelvin wished him, but the "don't" part was said in a quieter tone than the rest of the phrase.

Kelvin led me to his car. Once I'd buckled in, he turned to me and said, "Are you sure about this, Lissa?"

CHAPTER 5

In the parked car, my best friend continued to pepper me with questions. "Is this really a smart decision, Lissa? Meeting with a man who's ignored you for three decades?"

"Two," I said. Geez. I wasn't thirty quite yet.

"Why is he here anyway?" Kelvin asked.

I couldn't look him in the eye, so I focused on the top of his head. I've always wanted to have curly hair . . .

Kelvin snapped his fingers in my face.

I sighed. "Maybe he happened to be at the wedding." Inside, though, I wondered if it was destiny.

"Or maybe he's stalking you."

Ridiculous, but I humored my best friend. "How, and why?"

Kelvin drummed a beat on the steering wheel. "Maybe he heard Jin Bakery was catering—and now that you're successful, finagled an invite."

"News flash: That's not how wedding invitations work. Odds are he's probably connected to the bride or groom somehow. Once I go to the diner, I can find out more."

"Do you really want to go?"

"Yes." Only all my life. But I didn't dare say that part out loud. I couldn't tell Kelvin, I could barely admit it to myself, this deep wish to find my dad.

Wait a minute. A wish. I'd wished upon my godmother's glittering candle about longing for my dad. Had my desire come true? I'd asked something of the appropriately named Wishes candle before, and then a magical bunny had hopped right onto our stoop.

"I want to meet him," I said in a firm tone of voice. "Talk face-to-face."

"Okay," Kelvin relented. "But I'll be in the diner, watching."

"Now who's the stalker?"

"Uh-uh. I know what you really mean, and *you're welcome.*"

I grinned as he started up the car.

As we drove off, he added, "Just be aware that what we want as children might be different when we're adults."

Sometimes I thought Kelvin had a special talent, too. He had such ease reading my mind, but I guess that's what happens when growing up so close together.

I chuckled to lighten the mood. "When'd you get so wise?"

"I'll have you know I *did* go to college."

He had. UC Merced. Thankfully for me, he'd also returned to Pixie afterward and stayed to start up his floral shop.

We soon arrived at Pixie's Old-Time Diner. It was a cute place with a flashing neon sign and peach-colored vinyl booths on the inside, but it'd been a while since I'd stopped by.

Kelvin placed a hand on my arm. "Hey, are you going to tell your mom about this?"

I took a deep breath and exhaled. "Depends on what I find out."

My dad (can't believe I was actually using that word in real life and not just in my imagination) and I sat across from each other in the peach-colored booth. The place smelled like I'd remembered: a heady combo of burgers and pies.

Now that we were beyond the adrenaline of a wedding gone awry, I wasn't sure what to say to this complete stranger. Would we make awkward small talk? Chat about the weather? Would he ask me how life was going?

I stared at my distorted reflection in the chrome napkin dispenser. My father fiddled with the salt and pepper shakers.

The waitress arrived and left with our orders: black coffee for him, hot cocoa with extra whipped cream for me. Once we had our drinks in front of us, we both started speaking at the same time.

"Never mind," he said. "You go ahead."

"I have one burning question." Might as well cut to the chase after all these years. "Why?"

He furrowed his brow.

"Why did you leave me? I mean, us?"

My dad looked into his coffee as though it held the answers. He remained silent for several beats before finally saying, "I had a really bad feeling about things, about being a father."

That was it? He'd gotten nervous and run away? I shook my head. "I just don't understand." A man who regularly brought flowers to his wife didn't reconcile in my head with one who'd flee from parenting. Something didn't add up.

"Honestly, I felt compelled to go," he said, glancing at a spot over my left shoulder. He seemed like he was hesitant to say more. "Compelled" was an interesting word to use. What if . . .

"Did someone force you to leave?" I asked. It couldn't have been Mom. My grandma maybe? "Po Po?"

"Your wài pó?" He even had the accents down right, unlike me. "No, it didn't have anything to do with her. Though that tiny apartment in Oakland did feel cramped, with all of us stuffed in it."

I knew Mom had moved to central California from somewhere up north, but she'd never mentioned the actual city. "Can you tell me more about Po Po?" I asked. "She died when I was a toddler."

"Sorry for your loss, Felicity," my dad said, lowering his eyes. "She was a very hard worker. Had a gift with languages, mastered both Cantonese and Mandarin. Enjoyed staying busy, so she was always taking in seamstress work even while making pastry deliveries."

I smiled at that. "Her famous pineapple buns?" I asked.

He nodded.

At least we honored her memory through our custom-baked goods. Each Jin family member had her own signature magical treat. And yes, everything passed down through the maternal line. "Our bakery still makes them."

"I'd like to eat one again . . ." He gave a sad smile. "They were amazing. I remember her taking the time to craft each bun, checking the recipe on the counter. Making sure she got everything just right."

Recipe? We didn't write things down. My mom said we Jins shared our recipes verbally and baked by apprenticeship. He must have misremembered.

Oddly, what he'd told me about that Oakland time sounded idyllic. "So, what happened?" I asked. "Did something change?"

He took a sip of his coffee, and I licked my pile of melting whipped cream. "Your grandmother's pastries were so good—and your mom's, too—that we wanted to start a business. Make a real go of it."

"Mom never mentioned having run another bakery before." Why hadn't she told me?

He took another glug of coffee. "That's because we didn't last long. Couldn't cut it, even after I quit my teaching—"

"You're a teacher?"

He held his hands up. "Guilty as charged. High schoolers. I went back to teaching after, you know . . ."

A pang hit my heart. He'd been a father to other kids. Lots of them over the years, but not to his own child. I drank my hot cocoa, hoping it'd warm my chilly heart.

He continued with his story. "Anyway, the trouble started when I quit my job after paternity leave was done. I wanted to help out at the bakery, make it a success."

I put my cup down. "Did you not realize . . ." I'd been taught that Jins had to be in charge of everything in the bakery, from assembling the ingredients to putting pastries in the oven. Otherwise, the magic didn't work. Or maybe he didn't even know about the enchanted goodies.

My dad lowered his voice. "I do know about the, um, special Jin talent. If that's what you're wondering."

I also spoke in a softer tone. "But did you understand that nobody else can help in the kitchen?" I'd once wondered if Kelvin might assist me, but Mom had nixed that idea based on her past experience.

"We didn't realize it'd be an issue—not until that point. I guess in China, no non-magical Jins had helped with the baking before."

I snorted. Patriarchy, go figure. Turning the now half-empty cocoa mug in my hands, I said, "But that doesn't explain why you ran off."

"It was the headaches," he said.

"The what?"

"Once I started helping your mom, this weird nausea came on me. No medication I took made it go away, and the doctors couldn't find anything wrong when I went in."

His face was pinched tight. "Then one day, I went to hold you, and I got this super-intense headache. The feeling of something terrible happening overwhelmed me. I almost dropped you."

"Did you tell them, my mom and grandma?"

"I shared about the headache, and how I had this awful feeling clawing inside of me." He drained his cup of coffee. "But I got scared. I knew I couldn't be around you anymore and took off in the middle of the night, leaving a note behind."

I couldn't look him in the eye, so I focused on the salt and pepper containers. "And you never came back."

"I did," he insisted. "About six months later. But your mom and grandma had vanished without a trace by then." So, who had done the real leaving—the man before me, or my mom?

I felt confused as I revealed, "Mom moved here to Pixie and went by her maiden name."

"To think, all this time you were only a road trip away." His eyes seemed to cloud over with an intense emotion I couldn't interpret.

Was he thinking the same thing I was? Hunching my shoulders, I said, "It *is* too bad . . . A real missed opportunity." Unfortunately, Pixie was so small, certain maps didn't even list it. Besides, Mom didn't exactly flaunt her whereabouts. She'd only very recently agreed to put our last name on the bakery's signage.

"Well, I'm glad I came to this wedding," my dad said.

"Me too."

He stared into my eyes. "Finding you was meant to be." An echo of my own thoughts.

Hmm, I reflected once more on the Wishes candle. Was it truly fate? Or something more magical? "So, why were you at the wedding?"

My dad leaned back in the booth. "Finally, an easy question. Colton was one of my former students."

"And you teach . . . ?"

"High school algebra," he said. "I was one of Colton's favorites. He even asked me for a college rec letter."

"The two of you must have clicked." I tried to keep any jealousy from creeping into my voice.

"Colton liked order. And at that level of math, all the equations have clear answers." My dad pulled at the collar of his dress shirt. *Unlike other things in life*, I thought.

He continued, "Even his friend Easton liked me. Though English—he loved Shakespeare—and drama were more in his wheelhouse."

With his posh accent, I'd no doubt Easton would've loved studying The Bard and being in those plays. "Easton and Colton knew each other in high school?"

My dad nodded. "Best of friends. Knew each other since elementary."

Not quite as long as Kelvin and me then. I glanced over at my own bestie. He was staring at me from a booth across the way. "Everything okay?" he mouthed.

I gave him a quick thumbs-up.

My dad cleared his throat, and I turned my attention back to him. His posture became more tense, and he leaned in. "Does she ever talk about me?" he asked in an almost whisper.

It didn't take a genius to know he was referring to Mom. But what could I tell him besides the truth? "No."

He drained his coffee mug. "Figures she wouldn't want to reconnect . . . yet."

I didn't want him to hold on to imaginary hope. "I'm not sure if she'll ever be open to meeting. She's pretty content with life right now, flying solo."

"Sure, makes sense. At least I still have a memento of her. And fond memories." He slid his cup to the side. "How about you? What do you think about me? I know I've made mistakes . . ."

A huge understatement. But he'd been younger than me back then—and I was still messing up, figuring stuff out at my age. I didn't forgive him, but I wondered what it would be like to have a "complete" family. It'd been my secret desire for so long.

"Would you want to reconnect?" he asked. "Or at least talk more?"

I licked my lips. My past hopes and dreams welled up inside me. I'd appreciate having a few more conversations with him. "Yeah, I think I'd like that."

"Me too." He took out a napkin from the dispenser,

pulled a pen out from his pocket, and wrote down his digits.

I hazarded a glance at Kelvin, and he raised his eyebrows at me. Should I have heeded his warning about a stranger coming to find me out of the blue? Well, too late now. I took the napkin.

CHAPTER 6

I summarized my meeting with my newly discovered dad as I buckled into Kelvin's car, and my best friend frowned at me.

"You agreed to meet with him again?" Kelvin said.

"I feel like I missed out, not having two parents around."

His eyes darted away from mine. "Yeah, I wished I'd had more time with my mom."

She'd gotten sick our sophomore year and passed not too long after her diagnosis. Cancer. "She was the best." Kelvin's dad had never been the same after; Mr. Love had disappeared into his busy surgeon's life with concentrated fervor.

Kelvin and I spent a few moments in silence in the car. Then I spoke up, shifting to a lighter topic. "So, want to know why my dad was at the wedding?"

"Definitely," Kelvin said as he started up the car.

"He was Colton's high school teacher. And Easton's."

"Something's off with that Easton," my best friend said. "He was way too chummy. It was 'mate, this' and 'mate, that' with him."

"Maybe he's just a friendly bloke," I said, aiming for a British vibe.

"Oh, don't you start now."

I raised my hands in mock surrender. "You're still the king of jokes—dad jokes."

"I *lilac* the way you think," he said.

"Uh-huh. I walked right into that one."

Kelvin drove down the main street to the neighborhood where we both lived. He and his dad shared a picturesque ranch house while Mom and I were crammed into a tiny but cozy apartment.

"You know what's *not* funny?" I said as he stopped at a red light. "Murder. Detective Rylan Sun was on the scene . . ."

"About that"—Kelvin took a deep breath—"she wasn't wrong to have shown up."

"What did you see?" I asked. "Scratch that. First of all, are you okay?" A few months ago, a man had died in the alley behind Jin Bakery. I'd been shaken up after only seeing the body bag.

Kelvin's grip tensed on the steering wheel, but he said, "I'm fine. I mean, it was terrible . . ."

We'd turned onto our street by then, and he pulled the car to a stop in front of my apartment.

"How did Miles die?" I asked, thankful Kelvin wasn't driving at the moment.

"He was stabbed."

No wonder there'd been blood. What a vicious way to go.

"A knife?" I asked. Given the proximity to the cake table, that's where my mind went. Then again, I'd set up egg tarts, which didn't need any slicing.

"Pruners. Floral shears—and they were mine."

I gasped, while Kelvin rubbed the back of his neck.

"Yeah, Detective Sun gave me a hard time about it," he said.

"But you've got no motive. You didn't even know Miles, right?"

"That's what I told her. But she said she had to check every possibility."

Including my best friend as a suspect. I gritted my teeth.

"And it took a while the last time for her to come to her senses," Kelvin added.

"Don't I know it?" I'd been on top of the detective's list for the last murder. A fortune I'd written had predicted the cause of a man's death. I couldn't explain it away by coincidence, and I definitely couldn't tell the logical Rylan Sun about my family's magic. I really wanted to trust that the detective would get to the truth quickly now. But I just might need to help her along, like I had last time.

Kelvin yawned then, and we wished each other good night. I crept onto the apartment stoop, trying not to jingle my keys as I unlocked the front door. Mom should already be asleep because we had to wake up early to run the bakery.

She wasn't sleeping. My mom sat in our living room—the half that wasn't partitioned off for my "bedroom" space.

Mom was resting in her cracked faux leather recliner that had seen better days. The television remained dark, so I knew she wasn't up watching her favorite dramas. She'd waited for me to return, like she'd done during my high school days, when I'd slipped in past curfew. Usually I had hung out with Kelvin for too long, but a few times, I'd been slogging through lengthy group study sessions.

"Felicity, you're home," she said upon hearing my footsteps. "How was the wedding?"

I froze. Should I tell her about my dad? We didn't keep

secrets from each other. Yet I wasn't sure I wanted to introduce that bomb into her life at this moment.

Mom sat straight up. "What happened? Is something wrong?"

I hesitated, then took another path of conversation because I was scared of how she'd react to my other news. "Actually, I found a dead body."

"Come again?"

"There was someone under the cake table." I neglected to mention the blood. Or that it'd been murder. No need to alarm her even more.

She placed a hand over her heart. "Did the paramedics come?"

"Unfortunately, it was too late for the guy. The police showed up. As did Detective Sun."

My mom seemed relieved at hearing the name. "Oh, great. She'll take care of everything, sort it out. That's what she did last time."

With some help from Kelvin and me, but maybe Mom had blocked out our useful amateur sleuthing.

My mom cocked her head at me. "Isn't it kind of far for Detective Sun to travel here?"

Fresno wasn't that far away, but Mom was probably wondering why the local cops hadn't taken care of everything. "Detective Sun lives in the area now. Near Pixie Park, actually."

"She moved to our little town?" Even in the dim lighting, I could tell Mom's eyes had a gleam in them. "We're neighbors then. You should bring her a housewarming gift."

Of course I should. Maybe oranges. The lucky fruit happened to be Mom's go-to gift of choice. "Sure," I mumbled. "I'll do something later." No need to be specific with the dates.

"Imagine, a dead body at a wedding." Mom tsked. "How are the bride and groom holding up?"

"Shocked," I said. "I figure I'd bring them new egg tarts, maybe tomorrow? Could help them feel better about the whole thing."

"That's very kind of you, Felicity. And I'll add in pineapple buns. It's better to have even more happiness to start healing their hearts." Our Jin treats offered people joy after they ate them, and Colton and Leanne would need a lot more smiles to bring them through this tragedy.

"Well, we'd better get to baking bright and early tomorrow," Mom said.

Yes. Although technically we got up when it was pitch dark to begin baking. When I checked the current time, a twinge of guilt hit me. "You know, you didn't have to stay up for me, Mom."

"I wanted to make sure you were safe." She pecked me on the cheek before leaving me to get ready for bed.

But my guilt only grew stronger in her absence. Maybe it wasn't that I felt bad about her staying up and not getting rest. What was really eating me was that I hadn't shared about my father being at the wedding.

As though sensing my anxiety, my pet rabbit hopped over to me.

"Whiskers," I said, picking up the fluffy white bunny. "You always seem to have answers. Especially about magic."

I stared into her dark eyes that reminded me of scrumptious chocolate chips. "Was meeting my dad fated? Through the Wishes candle?"

She twitched her nose at me, and I stroked her velvet fur. There had been times when I'd petted her and received visions and solutions in return.

Nothing came to me now. Maybe Whiskers only

answered questions about my own magic. Not others'. To be fair, though, I wasn't sure my godmother Alma was truly magical. Guess I could make a pit stop at her store tomorrow to ask about the Wishes candle she'd made for me.

CHAPTER 7

Mom and I walked to the bakery in the wee hours of the morning. I'd gotten so used to the early schedule that I no longer needed an alarm to wake me up. And I wasn't stifling a yawn despite the lack of caffeine. Mom told me long ago that tea or coffee interfered with our baking powers, so I had to rely on natural energy. (Thank goodness I could still eat chocolate, though. The small amount of caffeine in a candy bar didn't seem to negatively affect the magic.)

At this time of day, nobody was around, and I could even hear the hoot of an owl as we strolled toward the cul-de-sac of stores. We happily lived close to our workplace, so it was a gentle and brief walk that took us to the door of Jin Bakery.

I wished it were daylight, so I could see the close cluster of shops in all their glory. Our landlord had recently painted the stucco walls of each store in striking primary colors: Kelvin's Love Blooms was vivid red ("Roses are red," he'd said); Alma's Paz Illuminations was royal blue (in contrast to the always dark interior of her shop); and ours was yellow. It matched the meaning of our Jin surname, although I wasn't sure the landlord even knew about that factoid.

We'd been known as Gold Bakery for most of my life because Mom had been hesitant to use our Chinese name for the store. She'd had to acclimate fast to Pixie . . . and it wasn't the best globally representative small town around. In fact, this cozy cul-de-sac had the most diversity found in the area. But things were changing. I mean, even Detective Sun had decided to live here. Here's hoping that we'd have an Asian mart in Pixie soon. Fresno wasn't too far away, but it'd be nice to have ethnic grocery stores within Pixie's borders.

Plus, I'd been wanting to snag a bottle of matcha powder. Green fortune cookies would be a hit. Especially for next year's St. Patrick's Day. Not that fortune cookies were Irish or anything. They were Asian American, with Chinese roots—or so I'd thought, until Kelvin had informed me about some similar Japanese crackers called senbei.

Whatever their origin, at least I could actually make them. I walked into the bakery with a grin. I belonged here and could make my ancestors proud. It'd taken twenty-eight years of baking fails and being relegated to the register for a while, but now I was elevated to the inner sanctum of the kitchen.

Moving through the open archway into the back of the shop, I again marveled at the workspace. We'd combined the modern with the whimsical, mixing steel appliances (including an industrial triple-deck oven) with a tangerine-colored floor and teal pendant lights.

I went to one of our refrigeration units and pulled out a carton of eggs. Before long, my mom and I were up to our arms in flour and batter. We always used our hands and "crafted with love," as my mom would say. She couldn't abide stand mixers and thought they took away from the care we put into our pastries.

"What are you making today, Mom?" I asked.

She bent over her mixing bowl. "Pineapple bun with coconut filling."

I licked my lips. We'd recently been exploring variations on our treats. My fortune cookies came in the popular Neapolitan flavors of chocolate, strawberry, and vanilla, but I wanted to expand.

It'd taken a while for my mom to also realize that she could embellish our generations-old recipes. Grandma's pineapple buns could use a little something extra. Even Mom's egg tarts might need more pizzazz. "Have you ever thought about making different styles of dàn tà?" I asked her.

She didn't correct my pronunciation. My accents were off in Mandarin. Not like there'd been a Chinese school in Pixie, and Mom had always been busy at the bakery. Besides, she'd wanted me to fit in more.

Mom paused in her mixing and said, "I have been thinking about creating one that's Portuguese-style, with a cookie crust."

"Mmm. I can't wait to try it."

As I rolled out fortune cookie discs, she said, "Don't forget. I'm going to add extra pastries for your wedding friends."

I wouldn't label Colton and Leanne as anything more than paying customers, but I murmured my thanks. Once we'd gotten several batches of pastries done, and it was closer to regular waking time for people, I'd give the couple a call to set up a visit.

A few hours later, I'd stocked up our glass display case in the front of the store and sat down at the stool next to the register. I picked up the nearby phone and called the newlyweds.

Leanne answered on the second ring and sounded tired. "Who's this?" she asked.

"Hi, it's Felicity Jin."

She didn't respond. Maybe she couldn't place the name because of her exhaustion.

"I'm the egg tarts caterer."

"Oh, right. Unfortunately, we ended up tossing your stuff because it was too close to the . . . cake table."

Had she meant to say "dead body"? "No worries. I've baked a new batch for you and your wedding attendants . . . if they're still around." I wished I could've brought over my fortune cookies and used my magic somehow to figure out this case, but they had specifically craved and requested my egg tarts. Besides, I could still do snooping the old-fashioned way and ask a few probing questions.

"That's kind of you," Leanne said, seeming grateful for my baking generosity. "And we're all still here at Pixie Inn." It was really the only place for visitors to stay. I'd never been inside since I actually lived in town, but I loved their rustic ambience outside.

"Would it be okay if I dropped by later? Not that I want to impose if you'll be going on your honeymoon . . ." But it'd be great to clear Kelvin's name sooner rather than later.

"Nah. We were only going to take a few days' trip to Kingsburg anyway." A cute place known for its Swedish village and architecture.

She continued, "But I asked Colton to postpone it. What with the cops questioning us and my anxiety, I would never enjoy it." They were still being interviewed about the murder?

"What time should I come?" I asked. "Evening would be better for me, and the bakery closes at five."

"You can swing by at five thirty. That will give us a few hours before the photographer arrives."

"Okay." That should be plenty of time to give my condolences and make sure the couple had achieved emotional equilibrium, aided by Jin treats.

"Oh, actually," Leanne said, "can you bring Kelvin along? He's your best friend, right?"

"Sure. I can ask him to come." We closed up at the same hour, although sometimes he stayed longer because of last-minute customers. But I knew he wouldn't mind tagging along.

All settled with the appointment, I said a warm goodbye to Leanne and hung up. Perfect timing. We'd open in ten minutes.

I checked our display case of goodies again. We had a lot at the ready for customers, and more in the cooling racks in the kitchen. But a sliver of worry slipped into my consciousness. Even though Mom and I were starting to offer variations of our pastries, we essentially only sold three kinds of items: egg tarts, pineapple buns, and fortune cookies. Would customers get tired of the same things day in and day out? If only we had more Jin family recipes to lean on.

We'd also had a dip in business when the murdered man had been found in the dumpster behind our bakery. I wasn't knowledgeable about feng shui, but dead bodies probably didn't bring good luck to a business.

Over the next couple of hours, the steady stream of customers soothed my fears. The people were a mix of new faces and regulars, like Mrs. Spreckels from the library around the corner.

Even Sweet Tooth Sally, the town gossip with a heart of gold, came by earlier than usual to pick up some treats. "I'm off to a board meeting," she said with a cheery smile. *Which one?* I wondered. But the sight of her fiery red hair and freckled face always lifted my mood. She really should run for mayor. Sally had helped us out in the investigation last time by using her connections. She was from a family that had lived here for generations, and she was forward-thinking; we needed that kind of leader in town.

She grabbed her full box of goodies and left with a happy wave. After Sally, our line of customers dwindled. We hit our usual lull right around noon. People often had lunch during this hour and didn't want to fill up their stomachs with pastries. Then after one, more customers would arrive, those with a time-for-dessert mindset.

Since we had a current tiny slowdown, I asked my mom if I could pop by next door.

"Going to visit Kelvin?"

"No. Alma."

"Say hi to her for me. Tell her that we should get together sometime."

I didn't know when that would be since both my godmother and mom worked hard at their businesses. Alma also sold her candles on Etsy, so she fulfilled orders at all hours of the day. "Will do," I said as I marched over to the royal blue storefront.

CHAPTER 8

My godmother's shop, Paz Illuminations, looked closed, but I knew better. She liked adorning the space with dark curtains. Black velvet draped across the front door and over the windows. It gave privacy and offered a great opportunity for customers to fully experience the wonder of lighting one of Alma's sample candles.

I walked through the entrance and found my godmother at the counter typing on her silver laptop. Not unusual. Although she was in her sixties (or maybe seventies? I could never tell), she was savvier than me tech-wise. In fact, Alma often aided us by updating our bakery's website or Yelp page.

She looked up at me and smiled. "Felicity, what a pleasure."

"Thank you." I hesitated. "I'm here to talk about candles."

"Are you looking for anything in particular?" She came out from behind the counter, ready to serve me.

"Actually, I wanted to speak about a particular candle. The one you gave me."

I'd already told Alma that we'd gotten a bunny after I'd lit the candle the first time. But a father at the second go-around? That seemed unbelievable. "The Wishes candle. Is there something special you put in it?"

"Do you want there to be?"

The problem with my godmother was that she often replied to a question with a question. I studied her lined face, hoping to decipher some kind of answer there, but she was unreadable.

I shrugged. "It's just that . . . Well, things keep happening that seem related to wishes I have."

She chuckled. "You know, I name each candle myself. The inspiration comes from a certain prickling in my mind."

Now *she* sounded magical as well. "Do you have certain talents . . . ?" I'd almost added "too," but stopped myself in time. My mom and godmother were close, but I never could tell if Alma really knew about our true baking ability.

"My great-aunt," Alma said, her eyes flicking up toward the ceiling for a moment. "She was a great curandera. When she passed on, I inherited some of her herbs. I've used them in my candles."

"Really?" I glanced around the shop, trying to figure out which ones held mementoes of Alma's grand-auntie. Could it be that tall blue one in the corner?

"In fact," my godmother said, "the Wishes candle held a touch of tronadora powder."

"What's that?"

"A type of flower, bright yellow. A relative told me it helps with diabetes. I can't remember the scientific name." She inclined her head toward Love Blooms. "I'm sure Kelvin would know better than me."

He would, but my mind snagged on something else my godmother had mentioned. Alma had said it was a yellow flower. I thought about the Wishes candle, which had a lovely golden color and matching speck-les in it. I thought the little dots had been glitter, but maybe they'd been the powder of these brilliant flow-ers. Could that be why my wishes were coming true? Some remnant of power still carrying forth from Alma's great-aunt?

As though she'd read my mind, my godmother said, "There are different ways of healing. My tía abuela used herbs. You use baked goods."

I nodded. "Both are valid." Maybe Alma's great-aunt had helped people with their physical diseases and ill-nesses. We Jins treated the emotional needs of our cus-tomers.

"Did that answer your question, Felicity?"

Only on the most basic level. What I really wanted to know was if it was wise to reconnect with my dad. Was it safe to open my heart to him? I licked my lips. "Alma, do you think we should always act on our wishes?"

She came closer to me and cupped my chin with a ten-der touch. "Unveil your ideas," she said. "Be ready to act on them."

Alma had a penchant for giving odd tidbits of wis-dom. I swear I should write them down for my fortune cookies—at least for the generic ones. The customized, predictive messages I saved for special occasions. It'd mean trouble for me if Pixians around town found out I could actually foresee their futures. Although word was already spreading that I was giving out interesting, per-sonalized fortunes.

I pondered over what my godmother had said. Were my "ideas" the same as my wishes? Did "unveil" mean to bring forth my thoughts, or did it signify that my mind needed to be enlightened? "I really don't understand," I said.

"Wishes," she said, "are an extreme kind of desire and can be twisted different ways."

I'm not sure her explanation helped me any further. The door to the candle shop opened, and sunlight streamed in.

Alma straightened up, checking to make sure the silvery braided bun on her head was intact, and greeted the customer by name. I excused myself to get back to the bakery, having obtained no real answers.

At the end of the day, I went over to our other neighboring store, Love Blooms. I opened the door and waltzed in. "Knock, knock," I said when I didn't spot Kelvin in the open.

I took a moment to soak in the beauty of his shop. He'd gotten his love of flower arranging from his mom, who delighted in doing ikebana. But he'd expanded his floral artistry to encompass all types of flowers and plants. The entire store felt like a private jungle of sorts, with ubiquitous fronds everywhere. If he'd added a manmade waterfall, or a bubbling fountain to the shop, I could've relaxed in there for hours.

Kelvin walked out of the back room, where he kept the extra supplies. "Lissa," he said, "what are you doing here?"

"Two things. First, do you know anything about the tronadora flower?"

"Sure, it's in the trumpet vine family." His eyes got dreamy as he added, "Beautiful yellow flowers. Why?"

I pointed in the direction of Paz Illuminations. "Talked to Alma about this special candle she gave me, which features the plant. What's the flower symbolize?" Kelvin liked keeping track of floral symbolism and often gave me bouquets with meaning, though I always had to ask him to explain them to me.

"Well," he said, "the yellow elder, one of its common names, reminds me of sunshine. I'd say it represents hope."

"Hope and wishes go together," I said. "Makes sense."

"Huh?" He looked puzzled.

"That candle," I said. "The one Alma gave me? She'd called it Wishes, and now I know why. And guess what? It brought my dad to me."

"Maybe," Kelvin said. "Maybe not. It's just a candle, after all."

I didn't know about that. Kelvin had met Whiskers but didn't know the bunny was magical.

My best friend continued talking, "You should be more careful. We don't know anything about your bio father."

I bristled. Why would Kelvin want to stop this reunion that had been so long in the making?

He stepped nearer, and I couldn't help but notice the care in his steady glance.

I put my hands up in surrender. "All right, I'll be cautious. And I promise to let you know when I meet up with him next."

"Good. So, what's that second thing you came to see me about?"

Grateful for a change of subject, I decided to tease him to lighten his mood. "I've come to whisk you away with me."

"Not that I mind leaving with a beautiful lady, but why?"

"It's Leanne and Colton. I'm going to see them." I

lifted a box of baked goodies. "And they specifically asked you to come along."

"Really?" he said. "But I already settled my bill with them."

I shrugged. "Guess we'll find out what they want with you soon enough."

CHAPTER 9

Pixie Inn appeared like a residence straight out of a fairy tale. It had a charming brick exterior and a slate roof painted a particular beige that mimicked the color of straw. A replica watermill, staged on dry land, decorated the side of the building. Adding to the manmade allure, a silver crescent moon in the sky hung just so above the inn, as though it, too, was a stage prop.

Pixie Inn's interior was also beautiful. It had lovely exposed wooden rafters and a roaring fireplace in the main lobby.

I measured the size of the place. It didn't qualify as an inn in my mind. Maybe more of a cozy bed-and-breakfast.

"Can I help you?" someone asked.

I stopped staring at my surroundings and focused on the person behind the check-in desk.

Recognizing the face, I stepped forward. "Mrs. Robson?" Her hair had turned all gray from its original brown, and she'd chopped it into a wedge haircut, but I remembered her tender smile and piercing blue eyes.

She took a moment to ransack her brain but soon came up with my name. Then again, we didn't have many

Asians around. "Felicity Jin," she said. "Why, I haven't seen you since sixth grade."

"I loved being in your English class, learning about sonnets and haikus and quatrains."

She chuckled. "It's been a while since I've taught kids. I run our family's inn now. This place has passed from one Robson to another throughout the years. One of us always seems to stay in Pixie."

I introduced Kelvin, who'd been standing behind me, to her.

She glanced at both of us. "Do you need a room for tonight? A romantic staycation, perhaps?"

I blinked at my past English teacher, and Kelvin made a gurgling noise in his throat.

Recovering, I said, "My best friend Kelvin and I are here to visit a few guests of yours. We catered their wedding. Kelvin runs the floral shop, Love Blooms. My mom and I are in charge of Jin Bakery."

"How lovely, dear," Mrs. Robson said. "Sorry for the mix-up. I'm afraid I don't get to eat sweets much anymore myself, but I do bake them for guests. Trying to manage my diabetes. And I'm not into flowers."

"That makes sense. So, which room are the bride and groom in?" I showed her the box from the bakery. "I have a little gift for them."

"Ah, I put them in the Shakespeare Suite," Mrs. Robson said. "Down that hall. Third door on the right."

We thanked her and followed my teacher's directions. Sure enough, a bronze plaque beside the room read SHAKESPEARE SUITE.

I knocked on the door, and Colton answered.

"We come bearing gifts," I said.

He eyed the box. "Excellent. I'm starving. Come on in."

The room was set up with a sitting section with a long burgundy velvet couch and a matching cushioned armchair, partitioned off from the sleeping area by a tall golden folding screen.

I offered the pastries to Colton, and he took out an egg tart right away.

"Want any, Leanne?" he asked.

Her slim figure came around the screen, but she shook her head. "My appetite still hasn't returned."

The new bride did look pale, almost like the ivory silk blouse she wore. She perched on the antique armchair and added, "But I appreciate you bringing us snacks."

"Yeah," Colton said, his words slurred by his chewing. "These are delicious, and I'm feeling much better. We haven't had much time to eat, what with the police coming by and asking all sorts of questions about Miles."

"The cops grilled Kelvin, too," I said. "Think he might have done it." My best friend shuffled his feet while I let out a laugh of disbelief.

Colton chuckled, too. "Him? The florist who doesn't even dare tear a flower petal?"

"Right?" I said. "But I'm curious what you ended up telling the police. *Did* Miles have any enemies?" Because why else would a wedding get ruined by death?

While Colton gathered his words, Leanne gestured to the couch. Both Kelvin and I sat down as Colton replied, "Miles was a decent guy, but he didn't have any deep friendships. And he often held grudges."

"But *you're* close to Miles," I said. "Enough to have him at your wedding."

"Of course, since he's family. Obligation. You noticed that my parents aren't exactly on speaking terms." He gave a wry smile, and I remembered how the parentals had tried to physically distance themselves from each other.

He continued, "It was a nasty divorce, and people took sides. Miles remained neutral, so he was one of the few relatives who could come to the wedding. Or wanted to."

Made sense. I remembered the talk in the tea tent. "Did I hear that he had been thinking about officiating the ceremony?"

"He thought he could," Colton said. "You know, get deputized for the day."

Leanne piped up. "Miles actually offered to—when he first heard about our engagement."

"But, like always, he didn't do his due diligence. The local county doesn't allow day deputies."

"Well, he didn't know that," Leanne said.

"Keep on defending him, as usual." Colton finished his egg tart with another huge bite.

She blushed. It pinkened her cheeks and made her look healthier, but marital strife already? It didn't bode well for the two of them.

I studied Colton. How long had he been jealous of Miles? And could it have turned deadly on Colton's own wedding day? Then again, they were staying in a room wallpapered with Shakespeare quotes, including a line from *Romeo and Juliet*. Maybe the romantic tragedy was subliminally influencing me.

"Different question," I said, breaking the tense silence. "I ran into your teacher the other day. Richard Zhou. What's your impression of him?"

Colton closed the pastry box. "Mr. Zhou? My favorite teacher, but he was strict with grading. Easton didn't like him. Mr. Zhou never gave extensions on assignments, and he didn't give out half points or quarter points for effort or partial answers, either. Why do you ask?"

I fumbled for an answer. "He's an old family . . ." Relative? Friend? What would be true here? "It's hard to explain." Or maybe I just didn't want to explain the embarrassing connection.

Colton looked on the verge of asking me more, but Kelvin saved me.

"So, you wanted to see me?" he asked. "I thought we squared away everything with the flowers and the arch."

"Oh, it's not about your handiwork." Colton put away the take-out box on a side table before he went on. "You were there. I mean you saw . . . It's just that Leanne needs some closure."

Kelvin turned his head toward Leanne, and she gulped.

"How did he die?" she asked. "Was it suicide?"

I flinched but tried to disguise it as a small shiver. Who would stab themself with pruning shears? Not a pleasant way to go.

Kelvin didn't move a muscle. "No, Leanne. It didn't look like suicide to me."

"See, Leanne," Colton said. "Miles wasn't a depressed kind of guy. Besides, that detective was asking us those pointed questions. I think it was murder." He clenched his fists.

Poor Colton, hurting about his cousin.

"Someone deliberately went and ruined my wedding," Colton said. Oh. I quickly changed my mind about his empathy.

"*Our* wedding." Leanne whispered the correction.

Wait a minute. Why wasn't Colton sad or angry about the death in his family? He just seemed upset his wedding ceremony had gone awry. Was he mad about the murder? Or, rather, that it had been discovered? If I hadn't noticed something off about the cake table . . .

I glanced at my best friend, who also seemed puzzled by the misdirected emotions. I myself felt mixed-up, but I knew grief affected people differently. Maybe Colton was still in shock.

I stood. "Please let us know if there's anything else we can do for you."

"Uh-huh," Kelvin said following my lead.

"There is something," Colton said as I turned to go.

I paused.

"You're familiar with the local area. Can you find Nova, and help her get dinner for us?" Colton's stomach growled. "She's in the room two doors down. Faces west. The Dickinson Den." His priorities seemed misaligned, but hangryness often overrode everything else. Unless he deliberately wanted to distract Kelvin and me from his weird vibe by sending us on an errand.

After a moment's hesitation, I agreed.

Kelvin opened the door to the room to exit—and Haley stumbled straight into him.

CHAPTER 10

Papers flew everywhere after Haley's crash into Kelvin. He steadied her and asked, "Are you okay?"

"I'm fine," she said, staying in his arms a little too long before dusting herself off. "But I made a mess . . ."

I started gathering the loose papers. They seemed to all have a wedding attendant's name listed at the top.

"Thanks for picking those up, Felicity," Haley said, as she fixed the mussed twin side braids she wore. "Leanne and Colton asked me to print the speeches out."

"The ones for the toasts?" I guessed. I'd only been given an abbreviated version of the reception timeline. The parts that involved my help. And I didn't remember anything about speeches, but I figured that's what she meant. "When was that going to be?"

Colton rubbed his tummy and said, "After all the food was served, including the egg tarts. I hate it when people make you wait for dessert."

"Too bad you didn't get to hear everyone's speeches."

"That's why I wanted them printed out." Leanne came over and reached for the papers. "So I could read them and put them in our wedding scrapbook."

She checked the names on top of the documents and frowned. "How come there are only five?"

I counted in my head. Weren't there six people in the wedding party?

Haley tugged the end of one braid. "I'm sorry. Miles' toast disappeared from the shared doc. And I couldn't find his printed copy in our room."

"Another thing gone wrong," Colton mumbled.

Kelvin and I decided to leave the newlyweds and Haley to resolve the sticky situation. After all, we had our own appointed mission. Maybe getting a meal in everyone's stomach would lift up the general atmosphere.

In the hallway, I reminded Kelvin. "Colton said Nova would be in the Dickinson Den."

He nodded and wandered down the hall, studying the plaques. Kelvin generally had a better sense of direction than me. "Found it," he said after a moment.

I knocked, but the door was already ajar, and opened at my touch. The Dickinson Den was painted a lovely lemon shade on the inside, and I marveled at the literary decor. One wall featured a wide glass-fronted cabinet filled with manuscripts and leather tomes. A print above the queen bed had a colorful illustrated bird and the phrase "'Hope' is the thing with feathers."

Nova came up to me and crossed her muscular arms. "Hi, can I help you two?"

"Sorry," I said, stepping back from her. "Colton sent us over. To figure out dinner."

"That man is always harping on about food. But I guess we'd better get him something before he gnaws off his own arm. Or, even worse, his bride's."

"Well, I did bring some snacks to tide you over. Pastries we left with Leanne and Colton."

"You did?" Nova tried to peer around the door and into the hall. "Jada just went to talk to the owner to see if there was anything left over from breakfast to eat. I should tell her to go to Colton's."

Kelvin studied the cozy room. "You and Jada are sharing this?"

"Yes, the Dickinson Den." She jerked her thumb to the side. "Turner and Easton have the one next door, called Hughes Haven. And Miles—or just Haley now—have Plath Place."

"I've always wanted to stay at this quaint inn for fun," I said. "But there's no reason to because I live in town."

"It's a nice place," Nova said. "Plus, Colton and Leanne are paying for our stays. And Jada is a considerate roomie—all those years living with Leanne. It's just a shame they don't serve anything other than breakfast here."

"Which reminds me, what kind of dinner would you like?" I asked. "I can recommend several spots around town."

"Anything that offers takeout," Nova said. "None of us feel like going somewhere. And last night, we ordered delivery from Foo Fusion in Fresno. Owner's a friend of Leanne's parents. Hated the meal."

Both Kelvin and I had tried their subpar Chinese food. Its bad quality had inadvertently led me to creating my signature fortune cookies to make up for the disappointment. Bittersweet memories.

"We don't have too many ethnic food choices in Pixie," Kelvin said.

We'd have to work on that.

"No worries," Nova said, "I think we just want something quick and filling at this point. Burgers would hit the spot. You don't have an In-N-Out, do you?"

"Sorry. But we do have Pixie's Burger Joint. And they even have vegetarian and vegan options," I said.

"That'll do." Nova pulled out her cell phone and tapped on it. "No DoorDash or Uber Eats here?"

"Welcome to Pixie," Kelvin said.

"There's only eat-in or takeout," I added. "Not even restaurant-offered delivery."

"Seriously?" Nova said.

"The city council thought it'd make us a better community if we sat down next to each other and ate. Or at least saw each other's faces while getting food to go."

Nova tapped her foot on the floor. "I guess I could Lyft there and back."

"I can pick it up," Kelvin said. His mom had always drilled niceness into him. He couldn't help but volunteer his services.

"Great," Nova said. "Let me get everyone's orders, and then I'll come with you."

On the way to Pixie's Burger Joint, Nova rolled down the window on her passenger side. The wind blew through her short hair, and she stuck her arm out, making a waving motion.

"Feels so good to get away," she said.

I piped up from the back seat. See, I could be nice like Kelvin. I'd given her shotgun. "Pixie is pretty walkable if you're determined."

"Maybe I'll take a stroll one of these days. But compared to SF, Pixie's kinda boring."

Excuse me? I knew we were small since my mom had elected to come here to get away from the urban life, but I had loyalty to my hometown.

As if he knew I might say something snappy, Kelvin spoke up. "It's a slower pace of life, but I like it. Pixie—

and its people—is why I came back after college and decided to open up a flower shop here."

"Love Blooms, right?" Nova said. "I like the play on words."

Love was Kelvin's last name. He'd come up with the catchy shop title himself, and he grinned.

"You from San Francisco?" I asked Nova.

She moved her hand up and down outside the window. "Yep. Actually, all of us on the groom's side are from the Bay Area. The bride's group is local."

"From Fresno."

"That's righ—watch it, buddy!" Nova leaned over and slammed the palm of her hand against the horn.

Kelvin stiffened at her sudden move.

"I hate it when people don't signal when changing lanes," Nova said by way of explanation.

Maybe traffic was so horrible up north that people honked at one another all the time. Even if they weren't the ones driving the car. Could it be considered a usual practice up there?

"Uh," I said, "so you know Colton from college? You two majored in communications?"

She seemed to relax again as she answered, "Uh-huh. I like to say we lie for a living." Her mouth pursed. "It might even be a family trait with the Wus."

"How's that?"

"Their sweet-talking genes." Nova counted off on her fingers. "Colton's dad, Colton, Miles . . ."

Kelvin had pulled to a stop in front of the restaurant. Pixie's Burger Joint always reminded me of that Hopper painting, especially because it had a huge glass window that revealed a long red counter and barstool seating.

We got out of the vehicle and approached the entrance.

A small golden bell attached to the top of the door jangled when Kelvin opened it and waved us through.

I paused before entering and turned to ask Nova, "Did you know Miles before the wedding?"

"Unfortunately," she said. "And he was the biggest liar of them all."

CHAPTER 11

Inside Pixie's Burger Joint, the smell of French fries permeated the air. It was a heady mix of grease, potatoes, and belonging. Teens would often head over here after class got out since it was only a block away from Pixie High.

Kelvin and I even came a few times, except we kept getting strange looks from peers. Like we didn't belong. Kelvin was nice and on the track team, so people at least waved hello to him. They usually ignored me. Once others discovered I wasn't stereotypically nerdy enough to help them with their homework or ace their tests, they gave me a wide berth. Not that I'd had time to hang out with people (beyond the required group projects and study sessions). Mom and I kept the bakery humming whenever I wasn't in school. Kids my age never came around; our regulars tended to be older.

I checked the company now. The restaurant held a more mixed population. Younger people crowded on the barstools along the long red counter. Couples, families, and solos sat at vinyl booths scattered on another side of the burger joint.

At least I didn't get stared at, like I'd used to. The

conversation kept flowing. Maybe Pixie was changing. I noticed a bit more diversity in the patrons, and nobody clucked their tongues over Nova's vibrant purple pixie hair.

She went up to the register and showed the guy her order confirmation. "It's ready in the back," he said and disappeared inside the kitchen.

While waiting for the food, I asked Nova, "What did you mean when you said Miles was the biggest liar?"

She shrugged. "Had no conscience. He lied easily, whenever it helped him get what he wanted. Attention, a job, the girl, whatever."

"And Colton was close to him?"

"Eh. He's the only cousin that remained in touch." She nodded her thanks to the returning restaurant worker. "Plus, Miles had contacts in this area. Even landed them their photographer."

She double-checked the burger orders in the bag.

Both Kelvin and I helped carry the stash of food and drinks.

"I thought Miles was from Oakland."

"He is," Nova said, "but interned at a Fresno hospital."

We got back to the car and scrambled inside. "Miles was in the medical field?"

"Only briefly. He would faint at the sight of blood. I think he did the internship to appease his parents."

The Asian kid on the doctor or lawyer track. Guess it did happen. I was happy my family focused on baking as a profession. "He must not have lasted long then."

She smirked. "Not even a month. Didn't complete it."

Ding. Nova's phone. She read the text and said,

"Everyone's gathering in the great room, so we should go there with the burgers."

Pixie Inn's great room really was a grand space. It was a cozy affair, complete with a brick hearth and flanked with imposing armchairs. A crackling fire roared. Not a gas imitation either. Flames licked at the wood logs and threw real heat.

A plush faux fur rug cushioned the hard floor. Colton, Leanne, and their friends (minus Turner) were seated in the soft carpeting next to a sturdy oak table.

Turner was center stage, in front of the fire, pacing down the length of the mantel. He appeared to be in the middle of a soliloquy, and he didn't break his gush of words at our appearance.

None of them even glanced at us as we tiptoed in. Truth be told, Turner did make a dashing figure, especially embellished with a flowing cape, a top hat, and a cane.

"Never fear, milady," he said, tipping his hat at Leanne and flashing his wavy dark hair. "I promise to always protect you, from friend or foe."

He swiveled toward Colton. "And you as well, milord."

Turner twisted his cane in the air, and at once, it resembled a flashing sword. "I will fight for your epic love, a romance for the ages. Not a single obstacle shall tear you two apart. That is my vow to the august bride and groom."

He took a theatrical bow after his last sentence, and his audience exploded in whistles and cheers.

"And that, my friends, is how you perform a speech," he added.

Haley's green eyes widened. "I didn't even memorize mine." She peeked at her phone, a document queued up on it.

Leanne patted Haley's arm. "Don't worry. Turner's a showboat."

Turner whipped his cape off in a single smooth motion. "And you love it, dahling," he said to Leanne.

"I tolerate it," she said—but smiled. "Anyway, what kind of personal assistant would I be if I didn't put up with your idiosyncrasies?"

"I think you got confused and meant to say 'individual style.'" He wiggled his eyebrows, and Leanne laughed.

I wondered how long they'd worked together. They seemed close. Her "fearless leader," as Leanne had jokingly called their relationship at the tea ceremony.

Nova clapped her hands together. "Before we continue on with the show, I have your food." She started handing out people's orders. "And special thanks to Felicity and Kelvin for helping me get it."

The entire wedding party joined in on thanking us. Turner even bowed again in gratitude. Others murmured their appreciation and praised our efforts and care in making them feel comfortable during this time of upheaval.

"Well, seems like our job here is done," Kelvin said with a wide grin. He put a hand on the small of my back, ready to guide us away.

Haley popped up from her seated position and rushed over. "You're leaving already?"

"Yeah, we don't want to disturb your dinner," I said.

"But you didn't hear my speech." She spoke to the both of us, but her eyes were glued to Kelvin.

"Sorry," he said. "It's getting late, and I should get Felicity back home."

"Oh, you're such a good friend."

Had she emphasized that last word, or was I imagining it?

"If you can't hear my speech, at least read it," Haley said.

"I really don't have time right now."

"Then later. What's your email?"

Kelvin was polite, often to his detriment. He gave it to her.

"Sent," Haley said before she waved us off with a wiggle of her fingers.

Once we'd left Pixie Inn, I said, "Softie."

"Can't help it."

"I know." I squeezed his arm. "Are you really going to read it?"

"Maybe. If I can't fall asleep tonight."

"I'm sure it'll be sugar and spice and everything nice," I said as we made our way back to the car.

He caught my reference to the nursery rhyme. "Come on, Lissa. She's not *that* much younger than us."

"You're the one who mentioned her young age, buster. Not me."

Kelvin did the chivalrous thing and opened the passenger door for me, but I didn't mind it so much tonight.

CHAPTER 12

I didn't have a chance to connect with Kelvin in the morning to check on his sleep and speech-reading status. Instead, I was swamped with baking and readying for the customers at Jin Bakery.

Mom and I had a long line of people waiting for our special goodies once we opened up shop. At the very end of those patient folks was Jada. Her hair looked different than before, both during the wedding and back at Pixie Inn. She'd had it up previously, but now it was let loose, and her straight black hair flowed down to her waist.

She shifted her green glasses on the bridge of her nose. "Hi, Felicity. I need to order more pastries. Apparently, Colton hoarded the ones you brought over, so nobody in the wedding party got to try any."

Guess I'd miscalculated the amount they'd needed. "I can bring some more over."

She shrugged. "I'm already here."

I checked the clock on the wall. "But doesn't Pixie Inn serve breakfast? Shouldn't you be eating there right now?"

"Eggs, sausage, and English muffins for everyone. But I got voluntold to come over."

I raised my eyebrows at her.

Irritation crept into her voice. "Squeaky wheel gets the grease. I complained, and Colton challenged me to do something about it. Which I am."

Reaching into the glass display case and pulling out an egg tart, I said, "Maybe you should munch on this right now." Whether she was hangry or angry, it would help even out her mood.

"Thanks," she said, taking a few bites. She closed her eyes, and I could sense the magic at work. Happiness and butter scented the air. A smile appeared on Jada's face. "I do feel better."

"Great," I said. "So, what can I get for you all? Though that last one's on the house."

She checked out our display of egg tarts, pineapple buns, and fortune cookies. She scowled when she spotted my treats. "I don't believe in fortunes. They're silly, like horoscopes."

Some people relied on those for direction, but I knew better than to argue with a customer. Also, I knew that *my* messages could come true. I switched topics. "Too bad Kelvin and I couldn't stay longer last night and listen to all the speeches. We left after Turner did his performance."

Jada wrinkled her nose. "You didn't miss much. The rest of the speeches were boring. Well, besides Miles' intended one. His would have been a real show-stopper."

"You know what he wrote?"

She straightened her shoulders. "I helped him write it. After all, he doesn't know Leanne as well as me."

"You two been roommates a long time?" I asked.

"Ever since we got thrown together freshman year in college, and we never looked back."

"But I guess she'll need to move out now . . . unless Colton is moving in?"

Jada jammed the rest of the egg tart into her mouth. She seemed to calm down once she swallowed it. "Leanne's off to the Bay Area. Gonna work remote from there."

How would I feel if I was suddenly left alone? Not that I wanted to ever move away from my mom. We lived together and worked together, and it still didn't seem like enough bonding time. But mothers and daughters were different than roommates.

Jada tapped on the glass case and pointed out the items she wanted to order, and I complied. While tallying up her total on the register, I said, "If you need more, I'm happy to deliver to the inn. Don't feel like you have to walk over here."

"It was actually good to get out of the place," she said. "I've been feeling antsy, what with the police coming around and everything."

Jada paid for her purchase and left with a curt "bye."

Not a moment later, Kelvin burst through the door. "Was that—"

"Jada. Yeah. What's with the hurry?"

Kelvin's dark curls didn't look any messier than usual, but his blue Henley shirt had one arm rolled up and the other down. He must have noticed me looking at his bare brown arm because he fixed his sleeves.

"Been rough today," he said.

"It's still morning."

"First, it was Dad, who rushed out—" He started hyperventilating.

"Deep breaths, Kelvin." I demonstrated, and he followed suit. It seemed to help. "Your dad usually is running off to the hospital." A surgeon's life meant being on call a lot.

"But, Lissa, he wasn't in his scrubs. He was wearing a *suit*." Now that was weird. Mr. Love didn't dress up. The last time I'd seen him in a suit had been at his wife's funeral.

"Strange. But you can ask him when you see him next."

He shook his head. "When will that be?" They didn't get much time with each other because of Mr. Love's work. Kind of the opposite schedule from my mom and me.

A chime sounded from Kelvin's pocket, and he groaned.

"Is something else the matter?" I asked.

"Ever since I gave Haley my email, she's been sending me stuff. My phone keeps dinging."

"What's she emailing?"

"All kinds of questions. How to store a corsage. What color flowers go well with her hair."

I placed a hand on my hip. "You know, I think Little Miss has a crush on you."

His mouth dropped open. "What should I do?"

"Ignore her. She'll tire of it."

Another chime sounded. "I need to turn off my notifications."

"What's she asking now?"

Kelvin peeked at the message. "Wants to know what I thought of her speech."

"Did you do your late-night reading assignment?"

"No," he said. "Went straight to bed."

"You didn't miss much, according to Jada. Now if only we had Miles' speech on that doc. I heard it was excit—"

Mom walked from the back kitchen into the main shop area. "Kelvin," she said. "I thought I heard your voice."

He dipped his head to her in respect. "Mrs. Jin, always good to see you. And I love your new hairdo."

"Why, thank you, Kelvin." Mom preened a little. Her hairstylist had recently convinced her to add curtain bangs, and she still felt self-conscious but proud of them. While Mom went to the same hair person on a regular basis to maintain a consistent soft black tone to her strands as well as explore new haircuts, I went once a year. To chop off the dead ends and do a no-nonsense blunt cut of my long hair.

Mom added, "What are you two looking at on the phone?"

I didn't want to get into Kelvin's tagalong and her messages, so I skirted the truth. "Fiddling with an online document," I said.

Mom pointed next door. "If you're having problems, talk to Alma. She's a whiz at those things."

Although my godmother helped us with everything tech-related, even I didn't think she could pull up a speech out of thin air.

"Sure, Mrs. Jin," Kelvin said with his usual air of deference. I also nodded along.

"I haven't seen you at the house lately," Mom said. "We should have a trio dinner again."

The three of us ate together on a regular basis, and I cooked a one-pot meal for the occasion. "That would be nice," I said. One day, if childhood dreams really did come true, I wanted to expand the guest list and add my dad. My mind started formulating a family reunion fantasy, but then a shrill sound broke the silence.

Kelvin's phone was vibrating and ringing in his hand.

I lowered my voice, hoping Mom couldn't hear. "Did Haley get your number somehow?"

How had she done that? But when Kelvin picked up the call, he said, "Dad?" And his expression turned grim. "You're where? The police station?"

CHAPTER 13

Kelvin paced around our bakery, his Doc Martens scuffing up our polished wood floorboards. "Did the cops pull you over?" he asked on the phone.

"Without a suitable reason" was the added subtext. Mr. Love drove a sleek Jaguar, which a few law enforcement officers couldn't quite believe was his, but the local cops were familiar with him as an upstanding Pixie citizen.

"Was he driving around Fresno?" I asked, but Kelvin put up a hand to silence me.

"You agreed to go in," he said over the phone. "Why?"

I left my best friend to wander over to a side wall. Our interior walls were painted a golden yellow to match the exterior. They evoked more cheer than our previous white walls, but I thought we could hang some prints to spruce up the space. Maybe some enticing close-up photos of our baked goods?

The scuffling of shoes stopped. Kelvin must have finished his conversation. I turned around to face him. He was staring at the floor.

"Don't worry about the marks," I joked.

"Huh?" He looked up at me.

"Never mind. What's going on with your dad?"

Kelvin wrung his hands. "Figured out why he was wearing a suit this morning. He was asked to visit the station. By Detective Sun."

I tucked a strand of hair behind my ear. "Is this about the murder case? But he wasn't even there at the wedding."

"She wanted to talk to him about his work. What things he did, programs he ran, stuff he volunteers for."

"Why?"

"I'm not sure," Kelvin said, "but she started asking questions about me. At that point, he shut down the questioning."

"Good for him." Was Detective Sun trying to get to Kelvin by going through his father? What a roundabout way. I'd have thought she'd know better than to continue to believe my best friend was a suspect. Though that murder weapon didn't do him any favors.

"Maybe she's trying to work all the angles?" Kelvin always gave people the benefit of the doubt.

"Nonsense," I said, shaking my head for emphasis. "You're no killer."

My mom gave a sharp gasp, and I belatedly realized she was standing behind the counter. "You said some-one died at the wedding, but I thought it was of natural causes."

No. Miles' life had been cut short. Literally. "Guess not," I said, trying to soften the news. "That's probably why Detective Sun is on the case."

The mention of her name cheered my mom up. "Don't forget, you should bring her a housewarming gift. I'll find out where she lives." With Mom's small-town connections, I'd probably get the detective's new address within hours, if not minutes.

"Of course, Mom. Get me her contact info, and I'll drop something off." I couldn't deny my mom. Besides, I'd be able to pick Detective Sun's brain and maybe get her to swerve off the path leading to Kelvin.

Understanding I had an ulterior motive to being a good neighbor, Kelvin said, "Thanks, Lissa." He pulled me into a warm hug. Usually his strong arms created a protective cocoon around me, but this time, I squeezed back, hoping to give *him* some comfort.

He held me for a long moment, then sighed. "Guess I better get back to work. Staying busy will help."

Kelvin's dad also lived by that motto.

"I'll check on you later, okay?"

He gave me a weak smile, and I worried about my friend.

Despite my intentions, I didn't get a free moment until late afternoon. A couple hours before closing, we finally had a lull in traffic. My mom and I had been running back and forth from the kitchen to the register, depending on who needed to be baking, to restock supplies.

I now had an extra tray of fortune cookies at the ready, and Mom had about two dozen egg tarts and pineapple buns available for sale.

"What a rush of customers." I wiped pretend sweat from my brow.

"Satisfying people's souls will never get tiring," Mom declared.

Nevertheless, I offered her the seat by the register to rest on. "Do you think maybe I could drop by Kelvin's for a minute?" I asked.

Mom pulled out her pocket watch and checked it. She didn't like anything on her wrists while baking, but she appreciated a portable way to keep track of time. "You know what? Why don't you take off for the day?"

"I don't think Kelvin's feeling that bad . . ."

Mom pulled out a slip of paper from her pocket and handed it to me. She'd written an address down. "That's Detective Sun's new place. After you chat with Kelvin, you can visit her—with an appropriate gift."

Right. I'd promised to welcome the detective to our community.

"Do you think you'll need my Corolla?" Mom had just fixed it, so the car was finally reliable, but it wouldn't take me more than twenty minutes to walk to Pixie Park's environs.

"It's still light out. Should be fine, Mom."

She glanced out the window at the bright sun and nodded.

Pixie didn't have a high crime rate, but I think she felt better about me walking in the daytime. Especially with the recent happenings.

"Kelvin could go with you," she said.

I smiled at Mom but knew I wouldn't take her suggestion. How could I talk about Kelvin if he was right there? Besides, he had to work. Assuming he was still in the mood to do so. Guess I'd find out soon enough.

After checking to make sure neither my mom nor the bakery needed anything, I strolled next door. Kelvin was prettying up a display of lilies when I walked in, but there were no customers in sight.

"Feeling okay?" I asked him.

"For now. Honestly, I'm just keeping busy until I can go home and ask Dad some questions. Whenever he gets in."

"I'm going to do a little interrogating of my own," I said. "Of the detective."

As Kelvin watched me, I traveled around his store, my fingers tapping different leaves and petals. The shop had tight pathways because Kelvin liked to put out multiple floral displays to inspire people—and maybe entice them into a splurge buy.

"What are you doing, Lissa?" he finally asked.

"I need to bring a housewarming gift to Detective Sun. What would you recommend?"

He snapped his fingers. "Wait right here." After rummaging in his back room, he returned with a potted orchid in his hands. "From my home greenhouse."

It was a lovely specimen in a vivid purple hue. "I'm sure she'll appreciate it." I tried to pay him for it, but Kelvin glared at me.

"I'm not taking money from you."

"It's a wonder you stay in business," I grumbled but relented. We didn't charge him for pastries, either.

"See what you can find out," he said.

If only I could sway the detective's mind somehow. Lead her to a different suspect. "Wait," I said. "Can you send me that speech doc?"

"Sure." Kelvin pulled out his phone.

After he emailed it to me, I peered at the page. Ignoring Turner's, which I'd seen performed live, I skimmed the rest. Snippets of the intended speeches from each of the other attendants jumped out at me:

Nova: "There is no life without passion!"

Jada: "Colton is a compelling guy."

Easton: "Bet you two are chuffed you're getting married!"

Haley: "Soulmates are fated."

I thanked Kelvin and held the potted plant with care.

While walking over to Detective Sun's new home, I thought about what I'd read of the speeches.

Nothing suspicious in any of them. Unless Nova's line about being passionate extended to a crime of *passion*.

CHAPTER 14

Detective Rylan Sun's new abode was a charming California bungalow with gray wooden siding and a welcoming red front door. I walked up the few steps to the entrance and used the brass knocker to announce my arrival.

I heard her call out "I'm coming" before the door swung wide open.

Her penchant for browns remained the same off-duty, and the detective was dressed in a camel-colored suit. She even had her hair up in the usual tight ponytail. "Felicity," she said. "I wasn't expecting you."

"Surprise." I held out the potted orchid. "And welcome to the neighborhood."

"You don't live near me."

"All Pixians are fellow neighbors, as you'll soon find out."

She beckoned me inside. "Here's my humble place."

I strode right into the living room from the front door and had to dodge a stack of boxes.

"Sorry, I haven't quite settled in yet," she said over her shoulder as she headed toward a cozy kitchen.

It even had a cute breakfast nook with a window. She

put down the orchid on the center of the wooden table and motioned for me to sit on one of the padded benches. "Would you like something to drink? I have tap water. Or coffee."

I declined but said, "This is a really nice home." I admired the space around me with its serene sage walls, exposed wooden beams, and glass kitchen cabinetry.

She slid into the booth opposite me and said, "Double the space as my previous one-bedroom in Fresno, and cheaper, too."

"You should consider working for the Pixie police," I joked. "No commute."

"Well, with all these cases, maybe you *do* need a detective in the local department."

We only had patrol officers in our small town. Not enough crime to justify divisions for burglary, homicide, and the like. Except now, and since she'd opened the line of conversation about recent homicides and possible suspects . . . "You know where I got that orchid from?"

She quirked an eyebrow at me. "Actually, I'm surprised you didn't drop off oranges."

I gave her a wry grin. "Figured I shouldn't repeat myself." I'd already gone the oranges route once before at the police station in an act of contrition for butting into her previous case. "Anyway, this beautiful bloom is courtesy of Kelvin Love. Someone who's nurturing, caring, kind—"

The detective put up her hand. "Are you trying to say that someone who grows stuff can't also kill?"

"Kelvin respects life is what I'm saying. And I don't think he'd stab anyone with a tool of his trade." He wasn't that callous. Or stupid.

In a calm tone, Detective Sun replied, "He has strength enough to penetrate a carotid."

I shuddered. Wasn't that the big artery near the side of the neck?

The detective blinked at me. "Oh. I figured he would've told you what he saw."

I cleared my throat. "Not any specific details. Kelvin is considerate like that."

Detective Sun put her hands, palms up, on the table between us. "I'm gonna be honest with you. I know Kelvin is your best friend, so you're biased. But I can't be. I need to follow all possible leads."

"What about the others at the wedding?" I asked. "Kelvin doesn't even have a tie to Miles."

Her eyes shifted. "You might want to have a chat with him about that."

"What do you mean?"

"He's your best friend. I'm sure he'll tell you soon enough."

Oh, I'd make sure of that. I now planned on going to Kelvin's place after I finished talking with the detective. He never hid anything from me. She must have been mistaken about any sort of connection.

Detective Sun continued speaking. "And you're not the only one emotionally invested in this case. Miles' godparents want closure. They'll both be here to support their son and are also willing to stay in Pixie until everything is over."

Godparents? Son? The detective must be talking about Colton's parents: Mr. Wu and Ms. Hung.

I'd forgotten about the parentals—on both sides of the bride and groom. They'd been at the wedding and could've witnessed something important.

Detective Sun tapped her fingers on the tabletop, and my attention returned to her. "You seem deep in thought," she said. "I hope you're not planning on getting involved again. Because that would be ill-advised."

"Understood," I said to the detective. And it was. I got that my own investigation wouldn't be the wisest choice. But prudence went out the window if it meant she was continuing to keep Kelvin in her line of sight.

After sending my mom's well wishes to the detective, I practically sprinted out the door. I needed to find out what the cop had been alluding to about Kelvin before I planned my next steps.

As I got to Kelvin's house, I caught a glimpse of Mr. Love taking off in his Jaguar. I hoped Kelvin had been able to glean more info from his dad about the police station visit.

I rang the doorbell of the Loves' ranch house, which was painted a pretty aquamarine, as though we were steps from the ocean instead of being a land-locked town.

"We need to talk," I said once Kelvin opened the door.

"Don't I know it." He gestured to the side gate. "Meet in the back?"

In his calming oasis. We typically met in the lush yard. I rarely stepped foot inside the house, though I knew it had vintage popcorn ceilings and shag carpeting.

"Have you eaten yet?" Kelvin asked, and I noticed the bowl in his hand. Umami-scented steam rose in the air.

"No, and who cooked?" I asked.

Honestly, I didn't trust Kelvin at the stove. He had a utilitarian perspective on eating. As long as it filled his stomach, he seemed content. "It's my dad's stew."

"Then I'll have a large heaping."

He acted offended, but complied.

In the meantime, I wound my way over to the side gate and opened the latch. Like many Pixie residents, the Loves left their gates unlocked. Most Pixians didn't bother to bolt their doors, either.

Kelvin had turned on the patio lights, a string of glass bulbs hanging from the eaves of the house and secured to the wooden fence that marked the perimeter of the yard. It gave a firefly-like ambiance to his captivating garden. If I didn't know better, I would've thought fairies had planted the flowers around me. The plants always thrived in Kelvin's yard, with their abundance of greenery and soft petals. He also frequently supplied his shop with a number of truly locally sourced bouquets from his backyard garden.

The patio door to the back slid open, and Kelvin carried out two bowls of stew. "The swing?" he asked.

Not like there was anywhere else to sit. Kelvin wanted to maximize the yard area for growing. The small concession to human comfort was a bench swing on a narrow wooden deck; it featured a dark brown wicker back and tan upholstered cushions.

Once I had settled in, he handed me my bowl. Chunks of carrots and potatoes bobbed at me from the gravy. A sprinkle of parsley leaves decorated the top. And I noticed that it was laid on a bed of white rice. I didn't wait for Kelvin to sit beside me as I dug into it.

Mmm. Dr. Ansel Love had mastered not only surgery but stew as well.

"Glad you like it," Kelvin said as he sat down with

care so he didn't rock the swing. "My mom was the one who said to pair it with Nishiki rice. Dad used to eat it with mashed potatoes before he met her."

It was a sweet homage to his mom, and I'd always appreciated the tender love between his parents. It made me believe in romance and happy partnerships.

I let myself savor another bite of stew before I went into business mode. "You know, when I was over at Detective Sun's house, she seemed to imply you had a connection to Miles. Do you?"

He pushed his spoon around the bowl, rearranging the ingredients. "Sort of."

"You could've mentioned this before." I might have swung the bench in my irritation, because Kelvin wobbled a bit.

"I just found out tonight. From my dad."

I steadied the porch swing and turned to face Kelvin.

"I swear, I didn't know before." His brown eyes were opened wide in earnestness. "Turns out my dad had been in charge of a certain internship."

I snapped my fingers in remembrance. "The Fresno hospital." Hadn't Nova mentioned that on our burger run?

"But so what?" I continued. "Shouldn't that help your cause? I'm sure your dad was kind to Miles."

"Not exactly." Kelvin's gaze flitted to his house, even though it was dark and silent inside.

"Spill it. I don't think your house is going to tell your dad what we're about to say." Unless he had some sort of smart speaker device.

"Dad was rough on Miles. Even booted him out of the program."

"Wouldn't that mean that your dad is more of a suspect than you? Which is far-fetched."

He shrugged. "Maybe the detective thinks I'd hurt someone who'd messed with my dad."

Not wrong there. Kelvin would never resort to violence, but he definitely made sure to be there for his family and friends.

I finished my bowl of stew. "Still, the timing is off. The internship was when?"

"Last year."

"Why wait until now for your 'act of revenge'?"

Kelvin gripped his bowl tighter. "Dad's currently up for a promotion . . . and this internship drama halted his chance of advancement."

"I don't know why there'd be drama. Didn't Nova say Miles fainted at the sight of blood? He probably wasn't qualified to continue."

My best friend nudged the wooden deck with the toe of his shoe. "But Miles filed a formal complaint."

"What do you mean?"

He kicked his Doc Marten against the floorboard and rocked us backward. I didn't reprimand him. "Miles told the staff that he got cut unfairly. Because my dad had targeted him."

"Your dad? No way."

Kelvin shook his head. "The hospital must have believed Miles. They asked my dad to no longer be involved with the program."

"Geez, I'm sorry."

"My dad mentioned something about feeling stressed last year, but I didn't know why. I should've pressed him harder then."

I put a hand on Kelvin's shoulder. "How could you have known?"

Although Detective Sun certainly seemed to think

Kelvin knew a lot about it. This must have been the connection she'd hinted at during our conversation. When she'd unfortunately shared details about the method of the murder. And who better than a surgeon's son to know to stab the carotid artery for a fatal blow?

CHAPTER 15

Mom must have heard me approaching because once I let myself into the apartment, she stood facing me. She seemed out of sorts, and I felt guilt washing over me.

"Sorry, I'm a little late," I said. "Dropped by Kelvin's on the way back."

Mom repeated my words slowly. "You were at Kelvin's, huh?"

"That's right."

"Were you there to thank him for the flowers?"

I stifled my automatic response of "What flowers?" and peeked over her shoulder. Our tiny apartment allowed me to glance at the kitchen counter, where a generous bouquet lay, wrapped in cellophane. Kelvin didn't use the clear wrap and preferred more quaint methods of decoration, like brown kraft paper.

Mom continued to wait for my response, and I dodged the truth. "Oh, you know Kelvin and his green thumb. He even invited me into the yard, where I could admire his flowers."

Even though the timing didn't really work, Mom seemed relieved. Kelvin couldn't have sprinted over here to give me a bouquet after my admiration, and I doubted he'd dropped off flowers when he knew I'd be gone at the detective's house. But something about Kelvin's penchant for growing blooms created an acceptable answer in my mom's mind.

"Well, he must have forgotten then," she said. "That I don't like lilies."

"Um, yeah. I'll be sure to take care of them." I led my mom over to her favorite recliner and had her sit down.

"Speaking of flowers," I said, "I gave Detective Sun one of Kelvin's beautiful orchids."

"No oranges?" Mom asked.

"Maybe some other day. She has a lovely rental." I described the cute bungalow home.

"I'll go with you next time and bring the oranges," Mom said. Her lucky fruit. "I wonder if she'll have a housewarming party."

Honestly, it was kind of a Pixie tradition, but I wasn't sure if the detective was well-versed in our community ways. Once a new resident moved in and was showered with attention and gifts, they were expected to return the courtesy by hosting a tiny gathering for neighbors and friends.

Mom kept talking and seemed back to normal. "She wouldn't have to do everything herself. We could help supply the food at least. Your fortune cookies would be a huge hit, and you could customize them to read 'Thanks for coming to my housewarming.'"

I held my hands in front of her. "Wait a minute, Mom. I think you're getting ahead of yourself. I'm not sure the detective is even considering a party."

"Well, you could offer our help to her . . ."

Right. I was probably the last person Detective Sun wanted to hang out with. But I did like Mom's elaborate vision for a gathering. Those customized fortune cookies would be amazing, and people would really respond to being personally messaged.

Which gave me a brilliant idea on how to finally use my fortune cookies in a sly way. Maybe it was the loose tie between the detective, a party, and fortune cookies, but I got to thinking about a way to get more info from the wedding attendants. What if I gave them prearranged messages via my fortune cookies? I didn't even need to use my real prediction powers, which required direct physical contact and receiving a vision to work. Instead, I just needed to think of the right phrase, so I could mine their reactions for underlying guilt.

In my happy place in the back kitchen of Jin Bakery, I worked on my signature recipe. I figured I shouldn't get too fancy. The classic folded vanilla cookie would do the trick. I hoped.

I scooped some flour and evaluated my intended message again. It'd taken me a lot of brainstorming the night before to create a philosophical message that might induce someone to confess. I'd come up with: "The burden of an unrepentant heart is immeasurable." Seemed pointed enough to result in a clear response.

As I created these special fortune cookies, I found myself murmuring under my breath. Mom thought music or sound influenced our baked goods. She always hummed while baking, and my grandma used to sing while maneuvering in the kitchen.

I baked in small batches, two or three at a time, because the cookies cooled down fast, and I needed to fold them by hand. I'd thought about using a machine, but Mom insisted that the magic flowed into our creations through our loving touch and handcrafting of the goods.

I'd complete all four of the cookies in short time. I recalled their names in my head: Turner, Nova, Easton, and Haley. And there was Jada . . . Should I leave her out? She'd already indicated that she hated fortune cookie messages.

Although perhaps she'd enjoy a freshly baked cookie. I'd save hers for last, for the end of the day, right before I delivered them to the inn. Though if she did eat my cookie and we touched, her fortune would still bubble up inside me. I didn't employ the prediction side of my talent all that often—it'd be too suspicious—but once in a while, I'd help predict a lotto winner or a love connection.

I knew the restrictions of my power. It only seemed to work on strangers, not people close to me (I'd tried before on my mom and Kelvin). Also, unlike my happiness-inducing magic, prognostication was a one-and-done deal. I could only predict someone's fate a single time.

My mom tapped my shoulder. I'd forgotten she was in the kitchen with me. We worked at separate stainless steel tables in the middle of the space so we wouldn't get in each other's way. "Did you want to put something in the oven? It's preheated now."

We had a massive industrial unit near the back wall. "On it," I said, finishing making the thin golden discs from the batter.

Mom and I continued to work in baking harmony right up to opening time. We carried our trays of goods out to the front together and slid pastries into the glass display case.

Glancing at her pocket watch, Mom said, "It's time, and let's keep the door open." She'd gotten it into her head that if she kept the entrance to the bakery open, people would smell the enticing fragrance of our treats and come in.

I didn't notice any substantial increase in our traffic yet, but who knew? Walking around the counter, I swung open the door and put the stopper in place to keep it from closing.

It'd be one less barrier for someone interested in a morning treat. However, the only person I saw strolling toward the cul-de-sac at this early hour was my godmother.

I called out a hello, and Mom bustled over to my side.

She added her own greeting and said, "Alma, it's been a long time. How are things going?"

They exchanged pleasantries and swapped business details.

Then my mom turned to me. "Go ahead and ask her, Felicity."

I gave Mom a blank stare.

"That thing you wanted to know the other day. You and Kelvin were trying to figure it out." She prompted me. "On his phone?"

Ah, right. The wedding speeches. Mom had me cornered because Kelvin and I had agreed in front of her to reach out to my godmother. I turned to Alma, who did look very knowing with her silver braided bun and mysterious flowing caftan. "It was an online doc," I said. "Some information got accidentally deleted."

She cocked her head at me. "Online, you say? It should capture the saves. Did you check its history?"

"Its what?" She'd have to spell things out for me.

"The document's version history," Alma said.

I nodded like I knew what she was saying. "Got it. Kelvin and I will take a look at that later."

She maintained eye contact with me. "I'm always happy to help you with whatever you need in life."

"Thank you," I said with sincerity. Alma had always

been there for me, like a second mother with her loving (and inscrutable) ways.

"Today's preparation determines tomorrow's achievement," she added.

Another enigmatic saying from my godmother. Well, I sure hoped that today's fortune cookie prep translated to my success this evening.

CHAPTER 16

That evening, when I walked out of Jin Bakery carrying the fortune cookies in individual wax paper bags with the personalized, printed messages, Kelvin blocked my path.

He held a single black rose. "Lissa, I need your help."

"What's with the funereal flower?"

"It's a breakup rose," he said.

"For . . . ?"

"I mean, not us, clearly." He hid the flower behind his back. "Not like we're together. Er, in that way."

Kelvin was kinda cute when he got all flustered. But I'd better calm him down, get him on to familiar territory. "I didn't even know you could grow black flowers."

"You can't," he said, his sense of ease returning as he talked about his favorite topic. "They have to be dyed black. There are dark rose varieties, but never quite this unnatural color."

"Let me see it again."

He held out the flower for my inspection. Jet black.

"And you're giving it to?"

"Haley," he said. "I turned off my notifications, but

didn't have the heart to actually block her emails. Figured I'd chat with her and get rid of the misunderstanding."

I touched one of the black petals. Still amazingly soft. "Hate to break it to you," I said, "but giving a gal flowers is not usually a sign of ending things."

He jutted his chin out. "But it's black. The symbolism." An association with death and dying, I bet. Kelvin was really into conveying meaningful messages through his bouquets.

Which reminded me. "You didn't happen to drop off some lilies on our doorstep, right?"

He gave me a strange look. "No."

And they weren't just any kind of lilies. They had been stargazers. So I guess I'd have to talk to my dad about dropping unwanted gifts off at our home. Too much, too soon.

For now, though, I focused on the present mission. "Ready to go to Pixie Inn when you are," I told Kelvin. "I brought along some fortune cookies."

"You do?"

In Kelvin's car, I explained my brilliant idea of giving the fortune cookie messages out to the attendants and gauging their guilt based on their responses. "Except for Jada. She doesn't like the sayings, but maybe I can get a custom prediction about her."

"Sounds like a good plan," he said, obviously trying to encourage me.

We soon arrived at Pixie Inn, but when we entered, no one appeared to be around. I only found Mrs. Robson, who greeted me with enthusiasm.

"Always great to see you," I said. "But where are your guests?"

"Holed up in their rooms."

"Oh. Let me see if I remember . . . Leanne and Colton are staying in the Shakespeare Suite."

Kelvin piped up. "Nova and Jada are in the Dickinson Den."

"Yes, that's right. You both get gold stars." Mrs. Robson studied Kelvin. "Did you also go to Pixie Elementary? I don't think you were in my class."

"No, ma'am. I didn't have the pleasure."

Mrs. Robson gave him a warm smile and continued sharing info. "In the inn, we also have Hughes Haven and Plath Place. The gentlemen are in the former, and Haley is in the latter."

I thanked Mrs. Robson for her help and added, "We've brought over treats."

"Well, aren't you two the kindest?" Though I noticed she did a double take upon seeing Kelvin's black rose.

We wandered down the hallway whispering together.

"How should I tackle this?" I asked. "I'd figured I'd run into everyone together in a common space, but I guess not."

"I can approach the guys in their room," Kelvin said. "Might be less awkward that way."

"Great, that will work." And I trusted Kelvin's observational skills.

"But can we see Haley together?" he asked, focused on the black flower in his hand.

"Sure. We'll go together right now. Get it done with."

He breathed a sigh of relief. Walking down the hall, we checked the plaques outside the different rooms until we located Plath Place. The door was closed, so we knocked.

Delicate footsteps sounded, and the door swished open to reveal Haley. She wore her hair in long pigtails and had on a romper patterned with red cherries.

Haley squealed Kelvin's name. "Come on in." Then she noticed me. "Felicity, guess you can join us."

Sure. Thanks for the permission.

Kelvin gestured for me to go in first. Save the best for last, I guess. Or maybe he wanted the option of making a quick getaway after giving his symbolic rose.

I held out a bagged fortune cookie to Haley. "Thought you might enjoy this."

She patted her lean stomach. "I *am* getting hungry." Haley broke open the cookie and nibbled with delicate bites. "You don't know how much I needed this."

It was fascinating how different people ate their cookies. And they all had a certain methodology to how they approached eating a fortune cookie. Haley made sure to savor and finish the whole treat before reading the message.

Confusion spread across her features. "These fortunes are too generic. I never regret anything I do." Really? She had nothing she wanted to repent for?

"I brought something, too," Kelvin said, thrusting the rose in her face.

"You got me a flower?" Haley said it like she'd received a precious gift of jewels. She brought the rose to her nose and sniffed.

"I did it"—Kelvin rubbed the back of his neck—"because I'd, um, appreciate fewer emails from you."

"I had to make sure I got your attention," she said.

"Well, you did . . ."

Moving closer to Kelvin, she continued, "To let you know that I'm into you."

"The thing is, er—" All of a sudden, he sidestepped toward me and slung his arm around my waist. "Felicity and I are together."

I tried not to react in shock.

Haley pivoted to me, and her green eyes narrowed. "I thought you said you two weren't an item?"

"It was rather sudden," I said. Like about a minute ago.

She shook her head, in disbelief. "Wow, I could've sworn Kelvin was my soulmate."

"How'd you figure that?" I asked. "Didn't you just meet him?"

"But he had the potential," Haley said. "His physique, that captivating voice . . ." She spoke as if he wasn't in the room.

I felt Kelvin freeze by my side.

"I could be wrong," I said. "But don't soulmates share a special connection? Wouldn't they have to know each other first?"

Haley sighed. "Maybe. Like Leanne and Colton. I wish I had what they do."

"One day, I hope you will." I wasn't sure if it was my encouraging words or that my fortune cookie had finally kicked in, but she seemed more content at the moment.

"Thank you. And I've never gotten a black flower before." She placed it on top of a spindly antique writing desk near a bunk bed.

Kelvin loosened his grip around my waist. "Yeah, it's also known as a breaku—"

I spoke over him because now was not the time to rub it in. "What's with the bunk bed?"

Both mattresses appeared to have been slept in recently. Did she alternate sleeping on top and bottom?

"Miles had the top, and I had the bottom," she said.

I glanced around Plath Place, taking in my surroundings. The walls were painted a dark blue all around, and one side had a mural of a large, empty glass bell jar.

"Did you say Miles was staying here as well?" I'd

forgotten that fact. I wondered if there were clues still to be found in the room. "Mind if I take a look?"

That fortune cookie must have really kicked in. Or maybe Haley was a go-with-the-flow kind of gal because she said, "Be my guest."

CHAPTER 17

"What am I exactly supposed to be looking for here?" Kelvin asked as he surveyed the top bunk.

"A clue," I said.

"Right. I'll just look for the clearly marked label then."

I didn't even offer a strained chuckle in response to his dry wit. "Anyway, you're taller than me." If I had to search the contents of the top bed, it would mean climbing up the flimsy ladder and scrambling over the railing. No thank you.

Kelvin grunted but used his height to his advantage. He searched through the rumpled sheets, while I took the low ground. I'd circled the room twice and found nothing interesting when Kelvin also concluded the same.

I figured the police had come visiting as well. Who was I to think they'd leave a clue behind?

"Thanks for letting us search," I said to Haley.

"Sure thing."

Kelvin moved to follow me out the door and skirted around the luggage rack with Haley's raspberry-colored roller bag.

I halted in my steps and gazed around the room. Only one bag in sight. "Where's Miles' luggage?" I asked.

"The police checked it out before letting Ms. Hung pick it up."

Miles' godmother and Colton's mom. "Did she come over recently?" I asked.

Haley twirled the end of one of her pigtails. "Yeah, but she's here every day."

"Really?"

"Sure. Eleven in the morning on the dot. To check on Colton. And then she goes and works remotely in that local coffee shop all afternoon."

I knew the place. The Pixie Coffee Spot. It served daytime clientele and closed at four. Maybe I could go there tomorrow on my lunch break. It'd be helpful to chat with Ms. Hung since she'd been on site as a witness and might know if Miles had had a recent falling out with anyone.

Kelvin and I bid goodbye to Haley and moved down the hall.

"Should we split up now?" he said. "I'll get Turner and Easton, and you handle Nova and Jada."

I handed over two fortune cookies with pre-printed messages. "Meet back in the lobby in twenty minutes?"

He gave me a thumbs-up and went in search of Hughes Haven. I remembered the location of Dickinson Den from the other day and moved that way.

I knocked on it, and Nova opened the door.

"I'm here with treats," I said, and she let me into the lovely yellow room with its charming literary vibe.

I pulled out the bag with the plain fortune sans message but then realized something. "Is Jada not around?"

"She wanted some fresh air, stepped out back," Nova said.

I put away the hollow cookie and held out the one with

the message to Nova. She grabbed it, and I couldn't help but admire her toned biceps, highlighted by her tank top. Baking required some hefty mixing, but my arms sure didn't look like that.

"Have a seat," Nova said as she settled on the queen bed in the room.

Most of the space was taken over by a huge glass cabinet filled with ancient, typewritten manuscripts, so I perched on the velvet, bench-like ottoman at the foot of the bed.

"How's it going?" I asked, but she couldn't answer since she'd already started in on her fortune cookie.

She was crunching away and barely managed to pull out the slip of paper. Nova had eaten about three-quarters of the cookie when she paused to read the fortune. Suddenly, she started to choke, and I whacked her back on instinct.

Nova sprang up and twisted away. "Don't touch me," she hissed.

"Sorry, I only wanted to help." I noticed her dilated pupils.

"This message," she said. "Have you *also* been snooping on me?"

"Whoa. What? No." I stumbled back a step.

"It's just a generic fortune," I added. "See, it's pre-written." Thank goodness I'd decided on printing instead of handwriting the messages.

"Oh yeah." Nova sat back down, appeased. Suddenly, she noticed my shocked state. "You okay there?"

Not really. "I'm fine," I lied. "Want to talk about what got you riled up?"

She waved her hand in the air. "Something from a long time ago. It's over now."

I mulled over the previous words she'd said out

loud in anger. "Did you say to me, 'Have you also been snooping?' Has someone been checking into your history?"

She rubbed her hands on her jeans in a repetitive motion. "Don't want to speak ill of the dead, but Miles was always trying to one-up people. Mostly by taking others down a notch."

Interesting. It made me think of his missing speech. Perhaps he'd written down something incriminating. Something that had led to its deletion . . . and maybe to his death?

After getting directions to the backyard from Nova, I stepped outside into the warm sunshine. A slight breeze blew, and the scent of jasmine floated in the air. Green hedges rounded the perimeter of the back space, but the most coveted spot appeared to be the daybed where Jada was lying.

The bed had four posts with an attached gauzy canopy. The sheer curtains shifted in the soft wind. The daybed was located in the exact center of the outdoor space, most of which was taken up by lush green grass except for the cobblestone path I was standing on.

I strolled over. Happily, Mrs. Robson had positioned two sun loungers there as well. I leaned back in one of the cream cushioned recliners near Jada. Her usual green glasses were resting on a teakwood table between the loungers, and she wore dark sunglasses while soaking up the last of the sun's rays.

"Hello?" I said, not sure if she was napping or just so relaxed she hadn't moved when I'd plopped down.

She mumbled drowsily and sat up. Jada slid the sunglasses down her nose and squinted at me. "Felicity?"

"Hi again. I'm back so you don't need to take a trip to the bakery. I brought you a fortune cookie."

She started scrunching her nose, but I headed off her protests with "I remember what you said. No fortunes in this one. Just a freshly baked cookie."

Jada placed her sunglasses on top of her head. Then reached out to me with her right hand. Our fingers touched as I deposited the fortune cookie bag into her open palm. I'd discovered that my magical fortune-telling worked only if I made physical contact with the recipient.

As she brought the fortune cookie to her mouth, I prepared myself for the magic to happen. I no longer experienced waves of dizziness or nausea, like when I'd first become aware of my gift. No alarming buzzing or ringing of my ears either. Instead, I focused on the beautiful display of colored lines covering my vision.

After much trial and error, I'd already mapped out which hue corresponded to what type of fortune. I figured I'd choose orange this time around, a color associated with predictions about relationships. That might cover the network of wedding connections.

As I reached for the color in my mind, I noticed it shimmering. This hadn't happened before. I studied the orange color, and there seemed to be multiple shades of orange before me. A darker shade closest to me, receding to the lightest hue farthest away. I'd always grabbed at the spot nearest me, but now I used my mental strength to reach for something in the middle distance. It wasn't the part of the orange line from super-far away, but a little more distant than my usual spot. I plucked it.

While peripherally aware of Jada chomping away with appreciation, I also found a message starting to come to me. Usually, I carried around pen and paper to write it down. People appreciated my personalized messages, but since Jada didn't believe in fortunes, I couldn't gift her with one. And I thought it'd be mighty odd to reach in my pocket and start scribbling, so I concentrated on keeping the words in my head. Once the sentence had formed, as though written in the air before me, I memorized it.

Jada finished eating, and leaned toward me. "You okay there, Felicity? Got too much sun?"

I did feel out of sorts, but it wasn't because of the sunshine. "No, I'm all right. How are you?"

We spent a few moments chitchatting, but I didn't get any updates beyond how she felt trapped at the inn. But she was trying to keep up appearances for Leanne's sake.

I nodded my assent in all the right places, and Jada concluded by muttering, "I really wish I could take her away from all this trouble."

"Yeah, I'm sure she'd rather be enjoying her honeymoon right now."

A deep emotion flashed in Jada's eyes, but I couldn't figure out the feeling before she slipped her sunglasses on. "Speaking of enjoying, I'm going to get all the light I can before the sun sets."

Good thing it didn't turn dark until later. She could continue relaxing for a while. And avoiding my questions.

Retracing my steps on the cobblestone path, I raced inside Pixie Inn. I rushed down the hallway to reconnect with Kelvin. Was I late? How much time had passed already?

I ran smack into him as he came out of Hughes Haven, where a whiff of competing colognes leaked out.

Kelvin steadied me as I wobbled. "Why the rush?"

"Didn't want to keep you waiting. And let me tell you Jada's fortune before I forget it." I'd continued to recite it in my head as I raced back inside.

He pulled out his phone and clicked on an app to record me as the message spilled out: "You will feel betrayed when your closest friend reveals the secret relationship she's hidden from you."

CHAPTER 18

Kelvin and I decided to mull over my prediction in the picturesque great room of Pixie Inn. At this hour, the fireplace gave off a golden glow and languorous heat. We scooted the massive armchairs to face each other and settled in to analyze my personalized message for Jada.

"She's going to be betrayed by her closest friend. Do you think that's Leanne?" I asked Kelvin.

"Could be. Although I'm your best friend, but I'm definitely not your roomie."

"I get what you're saying," I said. That honor went to my mom. "Could the close friend be someone besides Leanne?"

Kelvin said, "And what's all that stuff about a secret relationship?"

"Beats me. Guess we'll have to wait it out." I stared at the flickering fire, willing for time to move faster, for the log to burn down quicker.

"How long does it take before your predictions come true?" Kelvin asked.

"It's pretty quick." I remembered when a customer found a windfall on the ground shortly after sending him off with a fortune cookie. "Within half an hour."

"I've got extra time to relax right now," he said, stretching out his long legs.

It was a lovely space. I surveyed the mantel, which held silver-framed pictures of Mrs. Robson and her family in different locations. I recognized one as a shot taken in front of Yosemite's Half Dome. I swiveled my gaze back to Kelvin, who seemed on the verge of falling asleep in his armchair.

To keep him awake and to help pursue more leads, I said, "Tell me what happened with Turner and Easton."

He stifled a yawn. "They share a cool room. Twin beds on opposite sides of the room separated by a desk with an antique typewriter on it. Easton was lying down, and Turner was pacing around."

"So, what'd you do?"

"Handed them both cookies. Turner had already spotted me with the treats."

"And their reactions?"

He shook his head. "I couldn't gauge Easton's, because Turner started putting on a show."

"Excuse me?" I pictured the man of honor shimmying across the floor.

"It's Hughes Haven, right?" He continued at my nod. "Well, there's a whole wall filled with the text from 'Harlem'—you know the poem?"

I racked my brain. "Sorry, didn't graduate from UC Merced like you."

"It's also known as 'A Dream Deferred.'"

"The one about a raisin in the sun?" I did take English Lit in high school.

"That's right. Anyway, Turner started spouting lines from it. He must have been so bored these past few days that he'd memorized the whole thing. I tried peeking over at Easton, but it's hard to figure out someone's reaction when they're lying down."

"What about Turner? I'm assuming he eventually ate the cookie?"

"Well, he cracked it open. Tossed the cookie aside but read the message. Snorted and said something along the lines of 'Don't I know it.'"

Ah, he was one of *those* customers. We had a few people come in who could care less about the cookie part. They bought my signature treat for the interesting message they'd find inside.

"Did Turner elaborate?" I asked as I fidgeted in the massive gilded chair, trying to find a comfortable position. Although a large portion of the chair was covered in velvet, the frame was made of thick wood.

"Nope, but he did rope me into rating his performance. Wanted my 'assessment of the oratory techniques'—his words, not mine." His lips quirked. "B+, in case you're wondering. Solidly overacted."

"Looks like we got a bunch of nothing from them," I concluded and glanced out the window at the darkening sky. "Hey, what time is it? Been half an hour yet?"

Kelvin checked the time. "It has."

I cocked my ear toward the rooms. No screaming or yelling. "Why isn't Jada reacting?"

"We can check in on her before we take off for the night."

I led Kelvin to the cobblestone path.

Jada was sitting up in the daybed, rubbing her eyes.

I approached her and said, "Everything okay?"

"Peachy," she said, stretching her arms above her head. "I really needed that nap."

How could she have fallen asleep when she realized

she'd been betrayed? "Glad you got your rest. Let me know if you need anything." Or want to tell me any secrets.

"You're too generous." She put on her eyeglasses and smiled at Kelvin. "You as well. Caring about us, checking in and bringing food."

At least we'd made a good impression on Jada. And, hopefully, with the rest of the wedding party. Still, I thought her reaction didn't quite fit the fortune I'd received about her. Could something be off with my magic?

If there was, I knew who I could turn to as a reliable source of wisdom. "I need to go home," I said. To his credit, Kelvin followed my directions and marched straight to the car.

He must have sensed my rising tension, because on the drive back he tried to get my mind off things by asking about my morning. I humored him, chatting about Mom: how she wanted to leave the bakery door open to lure in customers, how she'd put me on the spot with Alma about the online document.

Before I knew it, we were at my apartment. I thanked him for the ride and rushed in . . . to seek Whiskers' guidance.

The bunny would have the answers to my questions. Even though Mom knew about Whiskers' powers, I still wanted to talk to the rabbit alone. The living room was already dark, so maybe Mom had retreated to her bedroom.

I slid the curtain open to my bedroom area and carried Whiskers into my private realm. Honestly, there wasn't much furniture beyond my twin bed and a scuffed-up bureau, but I liked having my own defined space.

Sitting on the bed, I held Whiskers in my lap. "Is there something off with my magic?" I asked her.

She tilted her head as though concentrating on my words.

"Show me," I said as I started petting her. It was the motion of stroking her velvet fur that often led me to revelations.

It didn't take long before the images rushed at me. Whiskers worked by using my own memories to provide me with answers. There was a montage of selected predictions I'd made ever since I began crafting my fortunes. Thankfully, she'd chosen all the positive ones. Each prediction of mine had come true, and all my prognostications had occurred after the visual display of rainbow colors.

I stopped petting Whiskers. "Does this mean that everything is okay? If so, what happened with Jada today?"

She head-butted my hand, and I responded by caressing her soft fur once again.

A flashback came of the scene with Jada in the yard of Pixie Inn. An orange line swam before my eyes, and I remembered that there had been nuances in the color. I'd deliberately picked a lighter orange farther away from me. Did certain shades change the meaning of my fortune?

"Does the intensity of the color affect the prediction?" I asked Whiskers. I'd chosen a faded orange. "Does it make the fortune more or less true, depending on what hue I choose?" Perhaps the faintness meant that it wasn't as solid of a prediction.

I waited for the answer from Whiskers, but she didn't say or do anything. She didn't nod at me to confirm my theory. Instead, she sat there in my lap, staring at me with those Hershey's eyes. So no answer. At least not right now.

I let her go, and she hopped away from me. Best to get a good night's rest. I often found that sleep revived my mind and energy. It also gave me new hope. Maybe the answer would come knocking in the morning.

CHAPTER 19

It wasn't an answer that came knocking the next day. Instead, I found Kelvin on my doorstep in the early morning hours.

"What are you doing here?" I asked. Mom and I were about to head over to the bakery and start preparations.

"I needed to show you this." He waved his phone in my face.

"It's not a funny cat video again, is it?"

"Those *are* hilarious," he said, "but no, it's the online doc."

I gave him a blank look. My mind didn't function well in the pitch-black hours.

"The one with the wedding speeches?" he clarified.

"Okay, now I'm following."

"I recovered Miles' speech. Well, after you mentioned Alma's comments."

"Oh yeah, she said something about the version history," I said.

"Uh-huh. I restored the changes. Take a look—"

But Mom's voice floated from behind me. "Felicity, we need to get going."

"Talk as we walk?" I said to Kelvin.

He nodded.

Mom greeted Kelvin warmly and didn't even question his early presence outside our home. Once the three of us began moving, she walked ahead at a brisk pace. Guess she figured she'd grant us some privacy.

"Give me a quick summary?" I asked Kelvin.

"Miles wrote a speech. But he decided to toast not only the bride and groom, but all of the wedding party."

I stifled a yawn. "Hmm, that's nice of him."

"Not if you read what he wrote . . . Miles basically skewered every one of them."

"Ooh, juicy secrets?" I said as we neared downtown Pixie. "Do tell."

"How about Turner's unethical fast fashion? Or Nova's suspended license?"

I stopped short. "She did get pretty mad at the other drivers, even as a passenger."

"Her reaching over me and leaning on the horn—that was wild." And shocking. Good thing Kelvin had remained calm under pressure.

"What else?" I asked.

"Easton's juvie record. Jada's breakup plot. Haley's obsession with Leanne."

"All that in one speech? Geez." We'd reached our cozy cul-de-sac. The jarring content of what I'd heard made my head spin. I couldn't wait to get into the safe comfort of the kitchen. My mom was opening the door to our bakery even now.

"That's not all." Kelvin stepped in my path to stop my movement. "To the bride and groom, he wrote, 'Congrats on tying the knot. Too bad about Leanne's mystery man who she's still pining for.'"

"What kind of wedding toast is that?" I said, rearing back in disgust.

Kelvin cleared his throat. "Actually, it gets worse.

That's the version prior to the last one. The most recent was more shocking."

"Huh?" I peered at the screen.

Kelvin pointed to a specific sentence. The line read: "*I'm* the mystery man Leanne's pining for . . ."

My head whirled some more. Miles had been in a relationship with Leanne? Why was he at the wedding then?

"All these secrets," Kelvin said, "make for good motives."

To murder. "Any one of the wedding party could have wanted Miles to go away . . . permanently."

"Even the bride and groom," he said. Kelvin was right. The confession Miles made would have ruined the wedding.

"Speaking of the groom," I said, "did you want to go to The Pixie Coffee Spot later? To find Colton's mom."

"Excellent choice. Meet you there at noon," he said.

The Pixie Coffee Spot, a local institution, stayed true to its literal name. It had a no-frills atmosphere, heavy on the unvarnished wood furnishings. The only decorations displayed were the large burlap bags the coffee beans came in, slouching in a corner of the shop. A tight space, it only had a few wooden tables with hardback chairs to discourage loitering. It also had a long wooden counter placed against a large glass window with a few simple barstools.

Colton's mom, unaware of the tradition to grab and go her beverage of choice, lingered at the counter with her laptop. Kelvin whispered that he'd put in our order: black coffee for him, chamomile tea for me. At least the coffee shop had finally conceded to adding more beverage choices on the menu. They still, though, refused to stock their own pastries. Not that Mom and I at Jin Bakery minded.

Ms. Hung, just like at the wedding, wore a jumpsuit—but this time around, it didn't feature sequins. It was a simple cream number and sleeveless—smart, given the weather. She'd pulled her hair into a high ponytail and stared through wire-rimmed glasses at her computer.

"Hi," I said, coming over to her spot. "You're Colton's mom, right?"

She peered up, took off her glasses, and put them to the side. "I apologize I'm really bad at faces."

"It's Felicity Jin. I catered the dessert for the wedding. And helped out at the tea ceremony."

She mock-slapped her forehead. "You'd think I remember. Maybe if I had the photos in front of me . . ."

"Of the tea ceremony?" I searched my memory. "Was the photographer around then?"

"Yeah. Took the photos through the window. He specializes in candid and action shots."

The photographer. I wondered if I could track the guy down. But for now, I concentrated on the witness I had in front of me. "How'd you enjoy the wedding?"

"It was nice, except for—" She bit her bottom lip.

"Miles, I know." I adopted a solemn tone. "Sorry for your family's loss."

"My poor godson. A tragedy." She shook her head, and her ponytail swished. "And he's always been misunderstood."

"How so?" I asked.

"Well, he was my brother's last son. Being the youngest of six was hard on Miles. And he was a surprise baby. He was kinda forgotten in the shuffle."

"But not by you," I noted.

"I took him in when he was seventeen. My heartless ex didn't even think to offer Miles a home." She sniffed.

"Gracious of you," I said. Not many people would agree to house an older teen on the verge of adulthood. "And I know you've been visiting Colton every day to check on him, too."

"It's the least I can do for my boy. But"—she glanced at her screen—"I do have to fly back for a work meeting tomorrow."

I heard footsteps coming from behind and turned to find Kelvin with a pair of to-go cups.

"Just curious, Ms. Hung"—I made sure to use her preferred surname—"did you happen to see Miles before the wedding began?"

"Briefly. Earlier that afternoon. Said he wanted to greet my ex. Probably put Miles in a bad mood—not an unusual result with my *was*band. Figured that's why Miles never showed for the tea ceremony." So Colton's dad might have been the last person to see Miles alive.

A shrill ring of her phone. The other customers in the coffee shop gave Ms. Hung disapproving looks as she answered the call and spoke loudly.

Her mouth hung open for a moment. "Yes, I can help break up Jada and Leanne's fight. Be right there."

CHAPTER 20

Kelvin and I followed Ms. Hung to Pixie Inn. The usual picturesque cottage scene was disturbed by an upset Jada rushing out the front door.

I could tell Jada had been crying. Her cheeks appeared splotchy, and she lifted her glasses and rubbed at her eyes.

She wore shapeless gray sweats and had a backpack slung over one shoulder. Where was she off to?

Leanne poked her head out of the inn. "Don't go," she pleaded.

Jada jabbed a finger in her direction. "Why didn't you tell me your mystery man was Miles?"

Leanne spluttered for a moment before replying, "It just didn't seem important."

"Even after I met the guy?"

Jada secured the backpack on both shoulders and started marching down the sidewalk—toward us. Kelvin and I glanced around. We decided to hide behind a broad oak tree to avoid any misdirected anger *and* to continue secretly observing.

On the other hand, Colton's mom chose to step toward the entrance. "Ladies, we can work this out."

Leanne bobbed her head in agreement.

Jada kept on walking. In a few moments, she'd pass by our hiding spot.

"Come back," Ms. Hung commanded. She had the stern voice of authority, someone accustomed to people obeying her every order.

Jada paused on the sidewalk.

Ms. Hung said, "It was me. *I* told Leanne not to make a big deal of it."

"You convinced Leanne to keep things quiet?" Jada said, half turning toward Colton's mom.

Ms. Hung nodded. "Yes, even told her not to tell Colton. It's my philosophy that we should leave our troubled past behind, move onward and upward."

Jada pivoted back the way she'd come, and I noticed the bright orange patch attached to her fabric backpack read "Roomies 4 Eternity." Extreme. Could she have been overly attached to Leanne? Had Jada considered them best of friends?

While I mused, Jada and Ms. Hung retreated inside. The door closed with a solid click of finality, and I found myself alone with Kelvin.

"What drama," he commented under the shade of the tree.

"And betrayal." I paused. "Do you think my fortune cookie message was about Jada and Leanne?"

Kelvin checked his memo app and replayed the recording of my prediction: "You will feel betrayed when your closest friend reveals the secret relationship she's hidden from you." He whistled. "Pretty spot-on."

"But why didn't things happen right away? My fortunes usually work that way."

Kelvin and I discussed the delay on the walk back to

downtown Pixie. Could something have interfered with my fortune-telling? Had I changed my magic by accident?

By the time we reached the cul-de-sac of shops, I had a working theory. "I think it has to do with the color line," I said. "The more faded the shade I choose, the farther away in time the prediction happens."

I'd have to experiment on some of my customers to better understand this new subtlety to my magical predicting power. I wouldn't mind that. I loved spending more time at the bakery.

Except, when I entered the kitchen, I found my mom in a sour mood.

She stood at one of the silver prep tables, but instead of having any baking ingredients before her, there was an open cardboard box with bubble wrap overflowing out of it.

"Did we get some sort of delivery?" I asked.

Mom didn't speak but pointed inside the box.

I went over and shifted the bubble wrap so I could see the contents. We'd received a glass jar of XO sauce. "I don't understand." The spicy, seafood-flavored condiment was generally used in cooking, not baking.

"He must have found me," Mom said with an involuntary shudder.

"Who?"

"Your father."

I felt my face flush, and I didn't make eye contact with her as I said, "Why don't we let bygones be bygones? We can be the bigger person—people?—here, extend forgiveness . . ." And maybe my dad had changed. After all, hadn't he been glad he'd gone to the wedding and found me?

"No way." Mom sprang into motion, shoving the

bubble wrap back into the box and closing the flaps. "Your father is bad news. And I thought I'd covered my tracks so well . . ."

Dad had mentioned that Mom and Grandma had disappeared on him when he'd tried to reconnect. Had they actually fled on purpose? Was Richard Zhou a dangerous man?

What was with the gift then? I gestured at the box. "What's with the sauce?"

Mom sighed. "He used to do it when we were dating. Get me a tiny jar of XO. You know, a kiss and a hug."

Dorky but kind of sweet. "Seems like he's trying to make amends."

"He should've done that way earlier," Mom said. "Instead of stalking me now."

"Excuse me?"

"The stargazer lilies. This jar." She tapped at the label on the box. "Check out the postal code."

I peered at the shipping label. Sent from Pixie.

"He's here, and I don't like it." She drummed her fingers against the steel table.

I cleared my throat. "Is there something I can do? Maybe I could mediate?"

"No, definitely not." She stopped drumming. "I know what. You can go buy some oranges."

"Huh?"

"For Detective Sun. We'll go to her place tonight and get her involved."

"I'm not sure that's a good id—"

"Hello. Anyone here?" A voice came from the front of the bakery.

Mom shooed me out to help the new customer, but I couldn't help glancing back as I exited the kitchen and trudged through the open archway. She stood at the silver table, staring daggers at the cardboard box—and my fantasy of having a family reunion dinner dissolved.

Instead of thinking about the past or the future, I immersed myself in the present. It helped that we had a steady stream of customers. At the end of the day, Sweet Tooth Sally came and swooped up all the goodies in our glass case.

"I'm on the Parks Beautification Committee," she said. "And we'll be doing cleanups, so I've got to feed the crew."

"How often do you beautify the green spaces around town?"

She flashed me her signature happy smile. "Every month. To be equitable, we rotate through the parkettes and Pixie Park."

We only had three grassy areas, and the smaller locations were in the northern and southern parts of Pixie. The larger park stood in the optimal central location. "You really are involved in everything around here," I said, packing up her pastries.

She inclined her head at me. "I try. This town has given so much to me and my family, it's only fair."

Mom slipped out of the kitchen at this point, her bag slung over her shoulder. She really wanted to visit Detective Sun as soon as possible. But she took the time to greet Sally with a hug and said, "Couldn't help overhearing the tail end of your conversation. You know, the mayor's planning on retiring."

"You're not the only one who's mentioned that to me," Sally said.

While I rang up Sally's purchases, I encouraged her. "You should think about running." And I didn't need to write a fortune to predict the certain victory.

"Well, I'll think about it," Sally said and left with a cheery wave.

Mom turned to me. "Ready to go?"

Guess so. We'd sold out of baked goods, but I still dragged my feet as I did the closing tasks. How would Detective Sun receive me this time? Would she be mollified by the presence of my mom? Or upset, intuiting that I was trying to out-sleuth her once I walked through the door?

CHAPTER 21

Detective Sun's new home remained charming the second time around.

"A red front door," my mom commented. "Vibrant, and lucky."

I wondered if the detective had asked for the color. Pixie, in general, did not appreciate things that stood out. We even had an ordinance that the grass on our front lawns had to be trimmed to a certain height.

Detective Sun may even have heard the compliment because the door opened just then, and she welcomed us in.

Mom offered her the housewarming present, an entire bag of Song Hay Double Happiness navel oranges. She wanted to gift the detective with *a lot* of joy and fortune.

The detective thanked my mom, and even gave me a polite nod. "Why don't I cut up some now? Please, have a seat in the breakfast nook."

My mom first peeked at the kitchen, exclaiming in delight at the beautiful cabinets with their clear glass panes. Once she finally took her seat on the padded bench in the cozy dining space, Detective Sun had already sliced the fruit and displayed it in a circular pattern on a blue ceramic plate in the middle of the wooden rustic table, along with two smaller, matching blue plates. I sat down next to Mom.

"How do you like your new home? And Pixie?" my mom asked.

"It's so different from Fresno. Quiet, unhurried. Been a good change."

Mom reached for a few orange slices. She put two on a plate, passed those to me, and then took one for herself. "I used to live in Oakland. And you're right about it being a good change. But there's this reason I moved . . ."

Detective Sun raised her eyebrows at me. I could sense Mom's nervousness, so the cop probably realized this wasn't purely a social visit.

"Go ahead, Mom," I urged.

She fiddled with the orange on her plate and said, "Well, I left because of a difficult person. My ex. He wanted to hurt Felicity."

What? I jerked, slamming my shoulder against the back of the bench. I ignored the pain.

The detective held my mom's gaze. "What do you mean?"

"He wrote a note. Said he thought he would harm the baby"—she pointed at me, and it was weird to think of myself as an infant—"so Ma Ma and I fled."

"And you picked Pixie to live in," Detective Sun finished.

Mom's eyes misted. "It seemed safe. Small. He would never think to come here . . . but now he has. Found us, I mean."

My mom's words were getting garbled, and I placed a calming hand on her shaking knee.

In a stronger voice, she continued, "Can I file a restraining order against him?"

"Let's think this through," Detective Sun said, steepling her hands. "Do you have evidence of any harm? A history?"

Could my father, a high school teacher, be dangerous? He hadn't given me that vibe when we'd met.

My mom concentrated on her orange, pulling the peel away from the flesh. "Truth is, it was only the once."

"You mean the note?" Detective Sun asked.

Mom nodded.

"Do you still have it?"

"I burned it to ashes," Mom said.

"So, no history," the detective said. "And what about now?"

My throat felt dry, and I started in on the oranges on my plate.

Mom detailed receiving the stargazer lilies on our doorstep and the package delivery at the bakery.

"XO sauce?" Detective Sun asked, confused.

"A private joke between us," Mom said. "But it doesn't really matter."

"And you know for sure they're from him?"

"Who else would it be? But I don't have the flowers anymore . . ." Mom glanced over at me.

I quickly swallowed my bite of orange. "Er, I threw them away."

"What about the package?" the detective asked.

"In the trunk of my Corolla." Mom jerked her thumb toward the front door.

"Did it have his name on it?"

"No, but it has the local zip code," Mom said. "Could that be considered evidence of him stalking me?"

"I'm afraid that might be hard to prove," Detective Sun said, staring at the plate of oranges instead of at my mom. "But you could try." Her voice held doubt.

Mom waved her hand in dismissal. "Not worth it if the judge is going to dismiss my concerns."

"There's nothing else you have on him?" Detective Sun asked.

Mom shifted in her seat, while I began eating my second orange slice.

"He's a thief," she said. "Stole my most prized possession."

"Which is?"

"The Jin family recipe book."

I choked on the orange, and Mom thumped me on the back.

Once I could speak, I said, "We have a recipe book?"

She turned toward me. "I didn't want to tell you before. But, yes, all the recipes of past generations are in that book."

My head reeled. So what I'd been taught about our special magic and it having been verbally passed down was . . . a lie? But hadn't my father mentioned something like that, a recipe he'd seen my grandmother checking while making her famed pineapple buns?

Detective Sun pulled out a business card and scribbled something down. "My personal number," she said to my mom, pushing it across the table. "If you see him or find out his current whereabouts, I'll be only a phone call away."

I felt compelled to speak and cleared my throat. "Actually, I saw him already." Not at the diner. I wasn't about to admit that fact easily. "At the Lum-Wu wedding."

My mom's eyes widened while the detective gritted her teeth. "Who is he? What's his name?"

"Richard Zhou," Mom and I said at the same time.

"He was a guest there," I said. "In fact, you probably interviewed him."

Detective Sun pulled out her phone and started scrolling through it.

My mom placed a hand on my arm. "He didn't yell at or hurt you, did he?"

"No." My father had been nothing but polite to me at the wedding and beyond.

"But the murder took place near your cake table . . ." Mom wrung her hands.

Detective Sun tilted her head and studied my mom. "What exactly are you thinking?"

Her eyes wide, Mom forced the words out: "Could the intended victim have been . . . Felicity?"

"That's definitely a different angle," the detective rapidly whispered to herself. "Enough light in the tent, body not moved, stabbed at close range." She gave a firm shake of her head and said, "Please don't worry yourself. I think the killer knew the victim, and your daughter was not the intended target."

One point in my biological dad's favor: He *wasn't* a murderer. Not that that meant we'd have a happy family reunion anytime soon.

I pulled myself away from my thoughts and caught the last of the detective's sentence to my mom: ". . . and I'll see what I can do. Unofficially, of course."

"Anything would be helpful, Detective Sun," Mom said.

"Call me Rylan," the detective answered, holding out her hand to my mom.

"I'm Angela."

They shook hands across the table.

Detective Sun—I couldn't call her Rylan, not even in my thoughts—added, "If only I could do something for you right now."

Mom wore a sheepish expression on her face. "If you don't mind, I *do* have a package in my car I'd like gone."

"Certainly. I'll take care of it."

We all stood up from the table and marched outside. As the detective removed the box from the trunk of the car, I noticed my mom's grim expression and stiff posture.

I'd asked to meet my dad through the magic of the Wishes candle. Had I unknowingly invited trouble into our lives?

CHAPTER 22

When my mom and I arrived home, I suggested that we have our one-pot-meal trio gathering that night. I figured if Kelvin came over, it'd take Mom's mind off my biological dad. Plus, I wanted to talk to my best friend more about the investigation.

I called Kelvin, and he was game for dinner. He'd show up in half an hour, which gave me just enough time to cook. I foraged in the fridge and pantry, deciding to make a quick teriyaki stir-fry.

I'd boil some spaghetti, then add in pre-packaged veggies and rotisserie chicken. While I moved around the kitchen, Mom set the table, making sure to include a clear vase filled with water.

Despite being welcome at our home anytime, Kelvin never failed to bring my mom flowers on these special dinner occasions for the three of us. And he didn't fall down on his duty this time around.

He showed up thirty minutes after I called him, flowers in hand. He'd gathered a bunch of light purple lilacs. "For loyalty," he told me.

Mom grinned at Kelvin, and I was happy to see her feeling more at ease. "You look nice," she told Kelvin as she put the flowers in the prepped vase.

"Thank you, Mrs. Jin," he said while removing his shoes in our entryway.

He'd traded his usual Henley shirt and dark jeans combo for an Oxford with pressed slacks.

I gave him a quick hello hug. "What's with the fashion spread?"

He lowered his voice. "Need to do the laundry."

I chuckled as I returned to the kitchen and transferred the stir-fried noodles into a dish. Once we were all seated around the table and had served ourselves, we started chatting. I kept the conversation light and away from the topic of my dad.

Instead, I shared about my encounter with Sweet Tooth Sally and how Mom and I had urged her to run for mayor. Mom agreed with me and also talked about a few more regulars who'd visited our bakery recently. Kelvin talked about his newest gardening endeavors and waxed on about a compost bin he'd placed in his backyard.

At the end of dinner, Mom moved over to the living room to watch a TV drama she liked. Kelvin collected the dirty dishes, and I followed him into the kitchen.

"If you wash, I'll dry," I said.

"No dishwasher tonight?" he asked.

I mimed turning on the faucet, and he complied. "Mom won't hear us with the water running," I said.

As we washed up, I told Kelvin how Mom and I had visited Detective Sun for her help. I explained about the surprise delivery to the bakery and shared about the troubled history between my parents. Kelvin could be overprotective, so I didn't bring up the idea of my dad potentially harming baby me, but I did generally mention he'd written a disturbing note to my mom. Then I told him about the stolen recipe book.

Kelvin clanked a plate against the side of the sink. "He did what?"

"Shhh. Yeah, he took it."

"I knew something was off with the guy," Kelvin said. "You shouldn't trust him."

Part of me still wanted to give my father the benefit of the doubt, but the past evidence from my mom warned me against being so vulnerable. "Do you think I should contact him? Just to tell him I need some breathing space?"

Kelvin's voice became stern. "No, Lissa. That will only egg him on. I think you should simply ghost him."

I rubbed hard at the plate I was drying. "Really? Won't that be weird to all of a sudden not talk, especially after I agreed on chatting again?"

"That was before he started practically stalking your mom and scaring her."

I decided not to dwell on the sauce delivery but said, "He gave her *flowers*. Usually seen as a kind act, right, Mr. Florist?"

"Not when they're delivered to her front door unwanted."

Okay, he did have a point there.

Kelvin continued, "And if both you and your mom don't respond, maybe he'll get the message. To back off, obviously."

"Fine." For now. I cared about Kelvin's opinions and didn't want to rile him up. And I respected my mom's perspective. Besides, I had to concentrate on other things, like solving Miles' murder. "Hey, while we were at the detective's house, she let something slip."

"What?"

I shared Detective Sun's jumble of words involving Miles. "I'm not sure she even realized she was thinking out loud. Maybe she was still half-focused on my mom's problems. And guess what? She told my mom to call her Rylan."

"Aww, you got warm and fuzzy with the fuzz," Kelvin said.

I put the plate down and flicked my towel at his arm.

We continued finishing the rest of the dishes, Kelvin smirking at me the whole time.

Once done, though, I refocused us. "Detective Sun thought the killer knew Miles. But there were a lot of people at that wedding. Can we make a list of real potentials?"

"Let's draw it. Miles at the center, with lines connecting him to the others."

I found some scratch paper and a pen in the junk drawer. Then I mapped what we knew. "Because of his intended speech, all the attendants had issues with Miles. That's Turner, Nova, Jada, Easton, and Haley."

"Don't forget the bride and groom," Kelvin said. "I bet secret relationships are extremely toxic to a new marriage." I added Leanne and Colton to the paper.

Tapping the pen against the sheet, I said, "What about the parentals?"

"Sure. But add question marks near the godparents. Why would they want to harm their godson?"

"And why would Leanne's parents do anything either? Unless they knew Miles was the mystery man. But, still, that was in the past, right?" I put down the parents' names but with question marks.

"We can rule out all the other guests, including your father"—he said this begrudgingly—"because they didn't arrive until after Miles went missing."

"Right. But we should talk to the other parents as possible witnesses. Only I'm not sure where to find them."

Although something niggled at the back of my brain. A comment I'd heard in the tea tent, but I couldn't grasp it at the moment.

Kelvin snapped his fingers. "Don't forget the photographer. Not only would he be a good witness, but he took pictures."

"Maybe even incriminating ones."

"Do you have his contact?" I asked. Sometimes vendors spoke with one another, and Kelvin was a friendly sort of guy.

"No, but I think I saw his name on—" Kelvin searched for something on his phone. "Yep, it's on their wedding website."

"They listed the vendors?"

"No, but he's in the photo credits on the engagement pics."

Kelvin tapped some more on his phone. "Just filled out his online contact form. Said I wanted to meet up in case he had some good snaps of my flower arrangements."

"I'll come, too," I said. "He might have taken photos of my egg tarts display on the cake table." And possibly any clues surrounding it.

CHAPTER 23

With my mom's mind more settled because of Detective Sun's assurances and Kelvin's presence, I returned to Jin Bakery in the morning with a spring in my step. I wanted to experiment more with my magical predictions. Did the intensity of color truly matter in understanding when future events might play out?

To test my theory out, I'd have to promise personalized messages to new customers. My magic didn't work on those I was familiar with or too close to me. Besides my usual batch of pre-messaged cookies, I created a set of hollow ones. Vanilla fortune cookies. The strawberry and chocolate flavors were a hit, but vanilla was the most popular by far.

Customers wandered in, and it took me from opening until past noon to secure the right ones. They had to be strangers, interested in getting customized fortunes, and willing to spend some extra time at the shop.

I ended up with three takers. For the man in his early thirties, when my vision occurred, I chose the brilliant green line right in front of me. His fortune? "You will receive a message of love out of the clear blue sky." Within minutes, he got a text from his significant other to go outside and look up. I followed him out the door, and we were treated to a skywriter creating a message of "Will you marry me?" He texted back a thumbs-up. Ah, the wonders of technology.

My second test subject was a gentleman in his mid-fifties, and I picked a purple spot not too close to me. "Seek good health results and you will find them," I wrote. He got an email notification within twenty minutes that the lab work from his annual exam had turned out fine.

The third person who agreed to my special fortune cookie was a businesswoman, clad in a power suit. I picked a faint spot on the blue line, farther away from me. "A new work opportunity will not avail itself." But she never got a call or anything while at the bakery.

With that last test subject, I wondered if it was negligent of me to provide her with a prediction without staying there and supporting her. Was I being reckless? Or might it be better for me not to be around, to give her some space?

The bakery had emptied for the lunch hour, and Mom found me moping at the counter near the register. I couldn't control my predictions, whether they'd be "good" or "bad" or "meh." (I once actually predicted a pile of paperwork for Detective Sun.)

"Why can't all my predictions be positive?" I asked Mom.

She'd heard my thoughts on this topic before. "Fortunes are what people make of them."

At least those who received predictions got foreknowledge of things to come, sort of. That helped people to prepare—and potentially take action. "I guess so," I said. "And it's nice that I can choose how far down the road their fortune lies."

Mom stood before me, hands on the counter, and leaned in. "Really? How do you do that?"

"When their fate comes to me, it appears in colored lines. Seems like if I consciously choose a more vivid shade of a certain color, the fortune could happen to them earlier."

"Fascinating," she said. "My magic works the same way every time. Eat a pastry, get happy."

"That's a simpler equation, not so messy." I frowned. "You don't have the possibility of going around predicting people's deaths."

"True." She laid a hand on my shoulder. "Why don't you take a break, Felicity? You haven't eaten yet."

I *did* feel hungry. Maybe I could take a brisk walk and get some food? No, I'd rather take a drive. I asked Mom for the car keys.

"You going to Fresno? Checking on your orders there?"

"Yeah," I lied. It'd been a while since I dropped by the two grocery stores I supplied with fortune cookies. But really, I wanted the car so I could cruise around Pixie.

I took the keys, thanked my mom, and got into her Corolla. My ill-formed idea was to drive through town at a glacial speed so I could identify every pedestrian. I thought maybe I'd see Colton's dad or Leanne's parents wandering the streets and strike up a conversation.

No such luck. All I managed to do was waste precious gas and even more valuable time.

Might as well turn my lie around by visiting those Fresno grocery stores. I had loose contracts with a mart that sold Asian goods and a small shop with an international aisle.

At both places, I chatted with the owners (all stocked up with fortune cookies) and sent goodwill their way. After my last stop, my stomach let out a loud grumble. I still hadn't gotten lunch yet.

Where should I go? I wasn't too far from Foo Fusion, but I made a face. Hadn't Nova said something about the food there still being mediocre?

Wait, she'd also mentioned something else. They'd ordered takeout from the place because the owner was a friend of Leanne's parents: Michael Fu. He'd know where to find Mr. and Mrs. Lum, both eyewitnesses from the wedding day.

Foo Fusion remained impressive on the outside. I admired the ornate building with its sleek columns and the huge pair of Foo lions guarding the entrance.

Inside, there weren't that many customers. Maybe people had tired of his subpar Chinese cuisine. The restaurant, though, also offered hamburgers and doughnuts. I actually enjoyed their curry croquettes. I'd go order some of those.

Michael Fu spotted me in his establishment and wove his way toward me. "Felicity Jin," he said. "Been a while. Here for a business deal?"

He wanted me to be his regular fortune cookie supplier, and I'd taken missteps in that direction previously but had since corrected my course. As long as he sold inferior Chinese food and didn't appreciate handcrafted batches over mass-produced cookies, it'd be a hard pass.

"I'm here for the croquettes," I said.

"Those are very popular for some reason," Michael said.

Well, they would be, since they tasted way better than his main fare.

"Hey," I said, as though in afterthought, "do you happen to know Mr. and Mrs. Lum? They have a daughter named Leanne. I heard that you all were friends."

His eyes widened with delight. "Sure do. They hold a weekly casino night here."

I glanced around the room. "Do you have a special setup? Maybe a roulette wheel?"

"Nah. It's not so formal." He pointed at a few tables. "We just play some cards. And mahjong—you wanna join?"

I started to say no. I'd never been a great MJ player, even though I knew the basic rules. But didn't the game require four players? "You know, I'd be up for it if you could guarantee I got to play with Mr. and Mrs. Lum."

"I can arrange that."

"Then I'm in."

"It's happening tomorrow night," he said. "At seven."

"I'll clear my calendar."

"Be sure to bring cold, hard cash."

Uh-oh. What had I gotten myself into?

CHAPTER 24

When I returned to Jin Bakery, I was glad to find a steady stream of customers. I earned above minimum wage, but who knew what financial straits I'd gotten myself into by agreeing to a casino night with Michael Fu and his friends? I hoped the ante for a mahjong game wasn't ridiculous.

I continued to serve customers on automatic pilot (having no more brain capacity to do fortune cookie testing on them) until Kelvin entered the bakery in the late afternoon.

He stood in line with the others and even asked to buy a pineapple bun with coconut filling, though I waved his money away.

"You know you have a standing offer for free pastries," I whispered.

"Only way I could talk to you is to get in line," he said. I packaged his pineapple bun as he added, "I set up an appointment with the photographer."

"When?"

"This evening, around seven thirty."

"At his shop?" I said. "Or home?" The guy could be a freelancer and working out of his own residence.

"Neither." Kelvin jerked his head sideways to the east. "At Pixie Park. Figured being there might jog his memory."

Not a bad idea. "Sounds like a plan."

"Yeah, he readily agreed. Said he wanted some good sunset shots anyway." People *did* flock to the hill for the bird's-eye view of the surrounding land and to soak up the last of the sun's rays.

"Meet me back here at five thirty, and we'll go together," I said.

"Deal."

Pixie Park, despite being the location of a murder, still felt serene as Kelvin and I walked its grounds. Of course, the wedding tents were long gone. The grass was trimmed, and the smell of freshly mown lawn lingered in the air. The bushes appeared carefully shaped to show off their leaves and flowers, and I couldn't find a scrap of trash on the ground. I'd have to make sure to thank Sally and her beautification crew for making the place pristine.

The photographer was standing on the hilltop where Kelvin's flower arch had been. He wore all black, but less as an artistic fashion statement and more of a blending-into-the-shadows way. In fact, when he turned and greeted us, I didn't register much beyond timid features that retreated into his face.

He introduced himself as Ben Bond.

I stuck out my hand. "I'm Felicity Jin. I did the pastries for the Lum-Wu wedding."

"I know," he said. "I've got pictures of the cake table."

I glanced at the equipment bag at his feet. "Mind if you show them to me?"

"Not at all, but Kelvin's first." Ben proceeded to pull out his huge digital camera. "Tell me if there's anything you like."

I huddled closer to them to peer at the screen. Ben scrolled through shots of Kelvin setting the flower arch on this very hill, the corsages worn by the bridal attendants, and the boutonnieres the groom's side received.

Kelvin let out little exclamations of praise with the differing shots and ended up ordering a variety of digital photos. He tapped on his phone. "Sending the payment to you now."

Ben nodded, pulled out his phone, and tapped on it. Then he turned to me. "I don't have too many pics for you, I'm afraid. Thought I'd take more during the cake cutting ceremony but . . ."

I gave him a tight smile. "I'm sure nobody wanted to be near the table where a dead body was found. Not even you."

"Also took several during the tea ceremony," he said.

I didn't even know he'd been at the window until Ms. Hung had told me. He'd captured me putting together the tea and handing over the implements to the bride and groom. Plus, he'd gotten shots of all who'd been in the tent: the two sets of parents, the happy couple, and the two head attendants on each side.

No telltale clues there. "What about the cake photos?" I asked.

Ben showed me some beautiful angles of the golden egg tarts display. I almost wanted to reach into the screen and grab one.

"Do you have any with a fish lens?" I asked. "I'd like to get the full effect." Actually, I wanted to see not only the pastries, but the entire table. And maybe a leg, with a clue, jutting out or something.

But the photos that Ben had taken were clean. No splayed limbs. Not even that dripping rose petal I'd picked up. These pics couldn't tell me anything. But then again, he'd only gotten close-ups of the cake.

"When did you take these?"

"I went into the cake tent just before the wedding ceremony." Ben fiddled with something on the camera and showed me the timestamp.

Nobody should've been in the tent then anyway since the wedding had been about to start. But I knew for certain that there hadn't been a dead body until after I set up my tiered display; I'd put up the cake table myself on empty ground. So the murder would have taken place any time after I'd organized the egg tarts display until the actual wedding. Plus, we'd started the ceremony late. That meant I couldn't rule out anyone who'd been in the tent with me during the tea serving.

I took a step toward Ben. "I really don't know how this tragedy could've happened."

Ben's face blanched. "It's the first time I've ever had someone die at a wedding."

"You're a photographer," I said. "Observant. You didn't notice anything unusual?"

Ben scratched the side of his neck. "I wish I had. But, like I told the police, I was focused on capturing the joyous people who were there for Colton and Leanne."

Unfortunately, one of those same loved ones might not have cared so much for Miles. I thanked Ben for his time and went over to the side to confer with Kelvin. Behind us, I heard the subtle clicking of the camera as Ben captured the colorful sunset.

I expressed my frustration with the meeting to Kelvin, but he didn't seem to think it was a wasted effort. After all, Ben had provided him with some stunning photos of the wedding's floral pieces. Kelvin had chosen pics not only highlighting the flower arrangements up close, but some candids of the recipients in their tents.

To check out the photos on Kelvin's phone, I stood closer to him. We examined the screen together.

"Wait," I said. "Go back one." Something had flagged my interest in a group shot of the groom's attendants.

In the photo's foreground, Kelvin was helping Nova with her boutonniere, delicately pinning it to a lapel on the pocket of her dress shirt. But in the back, Easton hovered at the edge of the shot. "Zoom in right there."

Our heads bent closer—

"I got it!" Ben said.

We turned around, and he waved his camera in the air.

"Did you find an incriminating shot?" I asked.

"What?" Ben said, looking confused.

Kelvin took a more polite approach. "What's got you so excited?"

"These sunset photos." He clicked buttons on his camera. "And I got this amazing picture of you two."

The sunset was gorgeous, an orangey glow with hints of purply pink. And the silhouettes of us were enchanting. At first, it almost looked like an engagement photo, with our bodies near each other and our heads tilted together.

I blinked a few times. No, it was just Kelvin and me. Best friends caught in the reflected beauty of a brilliant sunset. Friends who were trying to track down clues in a murder case.

"I'll give this one to you for free, bud," Ben told Kelvin.

"That'd be great. I appreciate it," my bestie said in his typical kind manner. "Lissa and I don't have very many pictures together."

It was true. We had classroom photos where we'd

stood out among the monochromatic crowd. I think we also had a few playdate pics that Mrs. Love had taken long ago. My mom, though, wasn't one for documenting things. And while Kelvin and I had spent lots of time doing things together, we never stood still to pose, preferring to be present in and enjoy the moment.

Ben sent the sunset pic to Kelvin and then slung his camera bag over his shoulder. The sky was turning darker, the wind was picking up, and Ben wanted to get home.

I thanked him as he left. For both photos. The one of Kelvin and me, two best friends. And the other one, of a groomsperson caught in a strange motion.

"What do you think Easton's doing in that shot?" I asked.

Kelvin clicked on the image I referred to and enlarged it.

CHAPTER 25

The photo Ben had taken of the groom's attendants showed Easton in the background. He was a bit blurred, but I could tell he'd brought his index finger to his lips.

"Is he trying to shush someone?" Kelvin asked. "I don't remember it being noisy in the tent."

"The finger is parallel to his mouth. And the color there is . . ." I squinted at the image.

"Red," Kelvin said.

A burst of red on his finger.

"He must have pricked himself with the boutonniere pin," Kelvin said. "It happens."

"And naturally sucked on the injury. Or maybe he didn't want to get blood on his clothes."

I suddenly recalled the bloody flower petal under the cake table—and recoiled.

"Are you okay? Are you cold?" Kelvin pulled at his gray Henley, but he hadn't worn a jacket, so he slung an arm around my shoulder instead.

"It's not the breeze that's bothering me," I said, but I didn't ask him to move away. "I was remembering the crime scene. And the blood on the rose."

I followed my circuitous train of thought. Detective

Sun had mentioned that the body hadn't been moved. Could Miles have been knocked out in the tent, or . . . ?

I'd shuddered at the blood. But Miles? He would have fainted on the spot. And who had conveniently pricked his hand at the wedding? Easton.

I shared my emerging theory with Kelvin, and he nodded.

"Well, I would imagine it's easier to jab a man in the neck when he's already unconscious," Kelvin said.

"It has to be someone close to Miles then," I said. "Somebody who knows he'd faint at the sight of blood."

"Easton went to high school with Miles. Maybe it came up in biology class?"

"Perhaps." I thought back on Miles' intended speech. "But let's not focus on any one person just yet. Everybody on that doc had secrets they wanted to keep hidden."

"If only we could get them to talk to us."

Kelvin stared in the direction of Pixie Inn. From this vantage point, we could see the faint outline of the waterwheel. "They probably have cabin fever and are getting on one another's nerves. I can suggest a group outing, and we can be their tour guides."

"That could work. And I'll see Leanne's parents tomorrow." I explained about the casino night, and Kelvin snorted.

"Okay, Lady Luck," he said, "I'll be sticking by you." We walked down the hill together with matching strides.

The next day, I did have some luck. Leanne Lum-Wu walked into Jin Bakery the first thing in the morning.

I'd just taken a seat by the register when she stomped in with a clear purpose.

"I need pastries. Lots of them."

"Hi, Leanne." I held up a hand. "Wait a moment. I thought you got bed *and* breakfast at Pixie Inn."

"We do. But it's been awkward in the mornings. Tense. People don't even want to eat together any-more—"

"You know what? Kelvin was just talking to me about setting up a bonding activity for your group. To get you all out and about. Might help with the tension."

"That's a good idea. I'll touch base with him. Mean-while, I thought I'd get everyone some treats." She nod-ded at the display case. "The last time you dropped off goodies was helpful. But Jada—" Her voice cracked with sorrow.

I put some sympathy into mine. "Heard you two had a disagreement."

Leanne's eyes widened. "You did? How?"

I wasn't about to tell her I'd seen Jada rushing out of the inn. "Pixie's a small town. Word gets around." It did, usually. I probably would've heard about it before too long if I'd tapped into the gossip grapevine. Or had Mom do so; she got along better with the long-term, overshar-ing residents.

"Jada likes your pastries," Leanne said, gesturing at the egg tarts. "They calm her down." She wrinkled her brow and added, "Actually, everyone feels better when we fill our tummies with your goodies."

That's how the magic works, I thought but didn't dare share. "I'll give you a discount," I said. "I know it's been tough for all of you this past week."

She massaged her temples. "I should already be on my

honeymoon, not fighting with my roomie and trying to unruffle feathers."

"You and Jada are still at odds?" I asked as I bagged the various pastries she pointed to.

"Over a guy—a dead one no less." She half laughed and half cried.

"You don't mean Miles, do you?" Which of course she did, because I'd already read the incriminating doc. Not that she knew.

"Yes, but not in the way you think." Leanne sighed. "We said we'd never let a man come between us. And Jada and I didn't. I even told her about Miles, just not by name. He belonged in my past. BC."

"'BC'?" I echoed.

"Before Colton." She shook her head. "Summer between my freshman and sophomore year at Fresno State. Back then, I was a sucker for smooth talkers."

"Where'd you and Miles meet?"

"A local hospital I volunteered at."

I placed all the bagged pastries to the side. "Heard he had an internship in Fresno. Was this around the same time?"

She nodded. "It was a brief fling. He was there only a few weeks before he got booted from the program. Figures. Miles often felt queasy—the beeping machines, the snakelike tubing, fierce antiseptic smell. Everything bothered him."

Like seeing blood. "I know it was long ago," I said, "but wasn't it awkward having him at the wedding?"

She blushed. "He was on our backup tier of wedding guests. Figured he wouldn't make the final cut. Except Colton wanted to have a matching number of attendants and Miles volunteered to officiate, so that brought him to the top of the list."

"Well, it was a nice wedding despite everything," I said, trying to encourage her. I hadn't been to many ceremonies, but it had been a great setup in a lovely spot. "And Pixie Park has some beautiful grounds."

Leanne looked down at the floor. "It would have been perfect. Colton and I always wanted to have an outdoor wedding, and usually, Pixie is such a quaint town. Colton had been preparing for months . . ."

"And it showed. The flower arch, tea ceremony, outdoor dancing—"

"His own parents had a different kind of ceremony, a spontaneous thing."

"People have varying tastes."

"That's what I said. But he had a superstition." Leanne rummaged in her purse for her wallet. "Can you tell me the total?"

I gave her the discounted cost for the baked goods. "What was Colton's thinking?"

She sniffed. "That a perfect wedding would result in a perfect marriage. Unlike his parents. They can't stand each other. Won't even stay in the same town. His mom's at an Airbnb in Pixie while his dad's at a boutique hotel in Fresno." I made a mental note to call all the boutique hotels in the city.

Leanne paid in cash, and I counted back her change. "So, how are you and Colton doing?" I asked.

"Getting better. I mean, he was a little upset about Miles and me, how I'd kept that secret from him."

I studied Leanne. Her gaze didn't waver from mine, and I hoped she wasn't downplaying Colton's anger.

"He's more mad that his planning got ruined than anything else," she said. "But I told him that even if we had an imperfect ceremony, we càn still have an ideal marriage. And delicious pastries will only help heal our relationship." She cradled the purchased goods in her hands.

I hoped so. Someone in their wedding party, for sure, had needed a lot of healing.

CHAPTER 26

The casino night at Foo Fusion consisted of two tables set up for the attendees. One was a standard round table where six people were seated, their faces inscrutable as they played a hand of five-card stud.

The other table had been earmarked for mahjong. I could tell, since it was a special square folding table, brought specifically in for the event; other furniture had been moved back to make room for it. The surface was covered with something akin to butcher paper. If you wanted to play mahjong, you needed a smooth surface for mixing the tiles.

Michael beckoned me closer with a crook of his finger. "Sit down," he said. "And don't worry, the starting bid is only twenty dollars."

A few minutes after I sat down, Mr. and Mrs. Lum walked through the door.

They each gave me a reserved smile in a polite manner. She wore a black silk dress, and he wore a wrinkled dark blue shirt. Did they like to dress in somber colors, or was it out of respect for Miles' passing?

Mr. and Mrs. Lum placed ten dollars in the middle of the table, and I added my Jackson to the mix.

"Excellent." Michael rubbed his hands, selected a

sleek briefcase from the side and popped open the clasps. It contained his mahjong set, the tiles a vivid green against the dark brown leather of the case.

Michael exchanged the money on the table with the tiles. Leanne's parents and I started moving the small rectangular pieces on the surface, clicking them together and sliding them around. Meanwhile, Michael pulled out his wallet and double-checked that we'd put in a total of eighty dollars into the pot.

Then he sat down and joined in the process of shuffling the tiles. I always had a hard time remembering how to count off and distribute the playing pieces, so I let the others take the lead. As we built the long wall of tiles, I reintroduced myself to the Lums.

"Yes, I remember you," Mrs. Lum said. "You helped with the tea ceremony."

I bobbed my head. "Glad I could be at the wedding . . . How are Leanne and Colton holding up?"

Mrs. Lum thought about it while her husband grunted. "Well, they got married in the end," he said.

"And now they're stuck," Mrs. Lum said but without malice, like it was a plain fact of life.

Mr. Lum grunted again. "She could've done worse. Gone for that cousin instead, the black sheep of the family."

"Do you mean Miles?" I said. "You know about their relationship?"

"Sure." Mr. Lum picked up some tiles to create the hand in front of him.

"It wasn't a big secret," his wife added. "And Leanne was so moody during that time."

Mr. Lum shook his head. "Hormones. Plus, all that Hollywood happily-ever-after nonsense messes with people's heads."

"Better not to have the extra passion and poetry." Mrs. Lum collected her tiles. "Means no let-downs when you actually become a spouse."

Michael looked on with a bemused expression during our conversation but didn't contribute to it. He concentrated on the game. Maybe he figured if we talked, we wouldn't pay enough attention, and he'd be declared the winner soon enough.

We each glanced at our own set of tiles. Whoever had flower tiles took them out of the lineup and drew new ones. Then we started playing in earnest.

Like a novice, I rearranged mine in order. Sequential possibilities or matching options. To win, I knew I needed to have four sets and a pair. *Pairs.*

I turned to Leanne's parents. "How did you two meet anyway?" Probably wasn't through a poetry reading.

"We were matched," Mrs. Lum said, pulling a tile from the center and discarding one from her hand. "Our relatives set us up."

Mr. Lum grunted. "Everything was simpler back then. No need for these lovey-dovey relationships, elaborate weddings."

Michael spoke up. "Why didn't they pick Foo Fusion to cater their wedding?"

Husband and wife looked at each other. I wondered if the Lums came by to eat at the restaurant or just to play mahjong.

"Leanne and Colton wanted dumplings," I said, remembering the wedding buffet.

"Ah well." Michael rubbed his balding head. "Guess I should add some more items to our menu."

We continued playing. Mr. Lum discarded a tile, and his wife picked it up after saying "chi." She created a three-piece set of bamboos: a chain of three, four, and five stalks.

"Such fuss," she said. "We got married in a courthouse. A lot cheaper. And we only needed a few witnesses."

About those witnesses. "How did Leanne pick her attendants?" I asked. Maybe the parents could give me insight into their characters.

"Turner is her boss," Mrs. Lum said. "Couldn't help but invite him. He's a very showy man but always dresses nicely."

Mr. Lum tilted his head from side to side. "Of course, Leanne's roommate, Jada."

"They've lived together for a while now?" I asked.

"Ever since they got assigned as roommates in college. Inseparable pair," Mr. Lum said. "Almost like an old married couple themselves."

Mrs. Lum added, "Probably would've stayed that way, too, if she hadn't met Colton."

Michael tried to slide a play by me, but I noticed the tile and swooped in. "Pong," I said, creating a triplet of matching single balls.

I threw out a tile and continued with the conversation. "How did Colton and Leanne meet, again?"

"Some sort of party." Mrs. Lum touched the top of one of her tiles, considering her next move. "Related to work."

While waiting for Mrs. Lum to play, I turned to her husband. "I know Leanne also picked Haley as an attendant. Have they been friends long?"

"Ever since kindergarten," Leanne's dad said.

Mrs. Lum finally played a tile. "Almost didn't happen either. Only became friends since Haley repeated a grade."

So Haley was a year older than Leanne? Huh. She seemed to act younger, with a naive outlook on life.

Michael gave a sudden shout. He'd self-drawn his

winning tile. He laid his hand down with satisfaction: a mix of straights, triplets, and a pair of red dragons with the "middle" character in Chinese.

He scrambled up to collect his winnings. Sure, I'd lost twenty dollars. But I'd gained more knowledge about the bride and groom, and Leanne's friends.

CHAPTER 27

One game of mahjong was enough for me, so I excused myself and stepped outside. I'd just passed the pair of Foo lions when a dark shadow emerged from behind one of the statues. Someone jumped out at me and grabbed my arm. I yelped in fear.

"Felicity, it's me," a familiar voice said.

It was my biological dad, Richard. "Let go of my arm," I said, attempting to shake him off.

"Oh. Sorry." He dropped his grip.

In the nighttime, he appeared different, more of a dim outline than a real person. He truly looked like a stranger. And really, that's what he was. Even though I'd built up this idea of a dad in my head, I didn't actually know the man before me—whether he wanted to help or harm me.

I rubbed my arm. It hadn't been a tight grip, but it'd startled me.

Behind me, I heard noises from the restaurant: cries of glee from winning and groans from losing. At least I knew people were nearby. They'd come rushing to my aid if I screamed loud enough. I decided to stick around Foo Fusion while Richard and I talked.

He started first. "Did Angela get the flowers and the

XO?" Too little, too late, buddy. Where had he been with his apologies decades ago after he'd hightailed it out of our lives?

I made my tone aloof. "Yes, she got them."

"And?" He pulled a hand through his gray hair. I noticed he'd dressed up, like he had at the wedding. A sports coat, and a pair of black trousers with wingtip shoes. At least he still wanted to make a good impression on me. But what did I know? Maybe he dressed like this all the time.

He continued talking. "Do you think she forgives me? Wants to meet up?"

How should I phrase this? He seemed as eager as a puppy, his voice rising with excitement. "She's not ready," I said. *And probably never would be*, I added in my head.

"Ah, but I need closure." He hung his head a bit. "I knew I shouldn't have bought her the sauce. Maybe her tastes have changed."

Speaking of taste, I narrowed my eyes. "Or perhaps you should have sent her the recipe book."

He backed up a few steps. "It was a memento," he confessed. "Something to remember you two by. Besides, your grandmother could have written it again by recalling the directions."

"There were *generations* of recipes in there."

Even the closer Foo lion appeared to glare at my father.

He sounded untroubled as he went on. "I figured we'd reconnect soon enough. She'd come to her senses. I'm a good man, after all." The last line sounded like a mantra he often repeated to himself.

"Wait a minute. How? You were the one to run away. You distanced yourself."

"For good cause. I thought she would understand." He scrubbed his face with his hands. "I mean, the headaches, the predictions."

"The what?" My heart seemed to beat harder.

"Something triggered an intense headache, and I got this strong sense that I'd hurt you. I wrote Angela a note . . ." The one which alarmed my mom, that made her think of getting a restraining order even now.

"You said something about predictions, plural?"

"I only made two, but yeah . . . The first involved you, after I held you. The second was for a stranger at the BART station. He literally bumped into me, and I got this clear thought. That he'd lose his wallet. I even told him so."

"What happened?" I asked, thinking about my own fortune cookie messages turning true. Had the talent come from my dad and not my mom?

"The prediction worked," Richard said. "Not only that, but the guy turned back to accost me in the station. Said I was a pickpocket. I had to show him everything on my person to prove my innocence."

At least he hadn't been accused of murder by the cops like me. Still . . . "That must have been rough on you."

He nodded. "I didn't ever want that to happen again. For a long time after, I kept physical distance between me and anyone else. A huge circle of personal space, even with my students."

He'd had a semi-valid excuse to stay away if he really thought he'd harm others. "Do you still make predictions?"

"Nope, and boy am I glad that phase is behind me. Things just faded. My headaches, the troubling forecasts."

"You don't miss it?" I'm not sure how I'd feel without

my magical powers, both the joy-inducing one and the prognosticating portion.

"There's less stress in my life now," Richard said. "And who wants to be the bearer of bad news?"

I thought about my own predictions, which varied in tenor. "They don't all have to be bad."

He shrugged. "Not worth it to me."

I had felt the same way as him. Wondered whether I'd constantly give bad news, ill-fated fortunes. But if I'd stopped at that one dead man, I wouldn't have been able to help other individuals.

Predictions, I realized, were just that. I didn't need to label them "bad" or "good."

I patted the Foo lion on the head, trying to calm myself down as I asked, "Do you still believe your prediction about me? That you'll harm me?"

"It's why I left, to protect me—er, you." He rushed on. "Anyway, that was the past. I got the sense, for some reason, that the prediction was tied to you as a child." He cocked his head to the side and studied me. "And now you've grown up."

I hoped that was a compliment, that I seemed like a mature and successful person.

He continued, "Yes, I'm here now. And I'm glad that when I learned about your bakery catering the wedding I reached out, because that's what a father should do."

A warm glow infused me. Richard *had* contacted me first. Maybe something inside my dad *did* long for his daughter. Perhaps he regretted his actions and had felt compelled to attend the wedding to reunite with me.

My dad noticed the shift in my mood, because he said, "I'll give your mom more time. But how about you? We could meet again, for something small like coffee."

"Let's do a meal instead," I said. "Pixie's Old-Time Diner tomorrow night. At six. And bring the book." If he wanted to make amends, he'd have to do so materially.

"Of course, of course." My dad did a tiny bow before he shuffled off.

CHAPTER 28

The next day was supposed to be my time off from work (once a week to "socialize," according to my mom, but it really only meant hanging out with Kelvin). But once Mom told me about Sweet Tooth Sally's large order, I decided to help out at the bakery that morning.

Sally had requested two trays of *each* pastry for her Rotary Club (of which, obviously, she was president). Though I could've given her day-old cookies, I thought a fresh batch would be a nice gesture. Besides, I didn't have anything planned with Kelvin until the afternoon. He'd made me block out my schedule from two o'clock on.

Mom had her work cut out because she had to craft both her signature egg tarts and Grandma's pineapple buns. Each Jin baker had her own recipe to master during her lifetime. We couldn't help each other either with the baking; Mom had tried to before with Grandma, but it'd ruined the taste of the pineapple buns.

Only once a Jin could no longer bake (illness, death) did the magical recipe pass on. Mom said that receiving the blessing from Po Po to take on the pineapple bun-making had been a magical experience in itself. My grandma had placed her gnarled, arthritic fingers on

Mom's smooth hands and said a blessing. Mom claimed she'd felt a rush of warmth envelop her, like a tight hug from Po Po. Ever since then, she'd been able to add the pineapple buns to her repertoire.

Beep. The small sound brought my attention back to the bakery's kitchen. Our industrial oven had preheated, and I'd better get to work. Mom was already bent over her own mixing bowl at the table behind me.

I started gathering ingredients and got to baking fresh batches of fortune cookies. I'd already printed out encouraging comments about people who contributed to the local community in my fortunes, and I imagined how the Rotary members would feel after reading them. Double the happiness.

With our baked pastries prettily positioned in our glass display case (and a few in a cooling rack in the kitchen), we were ready to open on time. And the first customer who sauntered in was Sally, ready to pick up her huge order.

Mom first complimented Sally on being a pillar in the community.

I provided a recent example. "Yes, just the other day, I was at Pixie Park. Looks beautiful."

She crinkled her nose. "It took us some effort to tidy it up."

"Really?" I couldn't imagine local residents getting rowdy. Maybe kids who'd been messing around at the playground? "Was there, like, candy wrappers on the ground?"

"Definitely food wrappers and discarded napkins," she said. "People also stick random stuff in the bushes, thinking no one will notice: ballpoint pens, floss, lipstick."

"But there are trash cans placed in different areas around the park."

"Tell me about it. And don't get me started on the cigarette butts."

My mom slid in a positive comment. "Well, thank you again for all that you do."

And we both reminded Sally about the mayor's retirement. She gave us a sweet smile in response and left with her goodies.

I spent the rest of the morning happily playing with flour and butter. Jin Bakery was my place of contentment, and I'd better give myself a dosage of calm before the afternoon. Kelvin had asked me to clear my schedule because he'd managed to arrange an interesting team-bonding activity with the entire Lum-Wu wedding party.

Kelvin had chosen Storyland for our field trip. Wasn't that too childish? But he hadn't bothered to ask me before deciding on the venue.

Both he and I would drive separate cars and transport the entire wedding crew to Roeding Park. Whether the carpool was because he wanted to save on the entrance fee or because he figured that people would talk on our short drive over to Fresno, I didn't know.

I didn't learn anything exciting on our way over, except that Leanne and Colton had patched things up. They kept whispering to each other, reigning over the back seat. Turner sat on the passenger's side and fidgeted with the air-conditioning. Well, that's what he got for wearing a peacoat in this warm weather. On the other hand, he looked as distinguished as ever in the navy-blue fabric.

"You didn't have to dress up," I said to him as we maneuvered into the park entrance. I could already see Lake Washington in the distance, home to the many birds who enjoyed the large swath of water.

"Trust me, this is not dressed up," he said.

"Oh, okay. Because we're essentially going to a children's playground."

He stared at the colorful entrance with its peaked rooftops and flying pennants. "I gathered that."

After we got out of the car, I explained to them about Storyland. "Imagine being able to walk into a land of fairy tales. That's what you'll find here."

"Great," Leanne said. She held on tight to Colton's hand.

He swung their linked hands together as they walked up to the window.

Kelvin must have driven faster than me because he was already there with his entourage: Nova, Easton, Jada, and Haley (who'd insisted on riding with him). He paid for our entire group and said, "My treat. Enjoy."

He even bought a "magic" key. It was technological magic because the yellow plastic (I mean, golden) key unlocked the audio boxes that would retell the various fairy tales at different locations around Storyland.

Kelvin offered the key to the bride and groom, but neither of them showed any interest in it. Turner then plucked it out of Kelvin's hand and said, "Dibs. I want to unlock the magic. And with style."

He marched through the archway, and I admit that the coat draped his figure well. We all followed along, and Leanne tugged Colton toward the playground equipment. They stopped at a seesaw, and both sat down, one on either end. Although heavier than Leanne, Colton distributed his weight so that they could maintain balance and swing up and down. She laughed with glee.

"They seem to be getting along better," I said to Jada, who stood next to me.

"I know," she said. "Probably a combo of your tasty fortune cookies and forgiveness."

I gave myself a mental pat on the shoulder.

After Leanne and Colton tired of the seesaw, we ambled over to the castle. It was an impressive site, with imposing gray turrets. The interior had pretend-brick walls and an actual round table for knights. While others sat down, Easton made his way to the royal throne in the corner. The grand piece of furniture was embellished with a lion symbol.

"Blimey," Easton said as he held court.

Turner chuckled from his seat at the round table. "What would Charles say, eh?"

Easton gave him a puzzled look. Guess he didn't get the monarch reference.

Kelvin cleared his throat, and I knew he wanted to start the interrogating part of our trip. He gave them an easy question: "Anyone been here before?"

Colton's attendants shook their heads. The groom himself hadn't come before either, though he'd visited Leanne in Fresno. "It wasn't really something I thought about doing as a college student," he admitted.

Turner readily admitted that he'd come about a decade ago, but things hadn't been as renovated then. "Some of the stories didn't work or squeaked out nonsense words. But now I have the power."

Kelvin murmured, "He-man."

Turner raised the key in his hand like a sword.

"So, moving along," I said. "What about you? Jada, Leanne, Haley?"

"Never been," Jada said. "Family couldn't afford it."

"We went as a part of a trip in kindergarten," Leanne said. She touched Haley on the shoulder. "Remember?"

"Yeah," Haley said in a soft voice. "I've been here twice in total." That's right. She'd repeated a grade.

"That exciting, huh?" Nova said with a toss of her purple-haired head.

"It was fun," Haley said. Turning to Leanne, she asked, "Remember that slide that came out of a giant shoe?"

Leanne furrowed her brow. "Can't say that I do."

Haley tucked a strand of hair behind her ear. "We went down it together?"

"Sorry, I don't remember that," Leanne said.

"Oh." Haley grew quiet.

"Let's go see some of the other fairy-tale stories," I said. "I've never been here myself, so those of you who've been here before can be my tour guides."

Turner stood up at once and bowed. "I'd be delighted to."

We exited the castle and went strolling along the grounds. I noticed Hansel and Gretel, the Three Little Pigs, and the aforementioned Old Woman in the Shoe slide.

"Let's go over there," Kelvin said, pointing in the distance.

"What is that place?" I asked.

"A chapel," he whispered to me. "Maybe it'll make them think twice about their actions at the wedding."

Always the optimist, Kelvin. But I obliged. And the rest of the group trudged into the small place with its interactive musical organ and rows of wooden pews.

Turner played a rendition of "The Wedding March." Leanne and Colton hammed it up by skipping down the aisle. Meanwhile, Jada emitted a small sigh and slid into a pew.

I followed her. "Everything okay?"

"You probably already know about my plan. Miles spelled it out in his speech. And Kelvin viewed that doc."

I jolted back. "How can you tell?"

"You can check the activity dashboard, and he was signed in when he read it. And reverted the changes so that my secret was exposed."

I leaned in toward her. "I remember something about a breakup plot."

She shifted the glasses on her nose and stared at the married couple in the chapel. "Thought I'd spill the beans about her mysterious past love, and it'd throw the two of them for a loop."

"But why? Weren't you here to support their wedding?"

"Not really." She made a heart with her hands. "Roomies for eternity. I even had a custom patch specially made with our slogan . . . But romance over roommates, I guess."

"They do seem happy," I said of the smiling couple.

"Yeah. That's why my plan was always going to fail."

I thought about my own living situation. Basically, I roomed with my mom. If I ever decided to leave, how would she feel? I knew the answer straight away: She'd be fine with it, glad for me even. Because we loved each other. No conditions.

"You know," I said, "you'll always be roomies. Maybe not literally in the same home, but in your hearts." I also tried making a heart symbol with my hands, but mine looked more like binoculars.

She got the drift, though. "You're right. And if *I'd* fallen head over heels with someone at Fresno State, she would've supported me. I just wished she didn't have to move so far away."

"It's not too bad of a drive," I said. "And thank goodness for tech."

"Only a vid call away," she said as she got up. "I think it's time to go."

I glanced around and noticed that the others had already wandered out of the chapel. We needed to catch up with the rest.

CHAPTER 29

The group had wandered over to a grassy hill. On the side, I spotted two fallen statues: Jack and Jill. And nearby was the well where they'd gone to fetch a pail of water.

On the hillside were bright-colored plastic discs. "What are those for?" I asked.

"They're sleds," Nova said as she sat down in one. She wriggled the sled farther, but it barely moved. The synthetic grass didn't make for the best of surfaces to glide on.

Beside me, Haley clapped her hands with excitement. "Go faster, Nova!"

Nova grunted and used her arms to hurry along the little sled, but it didn't want to be rushed. She finally cried out in frustration, stood up, and flipped over the disc with a loud thwack. Nova stared at it afterward, arms crossed, a satisfied look on her face.

Easton smirked. "Road rage much?"

Nova glared at him.

"You should own it, Nova. We all know about your suspended license."

She came over to Easton and flexed her biceps. He gulped. "For your information," Nova said, "I'll be getting

my license back soon. And you're no stranger to trouble
yourself, delinquent."

Easton flinched. "My lawyer should have advised me
to seal my records."

"What'd you do, anyway?" Nova asked.

"Nothing too serious." He stuffed his hands in his
pockets and avoided her scrutiny.

It's no wonder the entire wedding crew needed an
outing. They were at each other's throats. Kelvin and I exchanged a glance. We were finding out more info this
afternoon, but I didn't want to instigate another murder
while doing so.

"Let's check out some more spots," Kelvin said. "And
make sure to use that magic key, Turner."

"Of course," Turner said, leading the way.

People didn't seem in the right mood to enjoy the fairy
tales—we sped through the Three Little Pigs, Hansel and
Gretel, and Humpty Dumpty. Before long, we'd exited
Storyland and gone into the attached main park.

Leanne pointed at a bust in the distance near the lake.
"That's the Founding Father," she said.

We made our way over to the appropriately named
Washington Lake. Birds soared above our heads and wad-
dled along the ground. A gaggle of geese honked at us,
either wanting us to move out of their territory or to feed
them. I wasn't sure which.

Colton pointed at the trees above the water. "See the
nests up there."

We saw white birds in those trees. Tons of them.

"Egrets," Leanne said, moving closer.

We hurried over to the water's edge and glanced upward. How could those thin trees hold nests? The whole
area seemed to be erupting in bird chirps and croaks.

"We should close our eyes to soak it in," Leanne said.

As others followed her suggestion, I did the same. Then I felt a hard shove on my back.

I stumbled, opening my eyes in time to notice I was pitching straight into dark water. I pinwheeled my arms, but that didn't stop my forward motion. Falling into the lake, the crisp cold hit me like a blow.

I'd been close to the edge, in the shallow part of the water, so it took me only moments to get back to shore. Besides, about ten arms dragged me back up.

"What happened?" Kelvin asked.

"Uh, that was clumsy of me," I lied, not wanting to give whoever had pushed me any satisfaction.

I took some time to wring out my clothes the best I could.

Turner tutted with concern. He whipped off his pea-coat and draped it over my shoulders. "Here, you need this more than me."

"Thanks," I said, drawing the sides of the jacket closed to block out the chill.

I continued to shiver, so I ended up actually wearing the peacoat instead of using it as a cape. No wonder Turner hadn't been too stuffy with this jacket on. The material wasn't even wool, like it looked at first glance. It was a thin fabric with a coating on top to imitate the woolen look.

"Good thing we're on our way home," I said as we trudged to the parked cars.

Everyone murmured in agreement.

I drove back in silence, focused more on not getting Mom's upholstered seats wet and less on engaging my passengers in conversation. They didn't seem to mind, maybe tired from the day's outing.

The longer I drove, the heavier the coat seemed, especially on the right side. I hoped it wasn't getting water-logged. I'd done my best to dry up at the lake's edge.

At Pixie Inn, I parked the car near the entrance. I was getting out of the driver's seat when the long peacoat caught at the edge of the frame, tugging me back.

Something in the pocket had snagged on the car. I retreated and pulled out the offending item. A small rectangular box: a mini sewing kit.

Did he carry this around with him all the time?

Turner noticed what I held and snatched the sewing kit out of my hands. "That's for my mending," he said.

"I'll go ahead and wash the jacket," I offered. "It's the least I can do for borrowing it."

His gaze softened. "Well, it's delicate material. It'll need to be dry cleaned."

"Sure, no problem." He seemed sensitive over the peacoat. Why? "Did you make this jacket or something?" I asked.

Turner straightened to his full height and emitted a short gasp. "I don't sew anymore. I manage creating products, like this one. It's much more efficient—and lucrative—to be in charge."

"You're in the fashion industry, right?" I asked, remembering something about that from Miles' undelivered speech.

"In affordable fashion," he said.

"Fast fashion" had been what was written in the document. I wonder who he managed and what kind of conditions they worked in.

Before I could ask him any more, Leanne beckoned him over to the entrance of Pixie Inn. "Turner," she said. "Leave Felicity alone. She's got to change out of those wet clothes before she catches a cold."

I thought that was a myth, but I nodded in agreement

and watched as the Lum-Wu group disappeared inside the charming inn.

Kelvin loped to my side. "Leanne's right. You should get changed."

I held up a finger. "Just a minute. What'd you think about the outing?"

"Sadly, people didn't fall over themselves to confess," he said. "But there's a whole lot of tension. And secrets *were* revealed."

"Someone must not have liked that . . . because I didn't just fall into the water, I got pushed."

Kelvin balled up his hands into fists. "Who was it?"

"I don't know. My eyes were closed."

He sighed. "So were mine."

"But something's going on with Turner." I told Kelvin about my conversation and the flimsy jacket Turner had given me. "I wonder if he might be doing something fishy with his fashion business."

"Perhaps. But that could be unrelated to the case," Kelvin said. "Anything else you find out?"

"What I found was a sewing kit," I said, explaining what I'd discovered in the pocket of the peacoat. "Before Turner snatched it away, I saw a needle in it. Stained brown. It may have been blood."

Kelvin whistled. "The blood that knocked Miles out?" He nodded toward his car. "On the ride back, I was trying to get info from Easton about his JV record."

"And?"

"No dice."

"Colton probably knows more about that," I said.

"He might not say anything because of their friendship, though." Kelvin paused. "What about someone else who's known Easton for a while?"

"Who?"

"One degree of separation. Colton's dad. Isn't he staying in a boutique hotel in Fresno?"

"He is," I said. "Time to make some phone calls."

CHAPTER 30

The early bird really does get the worm. After dialing up hotels in Fresno, we finally located the one Mr. Wu was staying in. The friendly staff didn't mind confirming his stay, especially since I'd been involved with the wedding; apparently, the manager and Mr. Wu had chatted all about his son's nuptials.

Moreover, I learned that the hotel did not serve breakfast and that poor Mr. Wu was often seen exiting the lobby at eight in the morning with a hungry look on his face. Which meant that I could swoop right in and offer Colton's dad some delicious baked goodies.

I told my mom I had to make a morning delivery, and since I'd replenished the supply of fresh fortune cookies at the bakery, she let me go. Mom probably assumed I was out stocking my goods at the Fresno grocers, and I didn't bother to correct her.

This early in the morning, I decided to drive Kelvin in my mom's old Corolla. My best friend did not do well without a substantial amount of caffeine in him, and I wouldn't trust him operating any machinery without his usual hit of coffee. He'd actually purchased a fancy espresso maker about a month ago and boasted about its stellar qualities.

When he came over, his hands were holding a thermos for himself and a disposable cup of coffee for Colton's dad. I had to open the passenger door for Kelvin to even maneuver into the car.

Once he settled in, we drove into Fresno to win Mr. Wu's affections through pineapple buns and coffee. And like the front staff had informed me, we found Colton's dad coming out of the elevator just past eight.

I waved to him. "Mr. Wu. Just the man I want to see."

He gave Kelvin and me a confused look, but I lifted the pineapple buns for him to admire.

Kelvin also jiggled the cup of coffee. "I got you some fine espresso."

Mr. Wu's eyes lifted heavenward. "Thank you," he said and then held out his hand for the cup.

I led the way to some cushy seats with a small round table in the corner of the lobby. "Let's take a break over here."

Depositing the box of pineapple buns before Colton's dad, I opened a flap to let its essence of happiness waft out. His eyes lit up, and he automatically reached for one of the buns.

I grinned at Kelvin. Nobody could resist the Jin charm. I held up a finger: one point for me. But Kelvin tilted his head at the coffee cup Mr. Wu was cradling like a lover. He also held up a finger. Fine, let's call it a tie.

Mr. Wu, settled in a plush armchair, studied the two of us. "How long have you been dating?"

"What?" I said. "We aren—"

Kelvin didn't quite kick me, but he tapped the edge of my toes with his shoe. "As we told Haley, we've only started dating very recently."

Right. I'd forgotten about our cover story. No doubt

Mr. Wu could be part of the gossip grapevine connected to the wedding attendants.

"Those are freshly baked," I said about the pineapple buns. "They're also from my family bakery. We do more than egg tarts."

He nodded, either now remembering me from the wedding or agreeing with the fact that we served more than one type of pastry.

"How are the newlyweds?" Kelvin asked.

"Okay. Considering." Mr. Wu squinted at my best friend. "You're the flowers guy, right? Also subbed in for Miles." His voice shook at the name.

"Sorry for the loss of your godson." I nodded at him to eat the pineapple bun. "The pastry will help you feel better."

"Miles reminded me of my younger self." Mr. Wu's gaze grew distant. "The outcast of the family. A pseudo-rebel."

"Pseudo?" I repeated.

"Acting out in harmless ways." He took a bite of the pineapple bun, and a small smile appeared on his lips. "This is really good."

"How did he act out?" Kelvin said.

"Well, for one, he filled out a complaint card after a hospital internship. As a practical joke." Mr. Wu chuckled at the memory.

Kelvin's jaw worked up and down before he said, "Heard a great doctor was let go from the program because of that prank."

Colton's dad put up both of his hands. "Don't know about that. Miles didn't press any official charges. Couldn't have been that bad."

Was this the old boys-will-be-boys routine? I kind of regretted giving Mr. Wu one of mom's precious pineapple buns. "What about the speech he wrote?" I asked. "Everyone was buzzing about the unkind things he had to say. It could have potentially stopped the wedding."

"Nah." Mr. Wu slurped his coffee with confidence. "The speech was for toasting—and roasting. The wedding would have gone on."

Colton's dad had a point. If Miles had truly wanted the wedding to not go through, wouldn't he have done something earlier to stop the ceremony? He wouldn't have waited until the last minute.

Yet someone must have felt threatened enough that they'd decided to kill him. "Tell me about the wedding party. Do you know everyone in it?"

He shrugged. "No, just met those on Leanne's side, even though Turner was the one who first connected Leanne and Colton. But I've known both Nova and Easton for a while."

"They wouldn't be mad at Miles for sharing their secrets?"

He took another bite of pineapple bun and grinned. I hoped it was the magic working on him and not his glee at Miles' ruining of reputations. "Maybe Nova would. She's got a short fuse. Always been the passionate type."

The turning over of the sled at Storyland. "Did she and Miles get along?"

"They had a common thread. Colton." That didn't answer my question. Could Nova have believed Miles was threatening Colton's welfare? So much so that she stepped in to permanently stop him?

"What about Easton?" I asked. "He's been friends with Colton a long time."

"Yeah, Easton and Colton have been friends prior to his Britishisms."

I leaned in. "Sorry. What?"

"That fake accent he puts on. Started that in high school. After his juvie stint."

"You know about that?"

"Miles uncovered the records," Mr. Wu explained.

"How?" I asked. "Is he a lawyer?" What did Miles do again?

"No, he worked at the DMV." Mr. Wu sat back in his chair. "Brilliant of Miles, actually. He accessed the info from his work. People complain about the DMV, but they keep detailed track of things."

"Like Nova's suspended license."

"And Easton's yanked driving privileges," Mr. Wu said, "on account of his sticky fingers."

Sticky fingers? Did Easton have a history of stealing? Maybe he didn't want that to become public.

Was that a strong enough motive to kill Miles? I glanced over at Kelvin to check in with him, but my best friend still appeared to be fuming. His hands gripped his coffee cup, and he was no longer drinking his happy caffeine. He must still be upset that Mr. Wu had sided with Miles about the fake hospital complaint. I'd better cut this interview short.

After one more vital question. "Did you see Miles at any time before the wedding ceremony?"

"Sure, but why? Are you trying to figure out what happened to him?"

I played the Pixie card. "Yeah. I just can't understand how this could have happened in our wonderful town."

"People are unfathomable." He slammed his cup down on the table. "I mean, take my ex—"

I needed to head off his spewing. "What were you saying about Miles? You saw him before the wedding?"

Mr. Wu blinked at me and recalled his previous thought. "Yes, I did. Right before the tea ceremony."

"Where and when?"

"He brushed by me as I was trying to get to the groom's tent. Didn't even say hello and was looking down at his watch, as if he was in a hurry."

"Do you know where he was going?"

"Toward the biggest tent."

Right into the arms of the killer waiting for him at the cake table. What had he been rushing off to do?

CHAPTER 31

Back in the car, I checked on Kelvin. "Are you alright? I know that prank of Miles' cost your dad a position."

"And a blight on his reputation." Kelvin shook his head. "It's already hard for him because . . . glass ceiling." My best friend rolled up the sleeves of his Henley, exposing his dark skin.

"That's awful," I said, reaching over and giving Kelvin a hug.

He soaked it in, but the trill of his phone made us jump apart.

Checking the caller ID, he said, "It's your mom."

Why would she be calling Kelvin?

Kelvin picked up. "Mrs. Jin?"

A torrent of words flowed through the phone.

"Slow down, Mrs. Jin," Kelvin said. "Yes, Lissa's done with her deliveries now."

A wave of shame swept through me. It'd been a lie of omission.

"Go back? To the bakery, right?" Kelvin said.

Did we have an equipment fail? Or maybe an onslaught of customers.

"To the apartment?" Kelvin asked. "And Detective Sun is there? We'll be right over."

Before he'd even hung up, I'd started the car. "What's going on?" I asked.

His forehead crinkled. "I'm not sure, but your mom sounds distraught."

I put my foot down on the pedal, pushing the Corolla as I sped back to Pixie.

The first thing I noticed in front of our apartment building was the cop car. The black and white marred the landscape, a stark contrast against the soft pastels of the flowerbed in front.

Detective Sun stood with her back toward me, semi-hunched. What was she looking at?

I exited the car and soon realized she was bending over my mom, who was seated on the curb. Mom looked almost curled up on the pavement.

"Mom, what's wrong?" I asked, hurrying over to her and crouching down.

She took my hand and squeezed it. "Sorry to alarm you. It was a big shock. But Detective Sun is taking care of everything."

I stayed close to Mom but glanced up at the detective. "What's happening here?"

Kelvin moved into view, creating an intimate circle of four.

Detective Sun cleared her throat. "We found someone breaking and entering your home."

"A burglar?" We lived on a safe street, in a safe town. Most people actually left their windows open and their doors unlocked with extreme confidence. My mom and I kept ours locked.

Mom hung her head. "It was my fault. This morning, I left the window open a crack. For Whiskers to get some air."

"It's not your fault," I said.

"This is on *him*," the detective added, her thumb jerking behind her.

"You caught the guy?" I asked.

Kelvin shifted his gaze to the cop car. "I see someone in the back. Is that . . ."

I stood up and stepped closer to the vehicle. There was a patrol officer in the driver's seat. And in the partitioned space in the back was someone familiar. "Dad?"

My mom made a choking noise.

"Neighbors didn't even notice because the window's on the side of the unit," Detective Sun said. "But I caught him as he was climbing out."

"Thank you, Rylan," my mom said.

"Anytime."

Why had he been inside our home? I was pretty sure he knew that we'd be busy at the bakery at this hour.

I scooted over to the back window. My father's brown eyes locked onto mine. Through the glass, he held up six fingers.

Six. Was that supposed to be significant? Wait a minute. I'd asked him to meet me at the diner the previous evening. What with being pushed into the lake and calling the Fresno hotels, I'd completely forgotten about the appointment.

A strong, warm hand landed on my shoulder. "Lissa," Kelvin said, "the detective wants to talk to you."

Did she know I'd been in contact with my dad? I turned back to the cop, who'd straightened up and was facing me.

"Your mom isn't ready to do a walkthrough of your home. Could you do that with me? Tell me if anything's missing or out of place."

I glanced back at my dad, but he was staring through

the front windshield, no longer focused on me. "Sure, not a problem."

Since the apartment was tiny, it didn't take us long to go through all the areas. Nothing was out of place, and there were no missing items.

"How long was he in here?" I asked the detective.

"Not sure." She tugged at her high ponytail. "I only noticed him coming out."

"You keep track of his movements?" I asked, biting my lip. Maybe she'd even seen my late-night rendezvous with him in front of Foo Fusion.

"No. I go by the apartment and your bakery to do check-ins."

"Why?"

"Because I promised your mom," she said simply.

"Oh. Thank you." That was considerate of her.

I checked our home one more time. "That's so weird. Why would he come in here for no reason?"

"You sure nothing's gone?"

"Everything's accounted for. Especially our valuables, like jewelry."

"Maybe he missed being part of a family." Sadness tinged her words, and I remembered the detective telling me once that she'd lost her mom.

"What will he be charged with?"

Detective Sun brushed off her cinnamon-colored suit, and her voice took on a brisk tone. "Breaking and entering is usually categorized under burglary. But in the meantime, take care of your mom."

"I will."

When I went back outside, Kelvin was sitting next to my mom. She seemed to draw comfort from his support. Like daughter, like mother. I wondered what they'd been talking about.

Kelvin pivoted to face me. "I'm going to walk your mom over to the bakery."

"Wait, what? Don't you want to rest, Mom?"

She crossed her arms over her chest. "I can't relax in the apartment right now. Maybe after work."

"I think I'm going to stay here," I said, "and clean things up."

My mom trembled a bit. "Did he make a mess?"

"No. He didn't leave a trace. Everything seems in order."

Which worried me. I needed to figure out why he'd entered our home.

First, the cops took off. Then Kelvin and my mom made their way to the cul-de-sac of shops, ambling down the sidewalk. Kelvin held her arm as she shuffled off.

I walked back into the apartment and stood in the middle of the living room. "What were you doing here, Dad?"

CHAPTER 32

My biological father had broken into my home, but even after I checked a second time, I couldn't find anything missing. Not a single item was gone. We didn't even have anything super valuable. Our money went straight to the bank—or probably more often, to the expenses the bakery incurred. And most of our jewelry tended to be costume pieces.

If our apartment had gone up in flames, I don't think there was anything that needed rescuing. Except for our own lives. Oh, and Whiskers.

Where was the bunny? I called her name. Was she okay? We let Whiskers have free access of the home, but I couldn't find her near her eating area or her litter box. I even checked under the beds. No Whiskers.

I'd circled the apartment twice when I heard a strange noise from the kitchen. Was it the fridge? The unit was old and made odd clanking noises once in a while. This rhythmic thumping was different.

Fur. I noticed a patch of white velvet at the side of the fridge, in the narrow crawl space between the refrigerator and the wall.

"Whiskers?"

She shimmied out of her hiding spot, and I placed a hand on my heart.

"Whew. I was worried about you."

Whiskers tilted her head at me, as though wondering why on earth I would have been concerned. She could take care of herself. True enough. All of us Jins could.

"What are you doing there?" I asked. "Were you scared by my da—by the man who was here?"

Whiskers came out in the open and hopped to one of our low kitchen cabinets. She nudged it with her nose.

"You want something?" I opened the door and saw the usual array of cookware. "There are only pots and pans in here."

She remained in place and stared at me with those dark, knowing eyes.

The shelf that housed the pots could pull out. I wondered . . . After sliding it on the track, I noticed a bundle wrapped in tissue paper in the far recesses of the cabinet.

"Is it safe to touch?" I asked her.

My bunny twitched her whiskers at me. She wouldn't invite me over here if it were dangerous.

I grabbed the bundle, which had a heft to it. And a rectangular shape. I laid the mysterious package down on the kitchen counter and proceeded to peel off the tissue.

Unwrapping it, I discovered . . . a book. Leather-bound. It read "Family Recipes."

Could it be? Hearing a soft humming, I bent my head closer.

I flipped open the tome and touched the edges of the book. For a second, the pages seemed to glow golden instead of white. A warmth infused my entire body, like a giant hug.

What was the first recipe? Would I even be able to read it? Instead of Chinese characters greeting me, though, the

familiar English alphabet was written in confident, bold
letters.

Po Po. It had to be her handiwork. She'd painstakingly
translated everything to English.

The "A" entry featured a recipe for almond cookies.
A side note indicated that this cookie came from an ad-
aptation of the Chinese walnut biscuit.

I flipped through the pages of the book before me,
delighting in the riffling sound. The scents of past
baked goods seemed to waft in the air, infusing me with
wonder.

A snuffle came from behind me. I turned around and
noticed Whiskers, who blinked at me as though saying,
"I told you it'd be good. Always trust me."

"Thanks, Whiskers," I said, patting her head.

She indulged in my affection for a few moments and
then hopped away.

I returned to the recipe book on the counter. Mom
would be pleased. I needed to tell her straightaway. Or . . .
I could show her.

These were our family recipes, right? And I did have a
kitchen at my disposal, though it wasn't as well-equipped
as the one at the bakery. Plus, the home kitchen felt
cramped if too many people crowded into it. Good thing
there was only me and Whiskers here.

I floated around the kitchen, grabbing the right tools
and ingredients. Before long, I'd mixed the batter and
placed the cookies, topped with almond slivers, into the
oven to bake. Unlike in the past, the baking flowed seam-
lessly. I didn't have any fails or spills.

By the time Mom returned home, I had three batches
of cookies cooling on the kitchen table. I'd run out of
room on the counter to leave them all there.

She sniffed the air a few times and closed her eyes.

"This reminds me of childhood. My great-grandma baking in the kitchen."

"I assume that's because it's her recipe."

Her eyes flew open. "What?"

I showed her the tome.

"How did you—" She ran her fingers along the cover. "The book is just like I remembered it."

"I found it in the kitchen," I said. "Hidden in the back of a cabinet. Left by . . . Richard."

She wrinkled her brow. "He gave it back? After all this time?"

"Well, I might have urged him to."

"You don't even know the man."

"Er, have a cookie," I said, offering one to her.

She accepted it but asked, "What did you do?"

I confessed to my mom, sharing about how I'd run into my father after the wedding and that we'd had coffee together.

My mom gripped my arm with her free hand. "He didn't hurt you, did he?"

I shook my head. "He wanted to talk, get to know me."

"Hmm." She took a bite of the cookie, concentrating on the task. "Just the right amount of almond flavor and elation."

I'd finally done it. Followed in the footsteps of my ancestors by not just baking my own signature treat but those of Jins before me. "We could add so much more to our shelves. People will flock to Jin Bakery now."

She smiled at me. "Maybe one recipe at a time, Felicity. Let's not overwhelm them—or you."

I held the book up. "We can do it together. Split up the recipes."

"Actually, no. I touched the cover, but I didn't feel the rush."

"The what?"

"You know, a sense of blessing. Like when Po Po passed on the pineapple buns to me. I think it's only you, Felicity."

"Me what?" I asked.

She studied me. "Did you feel warm when you held the book?"

"Yes, like a giant hug. And the pages appeared almost golden for a moment. The book even hummed at me."

"Our ancestors have chosen *you* to pass on the recipes to."

"All the recipes?" I held out the book to her. "Are you sure?"

She flipped through the pages and shook her head. "I don't feel a thing. Just the delicate paper. Nothing supernatural."

"But can't you just read the steps?" I asked.

"There's nothing there."

"What do you mean?" I pointed at the instructions.

"I don't see anything. It's all blank to me," she said.

"Really? Oh, that must be rough." My eyes started misting, but Mom waved away my pity.

"It's okay. Your grandmother was the chosen one before me. The recipes flitted to her. The sacred book never transferred its power to me. For good reasons, I'm sure."

"But the pineapple buns?" I said. "You can make those."

"That gift she *could* pass down to me. It was hers to share. But not the rest of the recipes." So that explained why we didn't offer a huge selection of magical pastries in our bakery.

I placed the recipe book down on the table. "Can I reverse the magic? Give it to you instead? I shouldn't have touched it. If I'd waited—"

"No, Felicity. The magic flows to whomever it wishes. A chosen one every couple of generations. The rest become keepers of the book." She flinched. "Some of us guard it better than others."

"You couldn't have known that Dad"—she flinched again at me calling him that—"would take it."

"I don't know why he took it, especially as the recipes weren't even visible to him. And why he gave it back to me, like this."

She finished her cookie as I reflected on the recent turn of events. My father had broken into our apartment, not to steal, but to return something precious to us Jins.

I remembered he'd flashed six fingers at me through the window of the cop car. Our appointment time at the diner. Which I hadn't shown up to. I'd ghosted him, but he'd kept his promise to me.

Guilt rose up from my gut. I'd inadvertently placed him in this awkward situation. Now he'd been arrested for breaking and entering because of my forgetfulness. Was it even a felony to enter a home if nothing was stolen?

I needed to explain to Detective Sun the complexity of the situation. If not for my dad's sake, then to assuage my own guilt. I decided to take over a plate of goodies to her place. I'd need cookies—charmed ones—to get a good resolution for the ensuing conversation.

CHAPTER 33

Detective Sun's home was as cozy as ever. She didn't greet me with much enthusiasm when I showed up unannounced at her door, but at least she didn't turn me away. And I knew her resolve would weaken once she saw the almond cookies I carried with me.

"It's a new treat," I said. "You'll be the first to try it before we start selling them tomorrow."

We sat across from each other in her breakfast nook with its window view.

She bit into a cookie and smiled. "Delicious. Much better than those packaged varieties."

"Thanks." I think. I hoped my freshly baked ones far beat out the processed versions.

"But let's be honest." She laid her hands out, palms up on the table between us. "I don't think you're here to have me try your pastries."

"It's about my father." I stared down at the plate of cookies. "I think it's my fault that he broke in."

The detective chuckled. "Nobody forces someone else to break into a home."

"Well, I was the impetus." I looked back up and into her eyes. After swallowing hard, I told her about the recipe book. How I'd ghosted my father for an appointment, and how he'd only come into the apartment to give the heirloom to me.

"Interesting." Detective Sun nibbled the cookie some more. "Breaking in and not stealing something does put a different spin on what happened."

"Will he be okay?"

She sighed. "I bet he'll be fine. No prior convictions, and he's lawyering up."

"Good," I said.

She finished her cookie and watched me for a moment. "Do you know what I think?"

Nope. I may be a fortune-teller but not a mind reader. "Please, feel free to share your thoughts."

"I wonder why you're working so hard to connect with a father who hasn't shown up for you in decades. Shouldn't you concentrate more on the parent who truly cares about you?"

I felt my throat dry up. "Mom got a shock, but she's fine now."

"Love is as love does."

I scratched my head. "Confucius?"

"Forrest Gump, tweaked." She took another cookie. "I mean, your genetic donor finally talks to you. But why now?"

"What do you mean? He searched for me at the wedding." I must have been wanted, like I'd always desired.

"He was invited to it, and you happened to be catering there. Luck of the draw," she said.

"I disagree." It was fated. The Wishes candle. I'd asked for my dad, and he'd come for me.

"Suit yourself. I'm stating the facts," Detective Sun said.

Was she? But the "why now" question *did* bug me. However, not about my dad. I'd already shifted my mind over to the investigation, whether it was to distract myself from my mixed-up emotions or because the wedding had been mentioned.

The "why now" also applied to the timing of the murder. Had the killer acted only because of the gathering? Due to the convergence of the wedding attendants, or to make sure witnesses were around for Miles' demise? Or maybe it had to do with the bride and groom and the impending marriage itself?

Leanne and Colton. How had they met again? Turner knew. He'd introduced them.

It was about time to return his peacoat anyway. The dry cleaners would have it ready for me the next day.

I decided to pick up the peacoat from the dry cleaners during my lunch break. I'd have time then to make a quick trip to Pixie Inn to speak with Turner face-to-face.

In the morning, I devoted the time to making fresh almond and fortune cookies. By the time the customers rolled in, we had more than enough for me not to be missed when I did my errand later.

I also wanted to see how the almond cookies fared. Regular customers appeared perplexed and then elated that we'd introduced a new baked good. In all my years at the shop, we hadn't added any new pastries. Now that we had the magical recipe book, though, we wouldn't be lacking in variety.

Although many people took their goodies to go, a few ate them in the coziness of the bakery. And their eyes went wide with delight over the new cookie. One of them even asked, "Who made this piece of heaven?"

My mom clamped a hand over my shoulder and physically walked me to face the customer and receive more praise.

Everyone who tried an almond cookie said they'd make sure to tell their friends and family about the new, tasty treat.

After the morning rush subsided, my mom turned to me. "Sales have been so good. We might do more than break even this month."

Something we sorely needed. The landlord had hiked up the rent, and it'd been hard to cover the increasing cost. If the almond cookies boosted our profit margins, that'd be wonderful.

At noon, when I took my lunch break, I left with a jaunty wave. I hoped that things would continue looking up as I made my way to Pixie Inn.

The place was silent as I entered, eerily so. No activity, but I saw Mrs. Robson behind the counter.

She must have noticed the dazed look on my face because she said, "Everyone's gone for the afternoon. Or checked out."

"What?" They'd all left.

Mrs. Robson tilted her head toward the front door. "The bride and groom are getting supplies for their long-delayed honeymoon. The out-of-towners are experiencing their last days of Pixie. And the locals have checked out and returned to work."

Guess it was about time people wrapped up their vacation. "The police are done with their questioning?"

She shrugged. "Can't keep guests locked in here forever. That homicide cop made a few trips early on, but that's stopped now."

Detective Sun hadn't mentioned anything about the case last night, but maybe she'd hit a wall. Targeting

Kelvin in the beginning—clearly a wrong suspect—must have drained her time and resources.

If she wasn't staying on the case, maybe I could help out. I could at least touch base with a certain witness—or possible culprit. Pointing to the dry cleaning in my hand, I said, "I'm supposed to give this coat to Turner."

"He checked out already," Mrs. Robson said.

I suppressed a groan.

Her blue eyes measured me. "Don't worry, though. I have his business card. Along with the other Fresnans, in case someone might need their services in the future."

She proceeded to comb through a pile of business cards on her desk: ones with logos of a broom, or scissors, even a top hat. Mrs. Robson stopped at the last one and read out, "'Manager of Fashion.' Looks like Turner's got an office at the Fulton Mall."

I jotted down the address, checked the time, and calculated in my head. I'd be able to squeeze in a quick drive and chat in Fresno during the remainder of my lunch hour.

CHAPTER 34

Fulton Mall was kind of a misnomer. There'd been a time when the area had offered a pedestrian mall; the streets had been closed to traffic, and people could mill about different local shops. Although it seemed like an interesting place to visit, Fresnans didn't frequent the place in droves. It was a far cry from our own quaint downtown Pixie.

Several years ago, the city had tweaked the original concept of the walkable mall and reopened the region to cars, and officials had completed some renovations. Now, I parked near the sidewalk close to Fulton Street.

I found Turner's office quickly by its vivid red awning hanging over the entrance. When I pushed open the glass door, a connected brass bell tinkled merrily. The office, appropriately named Turner Fashion, had two rooms. The front area held an empty desk with a nameplate flipped on its side. LEANNE LUM, it read.

Despite the large open area, much of the room was filled with stacks of cardboard boxes. A door at the rear was left open a crack. I could hear Turner's voice coming from the interior recesses of the back space.

"I'm up to my eyeballs in returns. Can't you hold off a little longer?"

I crept into the room, a tight space with a compact desk, a rusted steel filing cabinet, and a single guest chair. Turner was talking on the phone, an old corded affair that I was surprised still worked.

The single guest chair already had something piled on it. A shiny leather jacket. Faux, by the glare of its glossiness.

I picked up the jacket, and as I did so, I felt a familiar heaviness in one of its pockets. Turner was still occupied on the phone, so I pulled out the mini sewing kit with one hand. Then I slung the leather jacket around the back of my chair and draped the bagged, dry-cleaned peacoat on top.

While Turner discussed quality control with his caller, I studied the sewing kit in my lap. It felt awkward to stare down, especially when Turner cleared his throat at me.

I slipped the sewing kit into my pants pocket and pasted on a smile. "I'm back with your coat. All cleaned."

"Thanks," he said, "but how did you find me?"

"Mrs. Robson from the inn. Said you checked out, but she also had your business card."

"Unfortunately, vacation time is over." He tapped the phone before him. "Not that it was the most relaxing break I've ever had."

"Yeah, but I'm glad Colton and Leanne finally get to go on their honeymoon."

He glanced toward the front room, maybe in remembrance of Leanne's position. "They deserve their happiness, and we'll send them off with glee tonight."

"Speaking of the two lovebirds, I heard somewhere that you were the man who introduced them to each other."

"Inadvertently." Turner leaned back in his chair. "But do you want to hear about it?"

I motioned for him to speak.

He got to his feet. "Naturally, my designs are wanted everywhere, including the Theatre District."

"You mean, Broadway?"

He flipped his hand in the air. "The arts area in SF. Anyway, I was given tickets to opening night at a show. I took Leanne with me. And who just happens to sit beside us?"

"Colton," I guessed.

"Yes." He rubbed his hands together. "It was love at first sight. And I made it happen."

Not really, but I think Turner wanted to take the credit. "Small world," I said.

"Everything is about connections. If Haley hadn't connected me to Leanne who I connected to Colton, we wouldn't even have had a wedding. And you wouldn't be here in my office right now."

I gestured around me. "How did you get your own business?"

He winked at me and sat back down in his swivel throne. "Connections again. I shudder to think of still sewing my way without recognition or recompense." He gave a long, theatrical shiver.

"But not everyone believes in your business model of fast fashion."

He sniffed. "Ignorant people. I provide a benefit. Affordable, stylish clothing for the masses."

"Aren't you concerned about the environmental impact?"

"It's fine," he said. Which didn't answer my question.

I pressed on. "The greenhouse gases? Or clothes in landfills?"

He stared at me.

"Was that what Miles was concerned about?" I asked. He'd associated Turner with unethical fashion in his never-delivered speech.

"Thanks for returning my peacoat," he finally said. "Now if you'll excuse me, I have some phone calls to make."

I left Turner's office as he picked up his corded phone. He didn't appear to be dialing any numbers as I headed to the front room, though. Passing by the tall stacks of boxes, I checked out their postal markings. They'd come from overseas destinations. Interesting.

What was Turner hiding? I touched the mini sewing kit in my pocket. Was it really a blood stain on the needle?

All the way home, I worried that I'd taken the kit. Here's hoping that Turner wasn't attached to it. Maybe I could keep the sewing kit, and he'd be none the wiser.

Once I parked the car near our apartment, I took out the box. Oops. On the back of the sewing kit, Turner had placed a prominent sticker that read, "If found, please contact . . ." He must actually value it, so I'd better make a quick assessment.

I studied the needle through the box's transparent lid. Was it red? Or brown? What did the color of blood look like once it dried up? Maybe I could go online and use Dr. Google to help me out. Though sometimes the internet went all zigzag on information.

Glancing down the street, I wondered about a different doctor. A real-life one with expertise. I headed over to Kelvin's house and knocked on the door.

Kelvin opened up—he sometimes took his lunch break at home—and I peered around him. "Is your dad here?"

"And hello to you, too."

"Sorry," I said, holding up the kit. "I need to find out if there's blood on this."

Kelvin caught on. "Is that Turner's?"

"Yeah, and I need your dad's expert opinion. Is he in?"

"You should know the answer by now." About ninety-nine percent of the time, Mr. Love was not around and busy at work.

"Which hospital?"

"You're in luck today. He's at Pixie Medical Center."

"Then that's my next destination. I need to sneak this back to Turner before he gets suspicious." I showed Kelvin the sticker on the back of the sewing kit.

"Who would've thought that little box would be so valuable?"

I shrugged. "People have the strangest treasures."

"And, Lissa, you're not going alone to the hospital." Kelvin locked up and followed me.

Pixie Medical Center was a small hospital with a hundred beds. It boasted a clean look of glass windows and sandstone walls. Inside, we stopped at a nurse station, and I said, "We're looking for Mr. Love."

The uniformed nurse raised an eyebrow at me.

"Er, Dr. Love." Kelvin's dad didn't stand on formality, and something he often said was that being called "doctor" made him feel like a relationship guru instead of a surgeon. So I called him Mr. Love out of habit.

Kelvin sidled up to the desk, adding, "Can you let him know his son is here?"

The nurse must've seen the family resemblance because she paged Kelvin's dad, and he soon arrived.

Mr. Love glanced between Kelvin and me. "Everything okay?"

Why'd I think I should waste this man's time on my unimportant errand?

Kelvin nudged me.

"Um, we're fine," I said. "Just had a question. Is there blood on this needle?"

Mr. Love put on some gloves at my remark. As I handed over the sewing kit, I thought about the cause of the blood. Turner had probably pricked his finger to make Miles faint. But then a more horrid thought hit me. I blurted out, "Could it have been used to stab someone in the throat?"

Maybe Turner had tried to kill Miles with the sewing needle.

Mr. Love frowned at me, opened the lid, and peered at the metal item. "It's pretty small to do much damage to a person." After a slight pause, he said, "And this isn't blood. It's rust. You can tell by the scaly texture and the color."

I felt my cheeks turn a more convincing shade of blood red than the old rust. "Oh, thanks, Mr. Love."

He gave the kit back to me. "This wouldn't have anything to do with what happened at that wedding, would it?"

My best friend looked down at the linoleum floor while I mumbled, "The police were getting keen on Kelvin as a suspect."

"Only at first," Mr. Love said. "They questioned me, and then they bothered my son. But the cops were wrong. Someone else used those gardening shears."

Kelvin's lips moved, and I thought maybe he was whispering "pruners" under his breath. Not that he'd correct his dad out loud. Too bad he'd left that tool out in the open for someone murderous to scoop up.

Mr. Love placed his broad hands on my shoulders, and I refocused on him. "Felicity, the cops aren't messing with Kelvin anymore. Why don't you let things be?"

I nodded, out of respect, and he left us.

But my mind started working overtime. The pruners. They hadn't been left out for just anyone to grab, they'd been in a tent. Which one? Kelvin hadn't remembered exactly where he'd left them since he didn't have a photographic memory.

But something else did. . . .

CHAPTER 35

The answer was simple. A camera. "Kelvin," I said, "do you still have those digital pics you bought? From the wedding?"

He nodded. "I can show them to you right now."

We examined the shots in the lobby of Pixie Medical Center. "Those," I said. "With the corsages and boutonnieres." The pics showed the wedding party in their respective tents.

"What are we trying to find?"

"Your pruners. In the background."

Kelvin zoomed in and out on the screen across several photos before we found it. "I recognize the orange handles," he said.

I bit my lip. "Which tent is it? Bride or groom's side?"

"Colton's crew."

"Which means Nova, Easton, or the groom had easy access to the tool."

"Easier," Kelvin said. "The tents were pitched pretty close to each other."

"Still." Maybe seeing the pruners lying around had sparked someone's morbid imagination.

"We better get back," Kelvin said, and I noticed the time on his cell phone.

Nothing much could have happened during our quick lunch jaunt, right?

Turned out that we'd had a ravenous crowd at the bakery while I'd been gone. In fact, my own stomach was rumbling. That's what I got for skipping lunch. And I couldn't fill it up with almond cookies either. Because all of them had sold out.

"They're all gone?" I asked my mom, staring at the empty display case.

"Even the extras that were in the kitchen." She beamed at me.

"I better get right to baking then."

Mom touched my shoulder. "I'm proud of you, Felicity. And thank you—for restoring the Jin recipes."

I wriggled my fingers, the memory of the invisible magic coursing through my veins coming back to me. It'd taken me a long time to claim my birthright, when most before me had naturally dived into magical baking. Now, though, I was the keeper and maker of my family's most treasured treats. "I'm truly honored."

"Our ancestors couldn't have chosen a better recipient," Mom said. "One of your almond cookies made a customer literally dance out the door with happiness."

I was the holder of the secret family recipes. Me. The original klutz in the kitchen with more than a few botched pastries to show for it.

In the kitchen, under the cheerful pendant lights, I got to baking. As I mixed the ingredients by hand, watching the batter smooth out, I thought about the recipe book. The one only I could read. Whiskers must have guided me to its presence in our cabinet . . . because she'd seen my father place it there.

How was Richard doing? He'd gone to great lengths to return the book to me after my unintended no-show. I felt guilty about leaving him alone waiting in the diner. Although, truth be told, he'd bailed out for much longer on his own child, leaving me behind as a tiny baby. Nevertheless, maybe I should check on how he was faring.

I could contact Detective Sun and get the updated scoop. She'd reassured me that he'd be fine, but I needed to know for sure. I could just call him. After all, he'd given me his number at our initial meeting, and I was carrying the napkin around in my pocket like some kind of talisman.

Once I created two new trays of almond cookies, I asked my mom for a snack break.

"You must have had a light lunch," she said.

"Very." An *empty* lunch was more like it.

"Go ahead."

After I'd gotten her permission and a pineapple bun, I waited until her back was turned before I slid the cordless phone off its unit.

I ate on the sidewalk in front of the bakery, munching away. When I finished, I dusted the crumbs off my lips and made the call. I expected to leave a message since I figured he was still busy trying to extricate himself from the criminal charges. To my surprise, my dad answered, and I stumbled through an awkward hello.

He seemed to know why I was calling and thanked me for my concern,

After a pause, I said, "I feel bad about the way I left things." I envisioned how he'd been entrapped in the police car and then sped off to the station. "Can we meet up?"

"Where?" he asked.

I thought about it. Not the bakery. I wouldn't do that

to my mom. Or the apartment—too intimate. "Pixie Park," I said. A neutral location within walking distance.

We agreed to meet up after the bakery closed for the day.

I told my mom that I had plans after closing. It didn't hurt that I lingered near Love Blooms while Mom walked back home. She'd assumed I would be hanging out with Kelvin. He, in turn, was currently at his shop, bent over a bouquet of purple irises. Whenever he worked, he concentrated so hard that he blocked everything else out. It was easy to slip away from the cul-de-sac unnoticed and saunter over to the park.

It didn't take me long to find my father on a bench near some beautiful rosebushes in pearly white, brilliant yellow, and blushing pink colors. Their soft scents floated in the air as Richard patted the space next to him.

I sat down by his side, glad we weren't facing each other but looking off in the distance at the trees in the park. It made it easier for me to speak.

"Thanks for giving back the recipes," I said.

"Glad you found the book. I was gonna give you a note about its hiding spot, but I didn't have time before I heard the sirens."

"Why didn't you just leave it on the counter?" I asked.

"And have your mom realize I'd entered your home? No way. But I never should've taken the book in the first place. The recipes belonged to the Jin side." Did he think of family in terms of *sides*? Opposing sides?

He shook his head. "And I could never figure out its trick."

"What trick?"

He scratched his head. "Of the book. I figured the

recipes were written with invisible ink, and I know that heat reveals the writing. At first, I used a flame, but then I ended up tossing the whole thing in the fire in frustration—"

"Wait, what?" I scooted to the far edge of the bench. "You tried to burn our family's recipes?"

"Bygones," he said. "Come on, Felicity. Didn't I eventually give back the book?"

"After you tried to burn it," I repeated.

"Magic. Can't get rid of it so easily." His jaw clenched.

"Why would you want to?" I asked.

"I never signed on for this nonsense."

His tone of voice made the gooseflesh rise up on my arms. "What are you talking about?"

"The manipulating of feelings. The quote-unquote 'gift.'"

Was he talking about the *joy* we baked into our pastries?

He sniffed. "Your mother"—but he said the word like a curse—"only told me about the magic after we tied the knot. That whole first year, I went back and forth about it. Had she tricked me into marrying her? What was the real chemistry, and what was the magical chemistry between us?"

Had he taken the recipe book as a memento like he'd told me before? Or was it out of spite? I wanted to get to the truth about my abandonment, and I licked my suddenly dry lips. "What about me? Was *I* not real enough for you? A clear symbol of your love?"

He turned toward me and seemed to remember my presence. "You were a good thing. An innocent baby to balance out the confusion in our relationship."

"But then?"

"Then it turned bad." His spine stiffened. "I knew

something bad would happen to you if I stayed in your life."

"That horrible headache you had," I said, remembering his story from the diner. "Did you say you also got nausea?"

He rubbed his forehead as though remembering. "Dizziness along with a roaring in my ears." That's how I had felt before I had reined in my gift of prediction. My added special skill had come from the Zhou genes. Was my father magical, only he didn't know it?

"And you're here now because . . . ?"

I wanted him to say it, to let me know he'd come back for *me*. Wasn't that the hope I'd pinned on the candle?

"Of the wedding."

"Did you know I was a vendor?" I wondered if Colton had mentioned our bakery and treats to my father. And he'd made sure to be here. To reunite with his long-lost daughter.

"Sure," he said, "after I saw the cake table." He glanced off to the side where the reception tent had been pitched.

"Oh." Guess he hadn't actively searched for me. It'd all been a coincidence.

"The egg tarts are distinctive. That, and you had your business cards stacked on the table." With my mom and me listed as co-owners. How many Angela and Felicity Jins could there be in the world?

"The cards were a sign that I needed to connect with my little girl again." He glanced at the rosebushes before continuing. "It was fate."

He'd called it "fate."

"So, you actually want to reconnect now?" After a few skipped decades?

He tapped his noggin. "I don't have any more bad

premonitions. We can have a fresh start. I can prove to you that I'm a good father."

Could we have a redo? My thoughts swirled in my head. He hadn't really found me. Instead, he'd gotten invited to a wedding and found my business cards.

He clasped his hands together. "Where do we go from here?"

"I don't know," I said. "Will you be sticking around town?"

"Well, my job is in Oakland. But it's not so far away."

And what about Mom? They seemed to have a tumultuous past. But he'd tried anyway, sending the unwanted gifts, breaking and entering—"Wait, what happened to those charges against you?"

"I've got a great lawyer," he said. "There's a world of difference between trespassing and burglary. Or, for that fact, murder."

I shivered.

He misread me. "It's getting late and cold. You probably need to get going."

I agreed and walked home at a quick pace. Not only for warmth, but because I knew that a murderer was still on the loose in Pixie.

CHAPTER 36

Even after I arrived at my cozy apartment, I still felt unsettled. Mom was already seated on her comfortable recliner in the living room in front of the TV. She turned her head to look at me. "Did you have a nice time with Kelvin?"

I murmured something unintelligible that I hoped she'd take as a positive response.

"That's great, Felicity." She turned her attention back to her show.

I heated up some leftovers. Taking my meal and Whiskers, I snuck into my partitioned bedroom space while Mom was distracted. I ate a quick meal, then focused on the bunny.

I'd wanted her cute company, but I also wanted answers. Whiskers had provided insight into my magic before. Could she also help me understand my father's headaches?

I settled on my bed with Whiskers in my lap. She faced me, and I looked into her chocolate chip–colored eyes. "The headaches my dad had? Does he have magic, too?"

Whiskers purred at me. Wait, bunnies could purr?

I decided to stroke her fur, the usual way I got her to communicate.

It took some time petting her fur, which seriously calmed me, before a blurry vision formed. Maybe there couldn't be a sharp image without access to memories?

In the haze, I noticed two figures. Despite being unclear, I could distinguish my mom. A man stood next to her—my father, I figured. They seemed to be kneading dough together. And then the image blinked out.

"What was that?" I asked Whiskers, but she only stared at me.

His headaches. Could they have been from being close to my mom as they worked side by side? Too much magic for him? Or could some magic have transferred over to him? But then why did he have the headaches, and how come he hadn't crafted any joy-inducing foods?

"Ugh. I just don't get it." I banged a fist against my mattress, and Whiskers scooted off my lap. Then I jammed my hands in my pockets—only to have something jab at my palm.

The mini sewing kit. I still needed to return it. Could I sneak it into Turner's office? No. Showing up two days in a row would be suspicious.

Where else could the sewing kit "be found" without raising suspicions? Pixie Inn. He could have lost it there. Might have slid right out of his pocket, in fact.

I'd been by earlier in the day. I bet I could convince Mrs. Robson I'd stumbled upon it in the entryway or something.

"I forgot something," I told my mom. "Just popping over to Kelvin's."

"That's fine." She waved me off, trusting in me and the Loves.

It wasn't a lie either. I'd decided to ask Kelvin to drive me to Pixie Inn. No way was I walking over there in the dark.

As luck would have it, Kelvin answered on the first knock. He listened to my plan for giving back the sewing kit to Turner.

"At least there won't be any killers at the inn," he said. "Aren't they all gone?"

"Mrs. Robson said the locals are, but there are still a few more days for those from out of town."

Kelvin glanced at the dark sky. "Well, they should be in bed by now. It'll be easy enough to drop off the kit at the front desk."

"Exactly."

Pixie Inn did seem quiet when we entered. Mrs. Robson greeted us by name and asked, "Did you get the time wrong?"

"I'm sorry?" I asked.

"You missed the party." She gestured down the hall. "It was in the great room. A send-off for the lucky couple. They'll be leaving tomorrow morning."

I remembered Turner mentioning something about sending them off, but I definitely hadn't been invited. Maybe they wanted to put the (literally) killer wedding behind them.

"I'm actually here to return this," I said, holding out the sewing kit. "Found it in the lobby earlier today but forgot to show you."

Mrs. Robson took the kit and examined it. "It belongs to Turner. I'll give him a call later. He might be on the road right now. The party ended about ten minutes before you arrived."

"Can you tell me when you reach him?" Then, distracted, I sniffed the air. "Is that chocolate I smell?"

Mrs. Robson beamed. "My homemade chocolate chip cookies." She leaned in. "I have a little trick to them. See, I add a sprinkle of sea salt on top to bring out the flavor."

"They must be delicious."

"Not a crumb left," Mrs. Robson said. "It was a cookie and cocktails extravaganza. I baked, and the rest of them brought drinks."

Kelvin chimed in. "Too bad we didn't get to say goodbye to the bride and groom. I'm assuming they'll leave early in the morning?"

"Yes, but they might still be awake now. Let me give them a ring."

Mrs. Robson picked up the receiver of the phone on her desk and dialed. After a moment, she smiled. "Hello, Leanne. Kelvin and Felicity are here in the lobby and want to give their regards to you."

Kelvin reached for the phone first and passed on his good wishes.

Then I spoke with Leanne. "Hope you two enjoy your well-deserved honeymoon."

"Thank you," she said. "Let me get Colton. He's just resting on the couch. Said his stomach was hurting."

A muffled clunk as she put the phone down. I heard a shuffle. In the distance, Leanne attempted to wake up Colton. Her entreaties kept growing louder—until she screamed.

"Something's wrong," I said to Mrs. Robson.

We hung up and hurried over to the Shakespeare Suite. Mrs. Robson pulled out the master key, unlocked the door, and swung it open.

Leanne stood over Colton, who was resting on the couch with his back to us. Except Leanne was shaking him, and he wasn't waking up. He didn't let out any grunts of annoyance at being disturbed.

"Let me see, dear," Mrs. Robson said as she went to Colton.

She checked his still body, while I leaned against Kelvin for both physical and emotional support.

"Colton is alive," Mrs. Robson said. "He has a pulse, and he's breathing. But we'll need the paramedics."

I straightened up. and Kelvin pulled out his phone to make the call. Thankfully, the paramedics arrived within minutes.

"Unconscious," they determined.

They put him on a gurney while peppering Leanne with questions about Colton's medical history.

She seemed close to tears as she said that Colton was healthy—had just passed his physical with flying colors.

"No allergies?" a paramedic asked.

Leanne shook her head. We followed them out the door.

"We've got to take him to the hospital. What did he have to eat and drink tonight?"

Leanne named a meal from a high-quality local restaurant and then shared about their send-off party. Cookies and cocktails. He'd toasted the others with his favorite drink, a martini.

What had happened to him?

Leanne jumped into the ambulance with Colton.

Mrs. Robson, Kelvin, and I watched as the wailing vehicle rushed down the street. I hoped for the best for him, but I had a sinking feeling that someone at the party hadn't been sending Colton off to a honeymoon but to the morgue.

CHAPTER 37

"We need to call Detective Sun," I said as we reentered Pixie Inn.

Kelvin nodded while Mrs. Robson said, "You mean the homicide detective? But why?"

Then her face paled. "You don't think . . ."

I didn't answer her but instead asked, "Did you already wash tonight's dishes?"

She flapped her hands around. "I only cleared them away. Before you two arrived, I barely had time to tidy up the great room."

"Perfect," I said. "And where's the kitchen?"

Mrs. Robson beckoned us to follow her down a hallway. We entered a dining room with a polished oak table placed beneath a glass chandelier. She didn't give the area a second glance as she bustled through the adjoining swinging door.

The gallery kitchen was narrow but big enough for a cooking range, a midsize fridge, and a porcelain sink. Dishes were piled on the blue-and-white-tiled counter, along with glassware. I noticed cookie crumbs on the small plates. Peering at the glasses, I tried to distinguish which one had been Colton's.

Noticing my interest, Mrs. Robson drew close to the drinking glasses and reached for one.

"Don't touch a thing," I cautioned.

She flushed. "Oh, right. But aren't my fingerprints already everywhere?"

I shrugged. "Just in case." I didn't know much about crime scene protocol, but I didn't want the detective reprimanding me for messing up her investigation.

"Was it that one?" Kelvin said, pointing.

I followed his line of sight to a glass with a telltale green olive at the bottom. Bingo.

"Great catch," I said. He preened a little at the praise. "Thankfully, it's still here."

"I'll call Detective Sun," Kelvin said as we moved out of the kitchen together.

I agreed, but once through the swinging door, I said, "It's probably best if we stay here until she arrives."

Kelvin dialed up the detective, who agreed to meet us as soon as she could. After we hung up, we heard shuffling footsteps approaching.

Nova arrived in the dining room. She wore purple plaid pjs that matched her hair, and she rubbed at her eyes. "What are you all doing here?"

In turn I asked, "How come you're out and about so late?"

"Something woke me," she said. "And I couldn't go back to bed. Thought I'd get a glass of warm milk to settle me."

Mrs. Robson went over and patted Nova on the shoulder. "It must have been the ambulance that woke you up, dear."

Nova jolted at the words. "The what?"

"Colton was taken to the hospital," I said.

"Why? What happened?" She didn't look as sleepy anymore.

"We're not sure, but he was wheeled out of here unconscious." I watched Nova's reaction. Her jaw dropped.

"According to Leanne, his stomach had been hurting," I continued.

Kelvin added, "We heard there was a send-off party. Did he eat anything weird tonight?"

Nova's face scrunched up, as though remembering. "I don't think he ate anything at all."

"Not even one of my cookies?" Mrs. Robson said, affronted, her hand over her heart.

"Which were delicious," Nova said. "I had three of them."

Mrs. Robson smiled, appearing appeased.

"He didn't eat, but he drank something, right?" I asked.

"Sure. His signature drink, a martini." She shook her head. "Maybe he had one refill too many."

"What do you mean by that?"

She glanced down the hallway, in the direction of the great room, where the cocktail party had been held. Lowering her voice, she said, "Colton's my buddy, but he ended up saying some terrible things this evening."

"Like what?"

She ran a hand through her short hair. "Basically, he berated every one of us. Leanne tried to jump in and save the event. Apologizing that Colton had had too much to drink, that he didn't mean it, and insisted he get some water."

"Did he eventually calm down?" Kelvin asked.

"No, he kept on with the insults. Said he'd cut his

ties with everybody, and that Leanne would, too. Told us we'd ruined his wedding, but that we were 'never going to ruin his honeymoon.'"

But someone did, hadn't they? He'd ended up at the hospital. Who could have been the culprit?

Before I could muse any further, steady footsteps echoed down the hall. Detective Sun stood before us, radiating authority. She'd even had time to put on a suit (in a mocha hue).

She nodded at Kelvin and me. "Why doesn't it surprise me that you two are here?" Flashing her badge at the group of us, she said, "Who wants to enlighten me on what's going on?"

We all started speaking, and she held up a hand. "Wait, I changed my mind. I'll get your statements one at a time."

It took half an hour of interviewing us and recording our responses on her phone before Detective Sun was satisfied and said we were free to go. At this point, Nova seemed fully wide awake. "No way I can sleep now," she complained. "And I'll have to call to change my travel plans."

"That would be wise," Detective Sun said.

"Of course. I'm not going to leave Colton while he's in the hospital."

I didn't think the detective was concerned about Colton getting the support he needed; she probably was making sure a killer wouldn't be jetting out of Pixie.

Before Kelvin and I left, I whispered to the detective, "Can you do me a favor? Please don't tell my mom about this."

She raised an eyebrow at me. "Honesty is always the best policy."

I nodded, agreeing in theory, but how could I explain

meeting up with my father in secret? And then gallivanting off to the inn to pursue a murder case? I'd have to think of a good way to frame my actions.

Kelvin yawned. "You ready to go, Lissa?"

"Sure am." We walked out together, and once we were in his car, I said, "Two murder attempts, huh? What's going on?"

Kelvin blew out a breath. "I'm hoping that it's one actual murder and Colton keeps fighting for his life."

"You're right," I said. "And let's drop by the hospital tomorrow to check on his status."

"Easily done." It must be great to have connections with the local medical system.

"I just don't understand," I said as Kelvin maneuvered the car onto the quiet road. "Why were two people in the same wedding party put in danger? There has to be a connection."

I bit my lip and continued, "Could Miles' killer have felt threatened by Colton somehow?"

"If Colton's awake tomorrow, we can try to get the answer out of him."

I nodded and added another thought. "Or you heard what Nova said about Colton berating them. Could someone have been so bothered by his words that they lashed out?"

Kelvin slowed down for a yellow light. "Someone with a hot temper?"

Being in the car reminded me of a certain wedding attendant's road rage. "Like Nova? She was all, 'I'm here for warm milk,' but maybe she really wanted to make sure the cups were thoroughly washed. To hide any incriminating evidence."

The light turned green, and Kelvin eased forward with care. "Sounds like she's sticking around until Colton's all better. Why would she do that if she wanted to hurt him in the first place?"

"Out of duty?" Though more sinister thoughts came to mind. "Or regret? Or, perhaps, as a false sign of good character?"

Kelvin drummed his fingers lightly on the steering wheel. "What if it was the opposite? Not a spontaneous thing, I mean."

I turned my head and studied his profile. "You're saying that someone deliberately planned to kill Colton?"

"Why not? Or what if—hear me out—Colton was supposed to be the original victim all along?"

"Um . . ."

"Miles and Colton are cousins. They have a certain family resemblance."

"So the killer goofs up the first time? And then tries to knock off Colton now?"

"Well, it's their last chance, isn't it?" Kelvin pulled up to my apartment complex. "I mean, Colton and Leanne were ready to go on their honeymoon tomorrow."

Kelvin had opened extra lines of investigation to pursue. I'd figured talking about it in the car would help me gain clarity, but I felt even more confused now. And then another idea emerged. "The modes of attack were so different," I mused.

"First, the stabbing." Kelvin shuddered, maybe thinking of how his pruners had been involved.

"Then, the poison," I added.

"Two different methods, which might mean . . ."

"There were two entirely different killers," I said. My head started hurting from all the speculation.

Kelvin leaned over and touched my forehead. His fingers felt cool and soothing. "Your brow is furrowed," he said. "Maybe you should get a good night's sleep instead of worrying so much."

"You're probably right."

"Things will look up in the morning."

I put on a fake smile for Kelvin, but I didn't share in his optimism. Another day just meant more time passing without the murderer (or murderers) being caught.

CHAPTER 38

In the morning, I moved like molasses. I barely rolled out of bed in time to walk over to the bakery with my mom.

As she unlocked the door to the shop, Mom asked, "Everything okay?"

"Fine," I said, trying to hide my yawn. I didn't want to tell her about the emotional drama that had happened last night. "I just stayed out with Kelvin longer than planned." Hey, that was partially true. Only we'd been surrounded by paramedics at the inn.

Mom gestured me inside the bakery, flicked on the lights, and then turned to me. Her eyes searched my face. "You know, in my opinion, Kelvin is a very nice young man."

"Yeah, and?" Where was my mom going with this? If Kelvin wasn't "nice," I wouldn't have been friends with him for so long.

She shifted her head a fraction, glancing over my right shoulder. "If you want my opinion, I think Kelicity would be a great name."

Felicity *was* my name. Wait, did she say "Kelicity"? Was she shipping us together? At least she hadn't suggested Felvin.

I shook my head to clear it. "Mom, we were just up late talking . . ." To the police, among other people.

"About?"

Not murder. I couldn't say "murder." My brain latched onto the first thing I could reveal without repercussions. "The hospital."

She scrunched her eyebrows at me. "Why would you be talking about that?"

"Our friend went to the hospital last night."

"Oh no." Mom clapped a hand against her mouth.

"We'll probably check on him later today."

Mom started marching toward the kitchen without a backward glance. "We'd better get started then," she said as I trailed behind her. "You'll need to bring treats over to him. The more Jin pastries, the faster the recovery."

As we entered the kitchen with its cheery tangerine-colored floor, I said, "But we don't have any magical healing powers."

"We give happiness," Mom said. "What better medicine is there?"

Couldn't argue with that logic. Mom and I worked in tandem to create delicious treats.

We ended up stocking our glass display case at the front of the store, had several trays of pastries at the ready in the kitchen, and had extra goodies to bring to Colton.

"Take a long lunch hour," Mom said, as she glanced at the box I was preparing to take over to the hospital.

I put in a pair of Mom's new pineapple buns filled with vanilla custard, along with half a dozen almond cookies. Ready or not, here I come.

I managed to snag Kelvin on his lunch hour, so we could go together. Pixie Medical Center still smelled like a clean combination of antiseptic and waxed floors when we arrived.

At the nurse's station, we encountered the same individual as before. "Dr. Love isn't here today," she told us.

Kelvin shook his head. "Our friend's in the hospital. Colton Wu. We want to visit him."

She hesitated. "You mean he's your relative, right? The rules state . . ."

Kelvin hated lying, so I stepped up to the task. "Exactly. Colton is our, um, cousin."

She clicked her tongue. "That poor soul."

Her words didn't give me a good vibe.

The nurse retrieved a clipboard. "Please sign in, and I'll get your visitor badges."

We did as she commanded, and I noticed Leanne's name. The bride had clocked in an hour ago. I pointed at the list. "Leanne forgot to sign out."

"Actually, I think she's still in there." The nurse checked the database and told us Colton's room number. She started to give directions when Kelvin cut her off with a polite interjection.

"I'm pretty sure I know the way."

"Of course you do."

"Follow me." Kelvin took brisk steps, and I noticed we were heading to the ICU area. I gulped.

When we arrived in the sterile room, with its white walls and blond wood paneling, all I could focus on was the quiet figure lying in bed. Colton seemed to be sleeping and at peace. His heart monitor was emitting a regular beeping rhythm. Perhaps he was better?

A sniffling sounded from the corner, and I finally noticed Leanne curled up in an armchair. Kelvin murmured his well wishes for Colton, and I said, "I'm so sorry, Leanne. I brought you some treats. Maybe they'll help."

"Thanks for coming."

"Of course."

Her eyes flicked to the box I held. "Bring any chocolate?"

Oops. "No," I apologized, but she flopped her hand in the air.

"Not like I've been enjoying eating anyway."

"How is he doing?" I asked.

"The doctors aren't sure when he'll wake up." A tear slid from the corner of her eye. "But at least they think he'll wake up sometime."

A loud stomping came from the hallway, and someone burst through the door.

"Jada?" Leanne said.

Guess everyone had decided to come during their lunch hour.

"Colton isn't awake, but feel free to talk to him." Leanne glanced at the bed. Colton's chest rose and fell steadily.

Jada didn't spare him a glance. "I came here for you, Leanne. I couldn't care less about that jerk."

"Shh!" Leanne jolted out of her chair. "He can still hear you." She made to cover Colton's ears but hesitated, stuck hovering over him. Seemed like Leanne didn't want to accidentally mess with any of the tubes attached to Colton. Dejected, she sank back in her chair.

"Whatever." Jada shrugged. "He acted like a jerk last night. Must run in the family. Miles crashing the bachelorette party, and now this. What kind of groom makes a speech about threatening to cut you off from your friends?"

"He was stuck in the inn for so long," Leanne said. "We were all getting cabin fever. . . ."

"Speaking of being stuck in places," Jada said, offering a hand to Leanne, "why don't you get away from Pixie? Come home."

"Go home now? But I don't think my parents—"

"*Come home*," Jada emphasized. "Back to our place, with its good memories."

Leanne shook her head. "It doesn't matter. I won't be able to relax no matter where I am. Pixie Inn is as good as anywhere else, and it's a lot closer to the hospital."

Jada checked out the boring white walls of the room. "You've got to take a break from the stress . . ."

"No," Leanne said. "I'd feel better staying right here." She patted the armchair. "This actually folds out, so I'm going to ask the staff if I can sleep overnight."

"Are you sure?" Jada's voice took on a pleading tone.

"Very." Leanne crossed her arms over her chest.

"Fine." Jada backed away a step. "But I'm always here for you, roomie."

Leanne relaxed her arms a little. "I know—"

A shrill ringing sounded in the room. I glanced at the machines, but nothing seemed amiss. With a quick motion, Leanne pulled out her phone and answered it. At the same time, she waved goodbye to Jada, who reluctantly left the room.

I didn't mean to eavesdrop on her conversation, but Leanne hadn't dismissed Kelvin or me.

She blinked several times as she held the phone to her ear. "What policy? A document?"

A few beats, and then she said, "I really don't know what you're talking about, Detective."

Her voice grew sharper as she added, "No, I don't

have time to come to the station to chat." She clicked off and stared at the phone in her hand.

Kelvin cleared his throat. "Well, we'd better get going."

"Try and eat something," I urged Leanne. "It'll keep your spirits up."

"You're probably right." She rubbed her eyes, and I wasn't sure if she was trying to get rid of tears or exhaustion.

"I can check in on you again later in the evening," I said. "And I'll bring chocolate."

A small smile emerged on her face. "Thank you, Felicity."

One more promise to make. I scooted to Colton's bedside. Bending close to his ear, I whispered, "Please wake up, Colton. I'm going to catch whoever did this, but I can't do it without your help."

CHAPTER 39

Kelvin and I left the hospital room in a somber mood. But maybe that was because we were both hungry. Kelvin grabbed us a couple sandwiches from the cafeteria. After I took a few bites and settled my stomach, I asked, "What did you think about what Jada said?"

He swallowed hard. "She was kinda heartless, don't you think? I mean, the guy was in a coma."

"Probably put there by one of them." I thought back to the glasses from the "celebratory" toast at Pixie Inn. "Leanne said his stomach had been feeling funny." Would the detective share any info about what had been in that martini glass? Doubt it. She'd probably tell me to concentrate on my own kitchen and not the one at the inn.

As if we were on the same wavelength, Kelvin said, "Wonder who assembled the drinks last night."

"Do you think Jada is still around?"

Kelvin took a few giant chews and finished his sandwich. Wiping his hands against his dark-rinse jeans, he said, "Let's take a peek."

We wandered down several hallways and circled back to the main lobby. By this time, I'd also finished my sandwich.

"Guess she's long gone," he said.

"Too bad. I wanted to ask her more questions about the send-off. And the bachelorette party."

"The party? Why?"

"She talked about the drama there," I said. "From Miles. Could that have been a factor in his death?"

Kelvin rubbed his chin. "If only we could get more info. But I'm not close friends with any of them."

"What about Haley? She was crushing on you. And you've got her email, right?"

Kelvin closed his eyes. "Don't remind me about that awkwardness."

"She was bound to have been at the bachelorette party. And last night's shindig, too."

"I'll contact her—after I figure out a fake reason." He shuddered. "Don't want to give her the wrong idea again."

I smirked. "Yeah, Romeo."

"I'll catch you up after you close shop, okay?"

"Agreed."

Back at the bakery, the air smelled like serenity. At least that's what whipped custard reminded me of. From behind the counter, my mom beamed at me. "The custard-filled pineapple buns have been very popular today."

"Why wouldn't they be?" I licked my lips just conjuring the flavor profile in my mouth.

"I'll save one for you," she said, pulling out a bun from the display case and shuffling back to the kitchen.

When she returned a few moments later, she motioned for me to sit behind the register. "Here I am blabbing about sales when you've got more important things on your mind. How is your friend?"

I thought about Colton lying in the bed and all the

tubes connected to him. "He's stable but hasn't woken up yet."

"Your friend's unconscious?" Mom seemed to wobble, and I offered her the seat, but she waved away my concern. "I'm fine. What happened to him?"

I wanted to lie, say it was a car accident or something. But she looked at me with such care etched in her face that I couldn't. I licked my lips again, but now they were dry from my nervousness of withholding info from my mom. "Well, it's still under investigation . . ."

"Such a shame," Mom said.

I nodded and busied myself messing with the display case. Since she'd taken out the pineapple bun for me, there was an empty space that needed to be filled to balance out the arrangement of pastries. "I'll probably drop by again tonight to see if there's any improvement."

"Of course," she said.

My mom looked like she wanted to say something comforting, but what could she say? A man killed, and another in a coma? This was not the sweet Pixie town that she'd uprooted her prior life to raise me in.

The bakery's door swished open, and I welcomed the distraction in the form of Mrs. Spreckels. Usually the stoic librarian didn't look ruffled at all, but now she strode in with hurried steps. Her horn-rimmed glasses, connected to a beaded eyeglass holder, swung to and fro with her rapid movement.

"Hi, Mrs. Spreckels," I said. "No need to rush. We've got plenty of pastries left."

She didn't crack a smile.

"I'd like to purchase three vanilla fortune cookies," she said, pulling out her coin purse. "It's been a day."

"An afternoon pick-me-up?" my mom guessed.

"Speaking of 'pick-up,'" she said, "I had to reorganize the whole 615 section. The books there were in disarray."

For someone like her who loved order in the library, including hushed silence and aligned book spines, I could imagine the heartache she felt. I'd give her half a dozen cookies for the price of three.

"Mischief-makers," she grumbled and didn't notice the extra treats as she counted out the exact change to me.

"Thank you," I said with a cheery smile. "See you again soon."

She bustled out, and through the glass door, I noticed her already grabbing a cookie. Mrs. Spreckels yanked out the generic printed fortune without giving it a glance and devoured the goodie. I really hoped the happiness flowing from the fortune cookie would soon bolster her spirits.

Being a Jin meant bringing happiness to others, as my mom often reminded me. Even with my new gift of future-predicting, I couldn't—or shouldn't—lose that core foundation.

I went back to the kitchen and pulled out the ingredients I needed to bake more treats. Once I'd finished with another tray of vanilla fortune cookies to replenish the ones I'd given to Mrs. Spreckels, I concentrated on a batch of almond cookies.

The combined aroma of diligence and delight must have brought in more customers. We kept serving a steady stream of people until about an hour before closing. Just enough time to slip in the back and craft some chocolate-flavored fortune cookies for Leanne. How could I make it even better for her chocoholic craving? I know! Chocolate upon chocolate.

I'd create a cocoa-infused cookie and dip it in rich chocolate. Maybe that concoction could become something in our rotation. I'd have to give it a special name. Would I name it after her? Leanne's Longing or something like that?

Speaking of personalization, I wondered if I should give her a special fortune. I could predict something positive for her love life, assuming fate veered that way. But might it be too risky? What if I offered her a look into a grim future instead? Better not risk it.

I could tap some other line of destiny, but which one? My thoughts wandered into predictions of her finances, and I recalibrated my intentions. What if I gave her a pre-printed slip about being lucky in love while I used my own talents to siphon off a clue for the case?

Leanne's conversation with Detective Sun had centered around documentation and a policy. I bet it had to do with money, and if I could use my fortune-telling ways to get more information, it might unlock something in the case.

I mixed the batter and popped it into the oven. Six chocolate-dipped, cocoa-flavored fortune cookies later, I heard the door open. Kelvin's familiar footsteps plodded toward me.

He leaned his head through the archway into the kitchen. "Ready to go, Lissa?"

I grabbed the cookies—and a mini notepad and pen. "Yep. Let's do this."

CHAPTER 40

It was as though no time had passed at all since we'd stopped by the hospital during our lunch hour. Colton still lay in bed, looking very much asleep and hooked up to a number of machines. Leanne sat in the armchair, drooping.

"Did you get anything to eat?" I asked her.

"Besides your pastries, a protein shake." Better than nothing, I supposed.

I offered her the new box of fortune cookies. "I made these double chocolate."

A smile flickered on her face and then went out. She did, though, peek inside the take-out container. "Chocolate-dipped cookies."

"Cocoa-flavored," I added. "I'm thinking of calling them Leanne Lift-Me-Ups."

She giggled. "That's the first time anyone's named something after me."

Leanne pulled out a fortune cookie and split it open. The message inside had one word typed on it: "love." "What's this mean?"

"You know I make personalized fortune cookies, right?"

She nodded.

"Well, there's six of them here. Each has a one-word message. When you eat them all, you'll get the full sentence. Only you might need to shuffle the words around for it to make sense." I'd typed out the message "Your love life will soon revive" to encourage Leanne.

She quirked an eyebrow at me. "Cunning of you, Felicity. Now I'll have to eat the whole batch to find out."

"You said chocolate would help you feel better, so why not?" I went closer to her and patted her bare arm. "But I do hope Colton wakes up soon. That will truly make you happy."

She nibbled on the fortune cookie and perked up a bit. A rainbow of colors started creeping into the periphery of my vision. But I held out, wanting to watch her reaction.

Leanne turned to Kelvin. "And thank you for your support, too."

"You're welcome." He hung his head a little. Flowers weren't allowed in this level of care, so he'd come empty-handed.

As Leanne continued chewing and enjoying the fortune cookie, I decided to embrace my power. In my mind's eye, I hovered over the red line associated with finance. Where should I touch it? The line stretched out into the distance, with accompanying gradated hues. I wanted to make sure I landed on a spot that had to do with this policy the detective had been asking Leanne about.

My heart felt tugged to reach for a spot in the middle with a crimson shade. Once I grabbed it, the message formed, and my fingers itched to write down the words. Using my notepad, I jotted: "Your partner's life insurance policy will remain a safety net in your newlywed life."

Did that mean that Leanne had a newlywed life to

look forward to? Maybe Colton would wake up soon. I glanced at his still form. "You'll heal," I told him. With less certainty, I added, "And we'll figure out who tried to hurt you."

The big toe on his left foot, sticking out from the covers, wiggled at me.

I gaped. "Did you see that?"

"What?" Leanne and Kelvin asked in unison.

"Colton's big toe. I think it moved."

We all stared at Colton's feet, but he didn't repeat the action. (Assuming I hadn't imagined it in the first place.) But Leanne stood up, kissed Colton on the forehead, and said, "You can do it, sweetheart."

Then she turned to Kelvin and me, pulling us into a hug. "Thank you for your gift. Especially this one of hope."

We left Leanne with a more peaceful look on her face.

Kelvin brushed his hands against each other as we meandered down the hallway. "Our work here is done."

"Not only that, but I solved that mini mystery of Leanne's convo with the detective."

"How?" He cocked his head toward me, and I showed him the written prediction.

"Detective Sun must've been asking her about Colton's life insurance policy. Maybe it was a big payout."

Kelvin shrugged. "Getting a new life insurance or upping the amount when you're about to get married makes sense. A smart way to take care of your partner. I'd do the same."

I tripped a little on the smooth linoleum. "You thinking about marriage?"

He held up his hands. "Not yet. Only when the right gal agrees to it."

I swallowed, suddenly realizing how parched I was. Thinking about drinks reminded me of the unsuccessful honeymoon send-off from last night. "And did you ever get in touch with Haley?"

"Yeah, I did. She'll be able to talk to us tomorrow."

"Great." I strode with quicker steps toward the lobby. "Haley can share the details about the toast, as well as that bachelorette party gone wrong. What time are we meeting up with her?"

"Snagged an appointment at noon."

"You had to schedule something with her? She must be busy."

The automatic doors to the hospital slid open, and we exited into the hot summer air.

"Yeah, but I was able to shortcut us in." He let out a hearty laugh.

"What's so funny?" I said as we got into the car.

"Nothing," he said, but he wiped his eyes several times on the drive back to our cul-de-sac of shops.

Noon the next day found us in front of a hair salon in Fresno called Peace and Hairmony.

"This is where Haley works?" I said.

He nodded.

No wonder we'd had to cram in an appointment. People kept floating out the doors, looking fabulous in their new dos. The shop had a cutesy vibe with a pink exterior and its name sign done in cartoon lettering. Inside, it had pink padded salon chairs and heart-shaped wall mirrors. Two stylists were hard at work, bent over their customers; one trimmed a beard while the other added foil to someone's hair.

Neither were Haley, who rushed out of a side door straight over to us. "Welcome, you two," she gushed. Her hair, now wavy and looking gold-spun, hung past her shoulders.

I was happy for her nice greeting. Guess she'd gotten past our pretend love triangle fiasco. "Should we go in your office or something?" I asked.

"No, silly." She patted the back of a pink chair.

So that's how Kelvin had gotten us an appointment. I snuck him a dubious glance. The one time I'd offered to comb his curly hair for him in middle school, he'd asked me a filtering question: "Do you know what 3b means?" When I couldn't answer him, he'd quickly declined my offer.

I was surprised he'd made an appointment with Haley. But maybe she knew how to work with textured hair.

Haley clarified, "Don't be shy, Felicity. Have a seat."

Now I reared back and grimaced at Kelvin.

"You said you liked your mom's new cut and the way she just went for it . . ." I had. On my mom.

Haley added, "Time's a-wastin'."

True enough. Guess I'd take one for the team. I sat down in the pink swivel chair while Haley touched my hair. "What are you thinking about getting done?"

"Um . . ."

"And it'll only be a cut. There's no time for color, not that caramel highlights wouldn't suit you."

"A simple haircut will be fine," I said. "An inch off."

"How about adding some layers?"

"Okay," I said. The extras might mean we'd have more questioning time.

Once Haley had shampooed my hair and tied a cape

around my neck, I started asking away. "Did you hear what happened to Colton?"

She picked up a pair of scissors. "Yeah, from Leanne. We've been friends since kinder. She doesn't keep anything from me. It was food poisoning, right?"

Was that the story Leanne was circulating? As Haley started doing her thing with a comb and scissors in her hand, I said, "I think it was, like, drinks poisoning."

"You mean alcohol poisoning? But Colton could hold his own."

"That's not what we heard," Kelvin said. "Sounds like Colton drank a bit too much, made an off-the-cuff angry speech."

I watched in the mirror as Haley pursed her lips.

"Who brought the alcohol?" I asked. Maybe if we could pinpoint who'd purchased what, we could figure out which attendee had tampered with the martini.

"We all did," Haley said. "Everyone brought something to share."

It'd be hard to track, then. I stayed quiet, and Haley filled in the silence by asking, "Is this length okay? I can go shorter if you want."

"Sure, a bit more," I said. That would extend our appointment.

"Did somebody mix the drinks?" Kelvin asked.

"We mostly made our own," Haley said. "Though Turner mixed a few. On account of his past bartender stint."

Turner, huh? I'd have to keep him in mind. Even though the sewing needle had been a dead end.

"Did anybody else have a martini?"

"Nah. That was Colton's special drink. We all knew that."

"You did? How?" I asked.

"His close buddies probably knew from before, and we—Do you want layers all around or just in front?"

"Everywhere." I pressed her. "How'd you know about his drink of choice?"

She sighed. "It came out during the bachelorette party."

Haley seemed to hesitate on spilling more, so my best friend jumped in.

"You know, I've always wanted to know what goes on during a bachelorette party," Kelvin said. "What'd you all do?"

She gave him a saucy smile. "Wouldn't you like to know?" Okay, weren't we finished with this puppy love business?

Kelvin shuffled his feet, but Haley said, "I'm joking. It was all aboveboard. We had a typical karaoke outing except . . ."

"Go on," I urged. I'm not sure if Haley thought I was talking about the haircut or not. She snipped away but also spoke.

"Long story short, Miles crashed the party," Haley said. "Seemed like he'd been drinking, and he even serenaded Leanne."

"That's not too wild," I said.

"He sang 'I Will Always Love You' to her." Awkward but not alarming.

Maybe she saw the doubt in my eyes, because Haley continued, "And then he railed about how she'd picked the wrong Wu cousin."

"What happened after that?" I asked.

"Miles told Leanne that she still had time," Haley said. "To choose *him* instead of Colton."

"Whoa, talk about an awkward night-before-wedding moment."

"Tell me about it. We ended up calling him an Uber before he caused an even weirder situation." She paused and checked the lengths of my strands. "By the way, do you want bangs?"

Sure, why not. "Okay, side ones."

"Way to live large." Haley started cutting again. Before long, she said, "What do you think?"

I studied myself in the heart-shaped mirror. "It looks nice."

She beamed. "I've been working here ever since I could push around a rubber broom. The skill's in our family. I got the shop when my mom passed away. . . ."

Haley turned to the side, and I let her have a moment of grief. She then busied herself getting the blow dryer out and styling my hair. Guess our conversation was done.

When she'd fully finished, she spun the chair around and asked Kelvin for his opinion. He stared at me with a goofy grin. I'd seen that gobsmacked look before when we'd gone to prom together—*as friends*, which I'd insisted on.

I'd been wearing a teal satin mermaid dress and had felt effervescent, especially after his unspoken compliment. My cheeks heated again now. Was it out of embarrassment or something else?

I snapped my fingers, to get both Kelvin and me past this strange blip.

"Well?" Haley prompted Kelvin.

"It's shorter," he mumbled.

I groaned. A hair appointment, his joke. "I get it now. You found *a short cut*."

Haley looked between us with confusion but unsnapped the cape around me. She even gave me a discounted "friends' rate" for frequenting her salon. At her premium prices, I still had a lot more baking to do to cover the hair splurge. At least I'd gotten another special deal: two-for-one on info about the awkward bachelorette party *and* the poisoned honeymoon send-off.

CHAPTER 41

Mom actually clapped her hands with glee when I stepped through the bakery door. "You cut your hair, Felicity! It looks stunning."

I ran my fingers through the wispy, layered strands of my shorter cut. It did feel breezier in the summer heat. Maybe it was nice to change things up once in a while. My thoughts flashed back on my interaction with Kelvin—but then the front door swished open.

Sweet Tooth Sally waltzed in, stopped, and did a double take. "Why, who's this?" she said, an impish grin on her freckled face.

"Do you like it?" I felt shy, half wanting to run into the kitchen.

"Love it," Sally said and pulled out her cell phone. She motioned for Mom and me to stand together and started snapping pics. I usually hated being the center of attention, but then again, so many memories of me growing up in Pixie involved standing out for the wrong reasons.

"This will be perfect for my presentation," Sally continued.

"Huh?"

"I'm going to the city council meeting tonight to pitch

revamping Pixie's official website." She frowned, an expression not suited to her bubbly personality. "The site is really dated. And I think highlighting our wonderful local institutions and, um, breadth of residents would make this a more exciting place to live and visit."

"You really do have the best ideas," I said, encouraging her.

"Sally for mayor," my mom added.

We all grinned.

Sally's eyes twinkled. "Well, if I bring them your delicious treats, the idea will be a shoo-in." She selected an array of pastries to haul to the meeting.

As I packed the fortune cookies, I was reminded of Mrs. Spreckels. "Don't forget to highlight the library on the website."

"Already done," she said. "I was just there, taking pics, even as the librarian bustled around tidying books. She seemed upset that the pharmacology section was messed up yet again."

Oh. My mind stayed on this tidbit of info as Mom rang up the large purchase. I gave Sally a distracted wave as she bustled out the door with the pastries.

"What's wrong?" Mom asked me.

Could it be a coincidence? "Pharmacology" meant *drugs*, and what were the chances of someone rifling through that specific section after Colton had been put in a coma?

A sense of foreboding came over me, and the hairs stood up on my arms. I rubbed at them and said, "I just need to drop by the library after we close tonight. Do some research."

My mom's face appeared grim as I beat a hasty retreat into the kitchen. I'd busy myself among the baking sheets and mixing bowls to discourage further conversation. Good thing several customers also walked in then. Distraction worked wonders.

Several waves of customers later, my mom had either forgotten or dropped the issue. She nodded to me as I left the shop and wished me a good library visit.

I stood in the shadow of Pixie Public Library's brick building, feeling a sense of power flowing through its arched doorway. There was wisdom to be found in there, not only for me but for anyone who decided to enter.

Even though many modern libraries had a constant hubbub of conversation with multiple book clubs or fancy programming, Mrs. Spreckels insisted on a reverent hush.

She stood behind the curved oak circulation desk, her horn-rimmed glasses hanging on its beaded holder, and steadily watched as I made my way to the 615 section of the library.

Everything seemed in order as I brushed my hands against the worn spines. A soft shuffling sounded from behind me. "This topic has been popular lately," the librarian said in a dry tone of voice.

"I know," I said, my voice lowered to a tiny whisper. "Sally came by the bakery earlier and told me. Who would have left it in disarray?"

"An out-of-towner, for sure," Mrs. Spreckels said.

I turned to her. "You sound confident of that."

"Why, I caught him in the very act today."

Him? "What do you mean?"

"He fled the other day after leaving the shelves disorganized." She clucked her tongue. "So this time, I kept an eye out. Confronted the man and said if he really wanted to research, he should actually borrow the books."

She continued, "He mumbled something about already having a Bay Area library card and ran off."

The guy was from the SF Bay Area? That didn't seem like a coincidence. My gaze shifted to the tomes. "Which books was he interested in?"

She waved an imaginary wand over the middle shelf. "Pick your poison."

"Excuse me?"

"Stuff about toxicology."

I made a choking noise. "Can you describe him?"

"Sure." Mrs. Spreckels proceeded to share about a young biracial man who spoke with an "interesting" accent.

"What do you mean by that?"

She crossed her arms over her chest. "While I've armchair-traveled the world via books, I've also done some real travel in my days. And even though he said he was 'having a gander' at my books, the phrase seemed forced."

I thought *that* was "interesting." She definitely seemed to be talking about Easton. "Thanks for your help, Mrs. Spreckels."

"Don't know what I did, but you're welcome."

Easton had been nosing around books in toxicology and fled when a librarian had started questioning him. But I knew where he was currently staying, and I bet I could convince Kelvin to join me.

CHAPTER 42

"I'm not going back to Pixie Inn tonight," Kelvin said.

"What? You're my best friend. Pretty please with a cherry blossom on top." We sat in his backyard on the porch swing, watching the cotton candy colors splashed across the sky.

He ran a hand down his face. "I'm tired."

I studied him. No bags under his eyes, but guilt was written across his face. "Did something happen?"

He glanced to the side toward the direction of my home.

"Mom?" I guessed.

"She cornered me at my shop. Said she was worried. I bet she knows you've been snooping again."

I frowned. I'd left the conversation with Mom by saying that I needed to research something. It was for a good cause. A man had been put into a coma, and I needed to stop the culprit. "But what if Easton does a runner?"

Kelvin cocked his head at me. "Do you think he actually did it?"

"I don't know. Maybe. I mean, doesn't he have a record?"

He gave me a look of disbelief. "We don't know what for. We don't know his circumstances. You, of all people, should be wary of assumptions and labels. You've experienced how Pixie likes to categorize."

They sure did. In-towners and out-of-towners. People who fit in and those who didn't . . . Even the "good" assumptions about me—that I was excellent at math and piano (both untrue)—made me feel uncomfortable growing up here.

I let out a huff. "If Easton didn't do it, he'll stick around. But if he did, he'll take off."

"Nope. Because that would make him look more guilty. To leave after a man goes into a coma." Kelvin pulled out his phone and waved it in the air. "There's an easier way to get you answers."

"Siri?"

"Mrs. Robson. She'd know his intended checkout date." Kelvin dialed and had a quick conversation, giving murmurs of understanding.

After he hung up, I twisted my hands in my lap. "What'd she say?"

"He doesn't have a clear checkout date. Renting day by day, depending on how things turn out with Colton. Checkout is usually at noon, and he tells her around then."

If only I could figure out for certain Easton's travel plans. I snapped my fingers. How about guaranteeing the timing with a well-placed fortune cookie?

Pixie Inn in mid-day sunshine looked innocuous. It didn't seem like a place where a man had been poisoned. Then again, I would have thought none of its innocent-looking residents had been at fault, but I knew better.

Kelvin and I drove together to save on the time we'd be away from our shops. We'd both taken an early lunch, coming about half an hour before the appointed time so we wouldn't miss Easton. It took about ten minutes before we heard footsteps coming down a side hall.

My best friend and I waylaid Easton before he could approach the front desk and talk to Mrs. Robson. "We've come to check on you," I said, showing him the box of fortune cookies I'd brought.

He tried to peer around Kelvin to no avail and checked his wristwatch instead.

"Want to get some fresh air?" Kelvin asked.

Easton glanced at his watch again. "Only for a little bit."

"We'll be out of your hair in ten minutes," I said. Wouldn't take me that long to write a fortune for him.

"Fine," he said, surrendering to our insistence. "We can go out back."

The green hedges were like I remembered, neatly trimmed while offering privacy from the outside world. Kelvin and I gravitated to the cream-colored recliners, but Easton opted to stand.

"How are you doing?" I asked. "How's Colton? I brought sustenance for folks."

His voice wobbled as he answered, "Not well. Colton's still in a coma. I checked on him yesterday."

"Oh, was that before or after your trip to the library?"

"Before," he said on automatic before he blinked at me. "Wait, how do you know I went to the library?"

I leaned back in my chair and moved my hand in a lazy circle. "You know, small town. Word gets around."

He grunted. "Too small. I stand out here."

My best friend and I exchanged an understanding look.

"The librarian mentioned you left some books in disarray," I said, putting our conversation back on course.

Easton wiped his hands on his pant legs. Did he feel uncomfortable? Sweaty perhaps?

"Were you interested in something in particular?" I asked. "Because she noticed that they were all shelved in a certain section."

Easton hung his head.

Kelvin encouraged him to talk. "Maybe you wanted to do some research?"

"Yeah, that's what it was. After what happened to Colton. I wanted to know if—"

"Did you think . . ." I left it a fill-in-the-blank question for him to answer.

"My buddy was poisoned." Easton took a furtive glance at the inn.

I sat up straight in my chair. "Did you see something the other night?"

He licked his lips. "No, that's the problem. I wish I had, but I've got a hunch."

"You do?" Kelvin leaned forward in his chair. "Who is it?"

"I could be wrong." His eyes flicked back to the inn. "Colton's such a cool dude. Who would want to hurt him for real?"

"I heard he made an awful speech and alienated his friends," Kelvin said.

Easton shook his head. "No man, he was just blowing off steam."

I tilted my head. *Dude, no man.* Had his usual expressions changed? What happened to his Britishisms? "Where'd your accent go?"

He backed up a step. "Um . . ."

Kelvin looked him in the eye. "It's okay." To speak, to be yourself. I wasn't sure what Kelvin wanted to convey, but Easton nodded.

"Guess the jig's up," he said. "I'm not actually British. It's just that people will treat me so much better. At school, at work . . ."

I remembered what Colton's dad had said about the accent and what my father had mentioned about Easton excelling at English. And drama. Was he acting for us even now?

Getting up, I stood next to him, a smidge too close. My hand bumped into his bare arm. "Oh, sorry. I wanted to give you a cookie," I said.

Because *the pastry* wouldn't lie to me. I opened the box and watched as he picked one. The planted, typed generic fortune in each cookie was something innocuous— about having safe travels in the future. He took a tiny nibble, and I could feel the customized message unfurling in my head. It would declare the real truth.

Before Easton could finish the cookie, before I could write down his message, something in the atmosphere shifted. Banging sounded from Pixie Inn. Then a wail of frustration rang out.

CHAPTER 43

Easton, Kelvin, and I rushed inside the inn to figure out what was going on. We noticed Mrs. Robson straightening the dining chairs while Nova appeared to be fuming, pacing around like a caged beast.

"Something happen in here?" I asked.

Mrs. Robson gave me a tired smile. "Nothing much. A few chairs got knocked over."

I stared at Nova, who'd pulled out her phone and kept tapping on it. "Why aren't there more Uber drivers here?"

"Need to go somewhere?" Kelvin asked, while eyeing Nova's attire.

She wasn't wearing purple plaid pajamas this time of the day, but her current fashion could be summarized in one word: clashing. She had on a yellow-and-magenta-striped shirt with camo pants. And mismatched socks.

"I'm in a rush. To go to the hospital," she said.

"Are you feeling all right, dear?" Mrs. Robson asked, her brow furrowing.

"It's not me, it's Colton."

Easton gasped. "Did he—is he—"

"Same as before. Still in a coma," Nova said. "But

Leanne called. She can't watch him and asked me to come. I need to go and take care of Colton."

Kelvin piped up. "We can give you a ride. Lissa and I drove here."

"Why didn't you say so before?" Nova rushed toward the front door while Kelvin hurried to catch up to her.

I turned to go as well, but Easton grabbed my arm. In a trembling voice, he said, "It was *her*."

"Huh? What?" I tried to disentangle myself from his grip, but he held on tighter.

"Nova. She was the one."

I waited for clarification.

"I remember her bringing vodka to the toast," he said.

"Um, okay. Noted." I didn't know what he was talking about and wanted to catch up with Kelvin and Nova.

He seemed relieved to have gotten that off his chest, and let me go. I scrambled out the door and found Kelvin and Nova at his car. They seemed to be disagreeing about where Nova would sit.

Kelvin's face brightened at my presence. "Tell her, Lissa," he said. "You wanted to ride shotgun. And I need you to navigate."

I was about to retort that my sense of direction was horrible, but something about Kelvin's insistent manner made me pause. Instead, I said, "Oh yeah. True."

Nova grumbled but slunk into the back seat.

Kelvin could drive to the hospital blindfolded. I got into the car, not really giving directions but half-heartedly affirming whatever turns Kelvin made. "Yep, that's correct."

Meanwhile, I devoted myself to writing down the message that I'd gotten about Easton before we'd been interrupted by Nova's outburst. It took me time to recall, but I finally had it. On a slip of paper, I wrote "You'll be jetting out of here as soon as possible."

Easton *had* been antsy. Did that equate to guilt? And what had he been saying about Nova and vodka?

It hit me then. The martini, Colton's special beverage that only he drank.

I pulled down the passenger visor and slid open the mirror, like I was checking my hair. In fact, I was checking Nova's expression in the back. She appeared tense, her shoulders hunched. Her hands were balled into fists . . . and she was moving them, as though she were steering the vehicle, not Kelvin. I remembered when she'd grabbed at the wheel during our food run. Impulsive much? Enough to have flown off the handle when Colton had made his rude speech?

She was the lead groomsperson. Did that mean she was more forgiving of Colton or more heavily invested? She'd said she would "take care of Colton." Did that mean caring for Colton, or "taking care of him" like you would a problem?

I must have lingered in watching her because she noticed. "Why are you staring at me like that?"

How could I verify what Easton had insinuated? "Sorry, I was spacing," I said. "Thinking back about that cocktail party. Who brought all the drinks anyway?"

She shrugged. "We each brought something to share."

"Like what?"

"Sherry, tequila, vodka, beer, even water."

"What'd you contribute?"

But she left me unanswered and pointed out the window instead. We'd arrived at the hospital. And Leanne was leaving Pixie Medical Center, but not of her own volition. Detective Sun was close behind her, waving at her to move along on the sidewalk.

Once Kelvin turned off the engine, we all jumped out of the vehicle. Leanne spotted Nova first. "Good, you're here. Go see about Colton."

Nova didn't have to be told twice. She sprinted for the hospital entrance. I nodded toward the door, and Kelvin caught my signal. He hurried to catch up with Nova. It'd be best if she wasn't alone with Colton, just in case. I'd have to get to the bottom of the drinks situation later.

Right now I focused on Leanne. I hurried to intercept her before she made it to the detective's unmarked car. "What happened?" I said as I jogged up to her.

"Keep going," Detective Sun urged Leanne, but Leanne refused.

"Give me a moment to say goodbye." She pulled me in for a hug. At the same time, she said, "Cops found an email inviting Miles to meet up with me before the wedding."

The detective clapped her hands from a few feet away. "Okay, that's enough time."

Leanne lowered her voice and whispered, "It wasn't from my account. Someone framed me."

She let go, and I watched, in shock, as the detective led her away. How long could they keep her?

Detective Sun's grim face didn't hold any answers. I thought back on the evidence stacking up against Leanne: first, the insurance policy, and now, a signed email. She'd better lawyer up soon.

CHAPTER 44

When I entered Pixie Medical Center, Kelvin and Nova weren't around. Good thing I remembered which hospital room Colton was in. I sped through the hallways and showed up as Nova was bent over the tubes connected to Colton.

She wasn't gonna unplug them, right? "Hello," I called out, both to distract Nova and alert her to my presence.

Nova straightened up and turned around. "I don't know why he isn't better yet. Shouldn't all these beeping machines be helping him?"

Kelvin shook his head. "Comas don't work that way."

"I thought I might have seen him wiggle his toe before. That's hopeful, right?" I said, pushing past Nova and blocking her from access to Colton. She begrudged me the space.

I was holding on to my box of fortune cookies and wondered if my magic might work on someone who was comatose. After clearing my mind to open it to a message, I squeezed his limp hand.

No reaction. From him or me. His body didn't move a millimeter, and my hands didn't itch to write anything down. My magic was blocked in this situation.

I sighed and faced Nova. "Not sure when he'll wake

up. Maybe it depends on what was put into his system. Did you know that Easton went to the library to research—"

She sniffed. "Books, whatever. What we need is action." Nova moved away from the machines in the corner and began pacing the short length of the room.

I pressed on with the conversation now that she'd ventured farther away from the bed. "If only we knew how Colton got sick. He was complaining about a stomachache, and you said he hadn't eaten any cookies. Could it have been something he drank?"

She pursed her lips. "The bottle was new, sealed and untampered with." How would she know? She must have been the person who'd brought the vodka, like Easton had said.

"Something could've been slipped into his drink that night. He's the only one who likes martinis."

"I didn't notice anything, and I think Colton held the drink tightly in his hand. Except when he got a refill."

"Who'd been pouring?"

"We did it ourselves." She scrunched her nose. "Mostly."

An image of Turner came to mind. In her hair salon, Haley had mentioned he'd done some bartending before and had mixed a few of the drinks. We'd have to pursue that avenue next.

In the meantime, I wondered if I could truly leave Nova alone with Colton. My fortune cookies would tell the truth. I opened the box now. "You must be hungry. Cookie?"

"Yeah, okay."

I handed the box over, my pinkie grazing the side of her wrist in the process. She picked a cookie, broke it in half, and started crunching away.

The colorful lines came at once. I'd choose orange,

the hue for relationships. *If only I could focus on her re-lationship with Colton.* The orange line pulsed, and I grabbed it.

My fingers twitched, and a message also appeared in my mind's eye: "You will watch over your recovering college buddy for a few more days."

Once I wrote the sentence down in my trusty little notepad, I felt a wave of relief. "I'm thinking Colton will get better soon."

Nova halted her pacing. "I really hope so."

Kelvin cleared his throat from his side of the room. "And what happened with Leanne out there? Did you get the story, Lissa?"

"The police need to ask her a few questions." I glanced over at Nova for her reaction.

She sat down in the waiting chair and said, "That's fine. I don't mind staying with Colton."

Nova either wasn't worried for Leanne or didn't care much about the new bride. Her loyalties clearly lay with Colton.

My fortune-telling hadn't led me astray yet. I figured Colton would be fine with Nova keeping guard. Hadn't my fortune said we'd have a few more days? And besides, alarm bells would really sound if Nova disturbed any of the machines.

Kelvin touched my shoulder. "Actually, we should get going. Our floral and baking duties call."

That'd been an intense lunch hour. "I'll fill you in on the Leanne specifics in the car," I said.

On the ride back to the cul-de-sac, I let Kelvin know about the evidence stacking up against Leanne. "What with the insurance policy and now an email asking for a meeting with Miles—which she says she didn't send—it doesn't look good for Leanne."

Kelvin focused on the road, but his jaw tightened. "Three strikes, and you're out."

I stared at the passing scenery without recognition, focused on my churning thoughts. "Bet the meeting time happened to be right around when Miles was murdered."

My best friend grimaced. "Probably. But I've done flowers for many weddings, and when would the bride have a chance? Her schedule is accounted for, and she usually has an entourage."

"They could vouch for her," I said, as I thought back on the events of the day. "It had to have either been before or after the tea ceremony."

"Miles wasn't around for the actual tea ritual, right?"

"No. He was gone by then—or maybe in hiding, shirking his duties."

"Makes a difference in the timeline depending on which."

"Unfortunately, I don't think Detective Sun is going to share any details of the case with me."

"Agreed," Kelvin said. "Well, maybe something will come to us while we're working."

Possibly. Baking acted as a kind of meditation for me. It was like traveling to a different cozy world when I entered the kitchen.

In fact, I got so caught up with the soothing rhythm of putting items in and out of the oven, I didn't even notice my mom standing by a prep table until she called my name. What was she doing in here in the middle of the day? I glanced out the front. A lull in customers. Did she come by to chat?

Mom had an odd look on her face as she examined me. I wiped my mouth. Had I left some stray crumbs on my lips? That's what I got for using my lunch hour to investigate. Since I didn't actually get a real meal, I had had to gobble some of our inventory.

"Everything okay?" I asked her while she remained silent.

"I know what you've been up to," Mom said.

So many things could fit that bill. "Are you talking about . . ."

"Your friend at the hospital, who's in a coma. It's Colton Wu, isn't it?"

"Maybe."

My mom put her hands on her hips. "Don't fudge the truth. I've been talking to Rylan."

I jerked at hearing the detective's first name. What, were we going to start having family dinners soon? "It's just that this case feels so personal," I said. "After catering their disastrous wedding and having Kelvin accused."

My mom's face softened. She loved Kelvin and knew I'd do anything for him—she would, too. "That ship has sailed," she said. "Rylan is questioning a new suspect."

The grapevine. News traveled fast. Guess the detective was picking up our small-town ways. "Did she call you about that?"

Mom nodded. "To reassure me. And to advise you to stop snooping. She said things are getting dangerous, what with the use of a hard-to-detect poison."

"What was it, do you know?"

Mom shrugged. "A colorless, tasteless substance."

Detective Sun had let slip to my mom info about the toxin Colton had been exposed to.

Mom shifted, and her arms now hung at her sides. "I know you're an adult now, Felicity. You get to choose your own path."

Had her tone changed? I could almost taste the pinch

of sadness in her voice. "Are we still talking about the wedding party?"

Her gaze grew distant. "Your father. He came back, and I refused his attempts at communicating. I didn't want to reconnect. Moved here to get away from him after all, but . . . I'm not you."

"I did reach out a few times," I admitted.

In a quiet voice, Mom said, "I don't think I ever want to keep in touch with him, but you—you still have his contact details, right?"

I did. The napkin with his scribbled number lay on top of my dresser at home. My mom had given me her permission, but did I want to talk with him more? It hadn't been a fairy-tale reunion, especially with the weird packages and breaking into our home. A small part of me still wanted more closure, though. "Thanks, Mom. I'll have to think on it," I told my mom.

CHAPTER 45

Sometimes I did my best thinking around Whiskers. Back in the apartment, I gathered up the white bunny and cuddled her in my lap while sitting in bed. "What should I do about my dad?" I asked her.

The irony didn't escape me. Here I was, sitting with a bunny who had materialized out of thin air from the Wishes candle, and I was asking her for advice about my father, who I'd also wished for through the same magical candle. Whiskers nudged my palm, and I petted her. She'd been a true companion on my magical journey, as I continued to navigate the ins and outs of my baking talent.

She snuggled deeper in my arms, and I enjoyed the physical reminder of our mutual bond. A realization struck me. My relationship with Whiskers was totally different than the one I had with my father. While they'd both started off as enchanted wishes, the similarities ended there.

Richard Zhou wasn't a companion or a buddy. He wasn't even a true parent, not actually having raised me up. In fact, he'd been distant—had *voluntarily* distanced himself from me early on.

Ever since childhood, I'd thought of a dad in an

abstract way. My father had been a kind of fairy tale. My adult mind pushed me to forget about those childish dreams, but I glanced over at the napkin on my dresser and hesitated. Maybe I'd keep it there a little bit longer.

I stroked Whiskers' soft fur. "Thanks for helping me reflect."

She twitched her nose at me as if to say, "At your service."

Which reminded me. I'd had something else I wanted to think through and needed to get her expertise on. "What was with the color pulsing that happened with Easton?" I asked.

I petted Whiskers as the images tumbled into my mind. I watched myself give Easton the cookie. At the time, I remembered thinking of Colton and had noticed the orange color pulsating. I'd picked it, and the message I'd written floated back to me. It'd been very specific about Colton's recovery.

Could it be? Maybe I had the ability to fine-tune my predictions. After all, I'd done so with the timeline of my fortune-telling through choosing the shades of color. Now, it seemed that I could home in on a certain subject. Wow. The doors were swinging wide open on my magical talent.

I might not have control over the murder investigation—and poor Leanne was suffering the brunt of suspicion—but at least there was forward momentum on the magic front.

The next day, my mom and I had just finished with our morning routine when the phone rang. Mom was busy sliding a tray of goodies into our glass display case, and I picked up the call.

"Mrs. Robson?" I said upon hearing her voice.

"Glad I caught you, Felicity. He's on his way."

"What? Who?"

"Turner," she said. "He lost his sewing kit, and you wanted me to contact him and tell you."

"Yes, that's right."

"Well, I plumb forgot, with everything that's happened since that night. But I called him earlier, and he'll be by the inn soon. Wanted to pick it up before work."

From my peripheral vision, I noticed Mom staring at me with her brow furrowed. Did she know I was still trying to investigate? "Will be right there with the delivery, Mrs. Robson," I said.

A pause on the line. "I don't understand."

"See you soon," I said, hanging up with a smile.

"What was that about?" Mom asked. "We don't do deliveries. And why to the inn?"

I held my hands up in the air, trying for a picture of innocence. "Mrs. Robson can't step away from her desk, you know."

"Sure, but . . ."

"And wouldn't you want to treat yourself after a resident had to be carted off your property?" I hoped Mom didn't know that Mrs. Robson was diabetic. That would have put a hole in my plan.

Mom seemed to think about it, then nodded. "I see your point. Tell her the pastries are on the house. I can't imagine witnessing something like that."

"Thanks, Mom. You're the best." I started packing up a to-go box with pineapple buns, almond cookies, and fortune cookies.

"Well, I'm off," I said, marching out the door before she could change her mind or question me further.

It took me longer than I wanted to get to Pixie Inn.

The crosswalk lights seemed to be delayed even as I tried to hurry to my destination.

Turner appeared to be stepping away from Pixie Inn as I arrived. I stopped him as he passed the waterwheel at the entrance by calling his name. "Turner! Wait up!"

He halted his steps and pivoted toward me. "Felicity. What are you doing here?"

I held up the box. "Comfort food. Mrs. Robson ordered them because you know . . ."

His mouth turned down.

"How are you doing?" I asked. "Everyone has been a mess ever since the honeymoon send-off. And no wonder, what with Colton in the hospital and Leanne in for questioning."

Turner frowned even more. "You sure seem to know a lot."

I sidestepped his implication by turning the tables on him. "Speaking of knowing, I heard you have some great bartending skills. Mixed the drinks the night Colton fell ill. Did you happen to notice anything amiss?"

Turner stared me down. "Not with anything I made. It was easy. A sherry cocktail for Jada, a martini for Colton, and a margarita for Nova."

I counted three people. "What about the others?"

"Didn't mix them anything. Leanne had soda, Haley had water, and Easton had beer."

"And you?"

"A simple glass of milk, my beverage of choice when paired with chocolate chip cookies." Touché.

He continued, "Done with digging?"

"Excuse me?"

Turner pulled out his sewing kit. "I keep this in the pocket of whatever I'm wearing. It was last in my leather jacket at work, so I'm sure I didn't drop it in the lobby."

I could feel my cheeks heating up.

"Not to worry," he said. "I don't usually hold grudges."

What did that mean? Was he forgiving me or not? He turned away from me and began whistling as he walked off.

CHAPTER 46

I couldn't get a read on Turner. First things first, though. I walked through the entrance to Pixie Inn to deliver the baked goods. We Jins kept our promises, especially about pastries.

After waving to Mrs. Robson, I placed the box on her counter. "This is the delivery I was talking about. Goodies for you and your residents."

"Maybe I can have just a little bite," she said. Mini bites. What a great idea. While we didn't carry recipes using sugar substitutes, we could offer smaller portions for those who wanted a mere taste.

Back to the case. "Is Leanne around?" I asked, wanting an update from her.

Mrs. Robson blinked at me. "Actually, she didn't show up last night."

"Strange." Could the police have kept Leanne in a holding cell overnight? "And she's still renting a room here, right?"

Mrs. Robson nodded. "They haven't cancelled yet, and I have their credit card on file."

My mind flashed to the new marriage. Colton. If anything, once Leanne was freed from questioning, she'd have returned to the hospital to watch over him.

I made a mental note to visit Pixie Medical Center after work.

After giving Mrs. Robson my regards, I power walked back to the bakery. Despite the brisk walk, my mind hadn't cleared, and I was still concerned about Leanne.

"Welcome back," my mom said from behind the register. "Did you get more info?"

"Not really. In fact—"

"Caught you," Mom said.

How could I explain myself? "I didn't want you to worry" was the best response I came up with.

"I'm your mother," she said. "You can't hide things from me. And I get it, Felicity."

"You do?"

She shrugged. "Sort of. You're an adult now and your own person. You seem to enjoy the risk of investigating."

I wouldn't characterize myself as courageous or anything, but Mom had a point. It'd been nice to solve a previous case. "There's something about fixing things for others that I like."

Mom gestured around her. "That's what Jin Bakery is all about."

"Joy?" I said.

"Which comes from compassion. That's why we want to give to others, help them. I send joy through my baking. But you're not content like me to stay in one place and have people come to you."

"I want to take action," I conceded.

She moved around the counter and put her hands on my shoulders. "You and Rylan would actually get along. Same compassionate personality, same drive to do more for the good of others."

I managed to stop the laugh before it reached my lips. Barely.

Mom removed her hands from my shoulders and nodded toward the kitchen. "For now, though, I need you in there. We had a huge order come in for a birthday party."

"On it," I said.

We stepped through the archway into our baking sanctuary. For a few hours, as I created edible delights with my hands and served customers, I forgot about the outside world. Once the clock struck closing hour, though, I remembered the troubles. Ones with life-and-death stakes, especially for Colton lying in a hospital bed. After finishing my few cleaning duties, I left for Pixie Medical Center.

Like I'd surmised, I found Leanne in Colton's hospital room. Except she wasn't alone. Through the open door, I paused and watched.

Jada plumped a pillow and placed it on the armchair. "How does that feel, Leanne? More comfortable?"

Leanne rested back and gave her a thumbs-up. It almost seemed like Jada was here for Leanne instead of Colton. She didn't even spare him a second glance as she fussed over her ex-roomie.

I tapped on the edge of the doorframe. "Knock, knock."

We exchanged greetings.

"Thought I'd find you here, Leanne," I said. "Did you stay over?"

Leanne colored and snuck a glance at Jada.

"She needed to get a good night's rest after everything," Jada said. "Leanne came back home."

Home? "Back to the old apartment?" I asked.

They both nodded.

"It's familiar," Leanne said.

"Better for her," Jada added.

I studied Jada for a moment as she fidgeted with her

green glasses. She didn't seem menacing in her striped shirt and blue jeans. But could Jada have done something to waylay the honeymoon, to have Leanne back for a night or two? Or permanently?

Leanne sighed from her chair and rubbed at her head. My attention turned back to the bride. "How did the questioning go?" I hoped Detective Sun had been cordial.

"Intense," Leanne said.

Jada bit her lower lip. "If they treated you wrong—"

Leanne put her hand up. "No. They gave me water, even offered coffee. It was just long."

"Something about an email, right?" I asked.

"They showed it to me, to get me to talk. It wasn't from my email address. Close. But with an added digit."

I stepped near her. "Did they believe you when you told them?"

"Don't think so. I mean, it even had my profile pic."

Someone who had a photo of Leanne. It had to have been an inside job for sure. "Do you remember the time stamp on it?"

Leanne wrinkled her brow. "I was so nervous I didn't notice the fine details. Even skimmed the message, which talked about meeting in the cake tent."

My throat constricted. That's where the body had been found. Right under my dessert table. My voice came out rougher when I continued speaking. "What about their questions? Did the police ask about a specific timeline?"

Leanne squeezed her forehead with her fingertips. "Yeah, they wanted to know where I was around the time of the tea ceremony."

I snapped my fingers. "That's perfect then. You have an alibi. Clearly, you were busy then. There was a bunch of witnesses: me, Colton, Turner, Nova, the parentals."

"Well, it also could have been before the tea ceremony. Guess there was a loose range of time involved."

It would be harder to establish an alibi for Leanne before the tea ceremony. Where had she been again? I mentally retraced my steps from the egg tart display. "You were in the tea tent before me."

She gave me a sad smile. "And I don't know for how long. Wasn't checking my phone when prepping for the tea ceremony. And I was alone." That's right. No one else had been around when I'd gotten the water boiling for the tea.

Leanne let out a long sigh, and Jada stood closer to her friend.

"I think Leanne would appreciate a break from thinking about all this," Jada said.

"The sooner we understand what really happened, the better Leanne will feel," I answered back.

Jada glared at me.

"Fine, I'll switch gears. What about you?" She didn't seem rattled by my interrogating her. "Did you notice Miles around before the wedding? Particularly near teatime?"

She thought back, closing her eyes. "I didn't see him. Since I wasn't needed for the tea ceremony—only family and head wedding attendants were invited—I was alone refreshing my makeup."

"In the bridal tent?"

"Yes, applying blush. My phone was streaming music. Oh." Her eyes popped open. "I didn't see Miles. But I *heard* him."

"How so?"

"The two tents for the attendants are close together. I heard him clomping outside the entrance. And then talking through the wall once he entered the other tent.

I could hear his rumbly, almost shouting, voice over my tunes." She waved her hand around. "But I figured he was practicing his speech for the big night. Only—"

"What?" I angled myself in Jada's direction.

"Once I finished my makeup and turned off my phone, I finally registered that his pitch had changed. He sounded irritated, angry almost, and mumbled something about gardening or dirt."

"Gardening?" I repeated. That was a weird topic to be mad about.

Jada said, "After a few minutes of debating, I went outside to find him, but I couldn't see him anywhere. I even checked the other tent. Figured he took a walk to blow off steam." She hung her head. "When the cops asked me if I'd seen him, I told them no because I truly hadn't. I'd heard him, and didn't remember until now."

What could Miles have been angry about? Not gardening, but perhaps dirt?

Not the literal kind. Maybe he'd been talking about getting dirt on people. What he'd put in that shared Google doc, gossip which had probably gotten him killed.

Thump, thump. My heart had sped up. No, wait. Those were footsteps plodding down the hall. A figure swathed in a dark hoodie loomed in the doorway.

CHAPTER 47

From behind me, Jada squealed, which turned into nervous laughter when the new arrival pulled down the hood of his jacket. Leanne, from her chair, reprimanded him by saying, "Easton, don't scare us like that."

My own jaw dropped. "You're still around?" I thought he'd be long gone already. Hadn't I written him a fortune that predicted a quick departure? Would've guessed he'd have boarded the plane by now.

I dug back in my memories. I'd definitely written Easton a fortune about jetting out of Pixie "as soon as possible."

Easton jammed his hands in his pockets. "Yeah, I thought I'd be gone, too. But I can't leave Colton behind. I chose to stick around." *As soon as possible*, I realized, could be subject to interpretation.

Despite my prediction for his future, he'd had a *choice*. Same as my dad, actually. The revelation struck me in the gut, and I wobbled. Leanne quickly vacated her chair and motioned for me to sit.

While I regained composure, I heard Leanne complimenting Easton in the background, telling him he was a good friend.

Easton said, "Well, Colton's a great guy."

Jada blinked at him. "Don't you mean 'mate'?"

Easton ducked his head. "Sorry, that was an affectation. I'm done being fake."

He probably meant his British accent, but my thoughts drifted to my father. How real had Richard Zhou's desire to reconnect with his daughter? Well, I had a source of character info here at my side.

Looking at Easton, I asked, "Colton told me you had Mr. Zhou as a teacher . . . Did he ever talk about having a child?"

Easton's eyes bulged at me. "No, never. He had a kid?"

"Does it seem difficult to believe?" I asked, a sudden sharpness appearing in my voice.

Easton shrugged. "He just didn't seem the type. Always complained that we were a handful." I remembered Colton mentioning that Easton and my father hadn't gotten along.

"Plus," Easton continued, "he liked the bachelor life."

Hmmph. I could feel a scowl forming on my face. "What do you mean?" Did he have a bunch of girlfriends he strung along? If Easton thought it odd I was asking a lot of nosy questions about his high school teacher, he didn't show it.

"Mr. Zhou went out all the time. Box seats at a game, a movie premier, a fancy club. He'd brag about his fun schedule to us."

I digested Easton's words. Had my own magical wish been founded on *wishful* thinking? Sure, my father had "found" me at the wedding, but only after a supernatural push on my part. He hadn't looked very hard for us all the prior years.

And did he want to connect now because I was an adult? I'd grown up and couldn't be the pesky kid ruining his active schedule. Given this new perspective of my

father, what kind of relationship did I really want to have
with him?

"I need to go home," I said, getting up from the chair.
How to deal with my father would require more reflection, and I wanted to do that in a private space.

As I walked to the door, I almost collided with the
nurse, who was carrying in a few gifts. She wasn't the
same person Kelvin and I had interacted with before, and
she narrowed her eyes at us. "Only three visitors, max,
allowed in this room."

I watched as she placed a plush bear with a Get Well
shirt along with two greeting cards on a nearby table.
Craning my neck, I noticed that they'd been mailed by
Turner and Haley. Rule-followers, those two.

The nurse placed her hands on her hips, and I backed
out of the room, saying, "I'm going now."

As I left, I heard her saying to the others: "And are
you all *family* here?"

I didn't know how they'd respond, but I was off to see
my own family. It'd be nice to be back at the apartment
brimming with warmth from my mom and Whiskers.
With occasional drop-ins from Kelvin.

Which reminded me. I'd need to update him on all the
happenings he'd missed out on.

My mom didn't feel like cooking that evening, so it was
easy to convince her to have Kelvin over for one of
our trio meals. This time around, I decided on doing a
simple soup of shui jiao water dumplings. I already had a
package of frozen ones I could just toss into the pot with
chicken broth and baby bok choy. Soon enough, I ladled
out the soup into bowls.

Everything was ready on our dining table when Kelvin arrived. He'd brought over his usual gift of a bouquet (yellow chrysanthemums). The vase was centered on the table, and I stared at the spot next to it. When we'd invited Alma over for dinner this past spring, I'd set out her golden Wishes candle. I'd had a fleeting thought about wishing my dad had been around . . . and it'd magically happened.

My mom interrupted my thoughts. "What about you, Felicity? Anything to share?"

We usually did updates around the table, and I'd obviously missed Mom's snapshot of her current life. Surely, I couldn't talk about the investigation during dinner. What could I safely share?

I chewed, taking small bites. Exactly. "Little bites," I said, recounting how I'd given Mrs. Robson pastries (and ignoring how it'd been a blatant excuse to get some gossip).

My mom nodded with enthusiasm. "Great idea. I knew you'd make an amazing co-owner."

I blushed.

Kelvin grinned and said, "Way to go, Lissa. Charging people more for less."

"Ha-ha." I mock-jabbed him in the ribs.

"Actually, it's not a bad idea. I could do tiny bouquets, too," he said. "I have friends who make a nice profit selling mini dried flower bouquets."

"Talk about brilliant," I said. "You'd be charging people for literally buying leftover old flowers."

He shook his head at me in slow motion. "I can't be-leaf you said that."

I groaned and focused on finishing my soup, not wanting to engage in a pun battle.

He continued, "You know you lilac my jokes."

"That's it," I said, pushing back my chair. "As punishment, you'll have to wash the dishes."

"Totally worth it," he said.

My mom chuckled in the background as we gathered the bowls and brought them to the kitchen. We talked about the case under the cover of the water. I was on dish-drying duty, so I also made sure to clink the porcelain and disguise our chatting.

I updated Kelvin on my adventures, including visiting the hospital and finding Jada by Leanne's side. I also mentioned how Easton had shown up at the end of my visit. Plus, I talked about Leanne's time with the detective and how Jada had actually heard Miles in the other tent while putting on her makeup.

Kelvin had me repeat that story twice. He finished washing and started rubbing his chin.

"What is it?" I asked.

"Something about the details and timeline of her story is bugging me. Let me sleep on it."

"Okay." I hesitated for a moment, remembering my other conversation from the hospital.

"Lissa, why do you look sad?"

I sighed. "It's about my father. I asked Easton about him. Turns out that he was living his best bachelor life all these years." I proceeded to share about how Richard didn't seem to even like kids, which would explain why he'd abandoned his own so easily.

"It was a foolish wish," I concluded. "He never really wanted to reconnect, but I forced it."

Kelvin held out his arms, and I collapsed into them. I wouldn't waste any tears on my bio father, but it was nice to be enveloped in a comforting embrace. Kelvin smelled like an intoxicating mix of Palmolive and love.

Where had that thought come from? I jerked back, out of his reach.

"Whoa, you okay?" he asked.

I stepped farther back, and a flash of white fur caught my attention. "Sorry! Hope I didn't step on you," I said to Whiskers.

I hadn't answered Kelvin's question and hoped he thought I'd just been startled by the bunny's appearance. Avoiding eye contact with him, I examined Whiskers at length for damage. She seemed fine.

I crouched down and petted her back. "What were my exact wishing words again?"

Whiskers flipped her ears, and an image floated in my mind. The dinner table from the past, with Alma there. Actually, I hadn't said a word. I'd *thought* something before the candle had flickered.

I closed my eyes and tried hard to remember the thought. A wish about how if only my dad had stuck around to witness my success.

Had I created things by magic that weren't meant to be? "Can I undo a wish?" I asked Whiskers.

I stroked her soft fur, but no more images appeared. Giving up, I rose to my feet.

A more alarming question came to mind. Had supernaturally asking for Richard Zhou to connect with me brought the wedding to the area? Was I indirectly responsible for a murder in Pixie?

CHAPTER 48

After the morning breakfast rush at the bakery, I took the quiet lull to go next door and visit Alma. I left Mom behind the counter, using her time to sketch out plans on how to successfully bake mini pineapple buns for the small-bites concept.

A quick peek into Love Blooms showed me that Kelvin was also free. I knocked on the shop door and beckoned him to follow me. I'd need his emotional support.

Kelvin and I walked into the dim interior of Paz Illuminations together. My godmother waved hello, and I stepped up to her.

"Do you remember that night we all had dinner together? How I put out the Wishes candle, and you lit it with that beautiful purple handmade matchstick?"

She smiled, and the crinkle lines near her eyes deepened. "A match passed down from my tía abuela." The healer. The flame could have sparked more magic. How many wishes did that candle hold?

"I was wondering about a wish," I said. "Can you take something back?" Who knew if Alma actually realized the candle was magical, but I figured she'd be the best person to ask. I wanted to undo what I'd wished for and the calamity that had ensued.

Alma's deep brown eyes seemed to look into my soul. "A human being is a deciding being," she said.

Why did she speak in riddles so often? "Translation, please."

My godmother studied me. "What exactly ails you?"

How to summarize what had happened since my father dropped back into my life? I wasn't sure how much, if anything at all, my mom had told Alma about the whole bizarre situation. "Let's just say, I wished someone into my life, and it's led to bad things. I want to undo it."

Alma tidied the back of her braided bun, making sure the ends were tucked in. "We're people. We make choices, and we have regrets. Sometimes we can be wishers, but we also must be doers."

Human beings are deciding beings. I mulled that over in my head. I'd wished for my father and had acted once he'd appeared. Taken the opportunity and met up with him at the diner. He'd given me his number, waiting for me to take the next step. Back then, I didn't know a thing about him beyond his first and last name. What to do now, when I had a wealth of information?

I felt a gentle touch on my shoulder. Kelvin. A sense of peace swirled around my heart.

"I'm here for you, whatever you decide," he said. And he meant it. He'd support me no matter what.

I thought about the wish that my father would be able to see my current success. He'd done that, hadn't he? I'd asked for his presence in my life.

He could be here temporarily for me. And that was okay, I realized. Richard had always only come for the wedding of a former student. Though he'd been reminded of me when he saw my name on those business cards.

Mine had been a one-way wish. And wishing from

one side in a relationship would eventually lead to disappointment. Even without making a fortune cookie, I could predict that the excitement (and his personal guilt) would die down for my father once he left. Out of sight, and all that. He'd happily revert to his bachelor ways without the enduring weight of parenting.

I envisioned my life without any more connections with Richard . . . and felt fine. Not hollow, like I was missing out on something.

Digging into my pants pocket, I unearthed his contact info. "I need to text someone, but I don't want to use my personal number." I glanced at Kelvin. "Or a loved one's cell."

Love. The L-word had cropped up again. But I tamped down my emotions and focused on the present moment.

My godmother distracted me by saying, "I've got just the thing. A Google Voice number I use, not my primary."

"Perfect." Alma let me into her account on her laptop, and I composed the message to my dad. Short and pointed, thanking him for his time but opting out of future connections. A breakup text, basically. It was cowardly, but I really didn't want to meet up in person.

I hit the send button. Done. In the back of my mind, I also thought, *Tit for tat.* He'd done a runner on me and my mom, leaving behind only a note.

Drumming my fingers on the base of the laptop, I waited. No response. "How long will this take? Doesn't tech speed things up?"

Kelvin wrinkled his brow at my words and pulled out his own phone. "Speaking of tech—Alma, I had a question for you."

He pulled something up onscreen and showed it to her. "It's about that shared doc you helped us with a while back. We got the restored version, but is there any way you can see who made edits?"

"Sure, if it wasn't an open link and set to anonymous. Let me take a look." Alma squinted at the words and tapped at Kelvin's phone. "There you go."

My best friend pursed his lips as he studied the details. "Interesting."

I checked for a text message again. Nothing.

"No response?" Alma guessed. "How about I let you know if a message comes through? That way, we can all get back to work."

Right. We had shops to run in downtown Pixie. "Of course. Thanks for your help, Alma."

"Anytime you need me," she said as we walked out the door.

Distracted by waiting on a response from my father, I was a baking disaster. I confused the ingredients, dropped the bowls, and made loud clanging noises in the kitchen. Mom checked on me several times over the course of the day and finally relegated me to the register. "At least you won't break anything out there," she muttered.

I hoped not. Actually, the position behind the counter calmed me. I could keep an eye on our entrance if Alma made a sudden appearance.

She didn't. I waited the entire day, thinking she'd drop by. Even after closing time, I kept on hoping.

Nope. So I took matters in my own hands. I rushed through our door just in time to see her locking up the candle shop. She turned her head at my footsteps.

I opened my mouth to ask, but before I could form any words, she shook her head.

"Sorry, nothing," she said.

"Oh."

Disappointment welled up inside me, but I gave my godmother a fake cheery wave as she walked away. Maybe I'd expected too much from my father. If he had skipped out earlier in my life, why wouldn't he do so without much fanfare the second time around?

I went back into the bakery, and even the faint scent of delight didn't cheer me up. Reaching into my pocket, I pulled out the napkin with my father's number on it. If he didn't provide closure, I'd make my own.

I was in the process of ripping the napkin to shreds when Kelvin walked in. Whoops. I'd forgotten to lock the door and flip over our sign to read CLOSED.

"What's that?" he asked, pointing at the shredded paper.

"Nobody important," I said.

"Ah, I get it."

"Are you here to check on me?" I asked. "Because, don't worry, my heart's still intact."

"Figured as much," he said. "It's always been filled to the brim with care."

He leaned against the counter. "Listen, I found something. I think I know who it was."

"Who what was?" My mind still lingered on my father.

"The kil—" Kelvin straightened up. "Mrs. Jin, so good to see you."

My mom greeted Kelvin with a smile, even as she held a broom and pointed the handle my way. "Could you give me a hand?"

"Yes, of course. Must have lost track of time," I lied.

Kelvin said, "I'll let you two close shop. But, Lissa, can we meet up tonight?"

"Sure. Drop by our place after dinner."

"You got it." He almost bounced out of the bakery with nervous energy. What had he been about to say to me? He must have uncovered something significant.

CHAPTER 49

Mom and I didn't have a magnificent garden like Kelvin's. We had a humble concrete patio. I also wanted a comfy porch swing like Kelvin, but we didn't have room for one. Instead, my best friend and I had to settle for a small mosaic bistro table. Whiskers nosed at a bush in the corner while we talked.

"What'd you find out?" I asked Kelvin.

His eyes sparkled. "Remember how we were talking to Alma? I got the editing history of the shared doc. Guess who erased the speeches?"

I tilted my head. "Could've been anyone from the wedding party. They all had secrets to keep under wraps."

"But the person's name who deleted everything was recorded—it was Easton."

I nodded. "His juvie record. Makes sense he wanted to hide it."

"Once a criminal?"

I raised an eyebrow. "We know better than to make assumptions." Hadn't Kelvin himself said something similar to me? "Just because Easton did something way back doesn't mean he's guilty of murder now."

"You're right. But everything's been an act with him, like the British accent."

"What about his loyalty to his friend?" I asked. "Easton stuck around when he could've left. He wanted to make sure Colton was okay." I appreciated people who stuck around. My mind flitted to my dad, and I frowned.

Kelvin shuffled in his seat. "Well, where was Easton at the time of Miles' death?"

"Beats me."

Kelvin rubbed his chin. "Or, if we don't think it's Easton, how about a different angle? Jada said Miles had been talking in the other tent, irritated. What if he wasn't practicing his big speech? What if he'd been pacing and plotting?"

"Plotting what?"

"Miles talked about gardening." He mimed scissors with his hands.

"The shears," I said. "They were in the tent with Colton's attendants."

"What if Miles grabbed them?"

"Why?"

"Dirt." Kelvin flashed his phone at me, the online doc pulled up. "To confront Easton, who'd erased all his hard work."

"But the doc could be restored if Miles knew how. Besides Miles could've winged the speech, he knew all the content."

Kelvin grunted. "You're right."

It was nice feeling vindicated, but that didn't advance our insight into the case any further.

Thud, thud. Whiskers hopped by. The sounds of the hops reminded me of what Jada had said. She'd heard clomping steps near the front of the tent but . . .

"Kelvin, what were the bride's and groom's tents like? Did they face each other?" I wanted to make certain of my memory.

He checked the photos on his phone. "Nope."

I'd remembered that the backs of the two tents were almost touching, making the entrances land on opposite ends. "How did Jada hear both Miles' footsteps outside the entrance? And his voice through the wall?"

Whiskers hopped up and down. "Thank you," I said, reaching out and petting her head. "You solved a riddle for us."

Kelvin spoke, a hint of wonder in his voice. "There must have been two people in the tent."

"Jada had been playing music," I said. "She probably didn't realize it at the time. The irritation or anger had been Miles arguing—"

"With Easton," Kelvin said with conviction. "He was spooked by the speech and erased it. Then Easton took it a step further. As a groomsman, *he* could have easily grabbed the shears from the tent."

But would Easton have done it? Stabbing Miles to make sure a juvie secret never came to light? I clicked my tongue. "Are we being too narrow-minded? If I could only make sure, look Easton in the eyes."

Kelvin chuckled. "You'd like a full-blown confession."

"That *would* make me feel more at ease."

A ding sounded from Kelvin's phone. He checked the screen. "Huh. You might get your wish."

"We're meeting up with Easton?"

"Everyone's gathering together."

My heart skipped a beat. "Is it Colton? Did he . . . ?"

Kelvin reached across the table to squeeze my hand. "He's fine. Getting better, in fact. Awake and moving into the step-down unit, according to Leanne. And he's the one who asked all the wedding attendants and us to come."

"Really?" I left my hand in Kelvin's grasp for its reassuring warmth.

"Apparently, he has an announcement to make."

"Where are we meeting?"

"In his new hospital room. Tomorrow evening, after everyone gets off work and before visiting hours end."

"Wonder what will happen," I said, giving a quick squeeze of his hand in partnership.

The next day, I felt jittery in anticipation of the gathering at the hospital. I woke up earlier than usual and even marched quicker than my mom to open up Jin Bakery.

Good thing I unlocked the shop door, because I noticed an envelope on the floor. My nerves were jangled even more when I found my name on it. I recognized the writing, too.

Though I'd thrown away the napkin with his phone number on it, my father's spidery handwriting graced the envelope. I swooped down, snatching it right before Mom made it through the door.

She moved into the kitchen while I busied myself out front. Once she seemed occupied, I opened the envelope. He'd added a few dried pink rose petals inside, like floral confetti. A small business card stared up at me—my own. I flipped it over. On the back, he'd written "Fare well." In two words, not like the usual goodbye, but more of a "hope the rest of your life turns out fine" way.

He'd returned the business card he'd taken from the wedding. Given back his means of communication. At least, symbolically. Of course, he knew where we worked and lived, but it felt like he'd respect my wishes.

I thought I'd feel a pang of remorse, but I didn't. Everything remained calm and okay in my world. I'd finally gained closure. Maybe he had, too.

Through the archway to the kitchen, I heard my mom call out, "You ready to join me, Felicity?"

"More than ever," I said, tossing away the envelope and its contents.

I headed for the kitchen, and the forward motion felt like moving on. Within the soothing rhythm of baking, I found contentment, and the day passed by in a happy, flour-dusted blur, complete with greetings to beloved customers.

When we closed shop, I hoped I could move forward in other areas of my life. Including a nagging mystery that needed resolution.

CHAPTER 50

The step-down unit in Pixie Medical Center proved nicer than the ICU space. The room was painted a muted blue, and a framed seascape print hung on one of the walls. Colton was still lying in a bed hooked up to a few machines for monitoring, but there was a small wooden bedside table with drawers for a touch of homespun comfort.

When Kelvin and I arrived, a few others were already in the room. Leanne stared at Colton's face, as though memorizing it, even as he sat up and smiled at her. Jada hovered near Leanne, and Nova was on the other side of the bed.

Kelvin inched forward and placed his vase filled with orange poppies on the bedside table. Flowers were allowed in this section of the hospital. "They're for health and regeneration," he said, but nobody took notice of the explanation except me.

"Great symbolism," I said, as he returned to my side. Voices coming from down the hall alerted me to more company. "Hey, how many people can be in this room?"

"Four, I think," Kelvin said.

"Er . . ." I stepped backward and bumped into a folded manual wheelchair resting against the rear wall.

The rest of the wedding party showed up, bringing our total number to eight visitors. Feeling the temp of the room go up, I fanned myself with my hand.

Colton eyed all of us. "Move closer."

We surged forward, and I could feel the crush of bodies.

"Thank you for your well wishes, and those"—he nodded at me—"seeking to uncover the truth."

His eyes glistened. "You've all come to visit me now, but I know one of you tried to poison me that night."

Leanne put a gentle hand on his shoulder, as though lending support.

"And I know who it was—"

Sudden darkness. The lights had gone off. A crash, then an ear-splitting scream.

Soon, a furious alarm sounded. The lights switched back on.

"I called for help," Leanne said, her finger still over the emergency button.

A nurse barreled in. "What's going on here?" he asked, turning off the alarm. "Is that broken glass I see on the floor?"

The crash. Someone had knocked the flowers to the ground. Who had been standing there?

"Out! All of you!" the nurse boomed.

We all jammed into the narrow hall, where another nurse hurried toward us. "This is a fire hazard," she said. Upon seeing Kelvin, she did a double take but insisted that we leave. "No exceptions."

As we beelined toward the exit, I slowed my pace to walk beside Leanne. She was dragging her feet, reluctant to leave her recovered groom.

I whispered to her, "Did you know who Colton was about to name?"

She looked at the backs of the wedding attendants ahead of us, "I do."

I stopped moving, while the others kept going. Kelvin glanced behind him once, but I waved him on.

Her voice came out gruff. "He told me right before the meeting. It was Nova. She'd handed him the poisoned water. The drink I'd asked for, to help him flush out his system after he made that awful speech. I can't believe it, but we have a killer in our midst."

Leanne started crying, and I patted her back in the sterile hallway of the hospital.

"Worse," she continued, "the police think it's me. Like I'd ever harm Colton. Or Miles."

Wanting to comfort her, I said, "I can put in a good word for you with the detective. Vouch for your character." Leanne was the least likely suspect, in my mind. Why would she want to kill her husband or one of his relatives, when she was newly connected to them?

Leanne wiped her damp eyes on her sleeve. "You'd do that for me?"

"Sure. Plus, Detective Sun doesn't know about this accusation from Colton yet."

"Thank you, Felicity."

"Of course," I said on automatic. But as we walked out of the hospital, I knew I'd need a lot of luck, more housewarming gifts, and maybe a special guest visitor to have a cordial conversation with the cop.

Once I got home, I talked to my mom about my plans for a surprise visit to the detective's home.

"That's a great idea," she said. "I'd love to see how she's settling in. And we'll make sure to bring oranges."

After a rushed dinner, we made a quick trip to the

store. We ended up securing a healthy stash of mandarin oranges.

At Detective Sun's house, I used the brass knocker to announce our arrival. The detective opened the door slowly. Through the gap, she took in my presence and paused. I almost wondered if she'd close the door on me when my mom spoke up.

"We brought more oranges," Mom said.

The detective took the fruit with enthusiastic thanks. "Come on in," she said, opening the door wider.

Mom said, "I hope you've been finding that Pixie is a lovely town to live in."

"It is," Detective Sun agreed. "My neighbor Sally even brought by pastries today. They might look familiar to you."

Indeed, on her breakfast table lay Jin Bakery treats. She had an array of our new mini egg tarts and pineapple buns.

"Would you like some?" the detective asked.

Although we sat down, we declined the pastries. "We get enough samples at work," Mom said as the detective settled across from us.

Sally, I thought. Reflecting on the blur of the day, I remembered Sweet Tooth Sally purchasing a box of baked goods. "Your neighbor is—"

"A force to be reckoned," Detective Sun said. "Sally's interested in running for mayor, and she's been picking my brain on how to improve Pixie. She's even talking about expanding local police services."

"Fascinating." My mom's eyes twinkled. "Would you think about working here then?"

"Possibly. There'd be zero commute, and I have a rent-to-own agreement with this house, Mama Jin."

I sputtered.

Mom rubbed my back, and the detective excused herself to get me some water.

I gripped the glass and took a few sips to calm down. "But don't they need you in Fresno, Detective Sun?"

"Sadly, I'm low on the totem pole." She continued, "That's why I get assigned to the cases in neighboring cities. Not that I mind."

I stared at the glass of water before me. Time to pivot the conversation. I'd promised Leanne. "Speaking of which," I said, "I saw Colton today."

Mom glanced at me from the side of her eye.

"As a friend," I said. "I wasn't sleuthing. He asked everyone from the wedding to drop by, and made an announcement. Leanne had nothing to do with his coma." I stared hard at the detective. She didn't flinch.

I kept talking. "I heard it was Nova who'd given him that drink. Did you check for her fingerprints on the glass?"

Detective Sun sighed. "Look, I'm not supposed to talk about an open investigation, but let me enlighten you. Unlike the cop shows you might watch, we don't have everyone's fingerprints on file. And things were a mess that night. The owner of Pixie Inn had cleared away the food and drinks. Evidence wasn't so clean-cut."

But my thoughts traveled back to the glass. I remembered Nova standing there late at night in her purple pajamas, before the entrance to the kitchen. Maybe *she* hadn't known about the unclear evidence and crept back to wash the glass. To erase her fingerprints.

"Does that mean Leanne is off the hook?" I asked. "She didn't hurt her husband, according to him." Plus, she could've poisoned him any old time besides the send-off party. I gathered my courage and added, "I don't think she did anything to Miles either."

Detective Sun hesitated before saying, "We don't need her for further questioning."

Was that a coded sentence? "You don't believe Leanne is a suspect anymore?" I asked.

"We're ruling out people based on the evidence."

"See, Felicity," Mom said. "We need to let the police do their job. Always follow authority. Because I bet they've made a lot of progress on the case, right?" My mom turned her head to look at the detective, a proud smile on her face.

Detective Sun seemed to melt for a moment under the praise and spoke quickly, like she couldn't help boasting in front of my mom. "It was the hot plate. Leanne had to get it from the park facilities manager, who noted the time, which was around when the email was sent."

"Excellent job, Rylan," my mom said.

The detective's cheeks flushed, and for a moment, I could imagine her as a little girl with pigtails, flourishing under the praise of her mother—Detective Sun must really miss her.

"So if you could re-create the movements of every attendant on that day," I said, "you'd find the killer." And probably Colton's poisoner.

Detective Sun blinked a few times, and her professional air returned. "Leave it alone, Felicity."

"It's a good idea, right?"

She gave a little laugh. "Yeah, if you could travel back in time."

If only I was magical in that way . . . But it did inspire me. I needed a visual of where everybody was around the time of the tea ceremony when Miles had gone missing. I'd have to call in a favor, but I thought all the key players would agree to it.

CHAPTER 51

Everyone agreed to gather at Pixie Park over the weekend. On Saturday morning, all the wedding attendants and I stood on the grassy hilltop, facing Leanne.

She laced her fingers together with nervous energy and addressed us. "Thank you for coming to support me. I do really need your help." At my request, she'd sent out an urgent invite to the attendants.

"What's wrong?" Turner asked, frowning.

"I bet you've all heard about my troubles with the police by now, how they took me in for questioning." She scrunched up her face.

Murmurs of sympathy echoed in the air.

Leanne continued, "I'll tell you something the police revealed to me. Somebody sent an email pretending to be me on the day of the wedding—to Miles. To make me look guilty."

Only Leanne, the mysterious sender, and I knew about the email (which no longer pointed to Leanne's guilt, I privately reassured her). I watched everyone on the hill for a reaction. They all seemed dismayed or stunned by Leanne's words.

Haley piped up. "If it's not really an email from you, won't the police soon realize that?"

Leanne unlaced her fingers. "The cops are busy. And other things about that email point to me as well, what with the local IP address and it being sent before the tea ceremony."

Jada laughed, a high-pitched squeal. "This is ridiculous."

Leanne held up a hand. "That's not all. Seems like I'm in even more trouble, given the fiasco with the broken glass vase at the hospital, which the nurse said had endangered her patient. I must have accidentally knocked it over in the dark. And then there were the removed tires."

This was news to me. "The *what* tires?"

"Someone must have pressed the quick release button for the axles on the wheelchair. Good thing the nurse checked before wheeling Colton out of his room for his morning ride around the hallways." She blinked back tears.

Easton crossed his arms over his chest. "The police think you have something to do with that?"

"Uh-huh. Since I was onsite in his room."

As were the rest of you, I thought.

Nova stomped her foot. "Well, the police are wrong. You and Colton love each other. You'd never hurt him. And you were too busy getting married to do anything to Miles on the day of the wedding."

"Thank you. I appreciate your vote of confidence." Leanne gave Nova a sad smile. "But I don't have an alibi. No one actually saw me in the tea tent at the time of Miles' death. Everyone was busy escorting the parentals or getting ready for the ceremony. Even Felicity didn't come until right before the tea-making ritual."

My cheeks burned. I'd been prepping the egg tart cake display. Maybe if I'd left earlier, I could have served as a solid witness for the bride.

Jada fiddled with her glasses. "How can we help you and prove your innocence?"

"Glad you asked," Leanne said, spreading her arms out to encompass the park. "If we did a reenactment of that wedding day, around the time before and during the tea ceremony, I think that would help."

I heard groans and grumbles, but Leanne persisted. "Please, humor me. A possible jail sentence is at stake here."

The complaints turned to compliance.

"One more thing," Leanne said, squinting into the distance. "I also called for a stand-in for Miles."

Even though I knew what was coming, I still turned to focus on the figure now strolling across the green space to meet us.

Kelvin looked amazing. He'd stuck to the original dress code of the groom's attendants and was wearing a dark blue dress shirt, accessorized with a red tie. He'd even pinned a white rose boutonniere to complete the effect.

"Thanks, Kelvin. You can start off in the groom's tent." Leanne turned her attention to the rest of us. "Everybody else, go to the place where you were just prior to the tea ceremony."

Jada quickly stepped to the center space, where the bridal tent had been pitched. Leanne moved off to where the tea ceremony had occurred, on the west side of the park.

I stayed in place, watching as Easton made his way to the groom's tent. So he and Miles *had* been together while Jada was busy with her makeup. As Easton whispered to "Miles," I headed north to the cake tent.

Both Nova and Turner moved in opposite directions from me. Nova beelined it to the parking lot on the southwestern side, and Turner left for the southeastern edge.

Haley joined me at the reception tent space for a few minutes before Leanne shouted more instructions. "Okay, now we're getting close to teatime."

While Leanne and Jada stayed in their positions, the rest of us started moving. I waved goodbye to Haley as I walked toward the tea tent. Haley, in turn, trotted to the eastern side of the park to the rosebushes.

Nova and Turner joined us in the tea area to create a cozy group of four. Meanwhile, Easton was the individual who moved the most. He appeared to be making a circuit, a large perimeter around the park.

Kelvin, as Miles, looked confused about what to do next. He tapped the toe of his Doc Marten on the ground, waiting.

"It's teatime!" Leanne shouted.

The four of us mimed the traditional wedding ritual. Jada stayed in her tent, and Haley walked to the restrooms. Easton continued on his loop stroll, pausing before the roses to smell them. Kelvin moved at a snail's pace to arrive at the cake tent.

"The tea is done," Leanne said, "and we can now go to the ceremony."

Everyone ended up at the hilltop.

Leanne clapped her hands. "Thanks. I appreciate you all participating."

"So, did that really help?" Nova asked, playing with a few strands of her purple bangs.

"Maybe. You went to the parking lot, right? Someone must have seen you."

Nova nodded. "I got the silk pillows from the car and ran into Colton's mom."

I remembered Nova leading the mother of the groom into the tea tent.

"You've got an alibi then," I said. As did Colton, who'd been walking around with his dad.

"Me too," Turner said, his voice booming. He thumped his chest. "I was in charge of bringing Leanne's parents to the tea ceremony."

Right. The head attendants *had* made sure the parentals showed up for the tea serving.

Leanne trained her gaze on those without alibis: Jada, Easton, and Haley. "What about you three? I understand if there was an accident involving Miles . . ." That was a lenient way to describe murder.

Jada flared her nostrils. "Come on. I'm your roomie, Leanne." *Ex-roomie*, I thought. Had she been angry enough to stop that change from happening—with violence?

Haley widened her doe green eyes. "You've known me since kindergarten, Leanne . . ."

Easton shuffled his feet and took out his wallet. From it, he pulled out an ear cuff. "I found this near the rose-bush. When I was taking a walk to cool off. Can't believe I told Miles to 'sod off.'" Jada gave a gasp of recognition— so *that* was the gardening remark she'd overheard, except she'd attributed it to Miles.

Multiple people leaned in to study what Easton held. I drew closer, too. In the palm of his hand was a small loop, adorned with a single row of glittering diamonds. I recognized it on sight.

So did Haley. "That's mine," she said with a whoosh of relief. "I wondered where it'd gone."

He reluctantly gave her the cuff. "Real diamonds, eh? Keep it safe." That reminded me of his old run-in with the law. A penchant for stealing, according to Mr. Wu.

I shook my head. This time, the situation was different. A finders-keepers scenario. And good thing he'd picked up the sparkling cuff, because it established that both Haley and he had stopped by the rosebushes.

Which left only Jada without anybody or any item vouching for her supposed presence in the bridal tent. She scowled at everyone around her.

Leanne touched Easton's arm. "But what about the music? Did you hear any when you were in the tent with Miles?"

Easton blinked and then started bobbing his head. "Oh yeah. Some great tunes coming from next door. Drowned out our argu—I mean, discussion."

Another person saved by Easton's testimony.

Kelvin turned in a slow circle. "If nobody was near me on that cursed wedding day, how did I—or rather, Miles—die?"

Death by shears definitely wasn't a natural way to go.

"Could it have been a stranger?" Turner asked. "Pixie looks safe and all, but—"

I interjected. "We're a cozy community and not known for serious crime." It was an ironic statement since I'd discovered two victims of foul play within a span of months, but I wanted to defend my hometown.

"Okay then," Nova said. "What if it was a wedding attendee? Someone who had a beef with Miles?"

"I guess," Leanne conceded.

"The police will eventually find them," Jada said. "And in the meantime, while Colton's healing, you're welcome to stay in the apartment."

"Thanks, but I'd rather be at the hospital."

Jada's shoulders slumped, but she nodded.

Everyone gave assurances to Leanne that the police would soon be investigating someone else. They also sent their healing wishes to Colton for a full recovery.

Leanne thanked everyone with grace. She seemed relieved but also puzzled. Before I left with Kelvin, she told me, "I just don't understand what happened. Nobody seems to be at fault. It's a total mystery."

CHAPTER 52

We were in Kelvin's shop, talking through the case since he'd had to get back to Love Blooms to open for the afternoon. I loitered there, hoping to untangle my thoughts.

"I don't get it. Who could it be if everyone was busy at the time of Miles' murder?" I asked.

Kelvin quirked an eyebrow at me. "You don't buy into the dangerous stranger theory?"

"Naw."

"What about the disgruntled attendee?" Kelvin rearranged some ivory-colored flowers in a vase.

"Not at a huge wedding," I said. "The timing doesn't work. Too many witnesses around. It must have been done in a lull, like the beginning or middle of the tea ceremony."

Kelvin placed a sheet of brown kraft paper and a pen on the long table near him. "Write down your thoughts. Maybe that will help."

I put down the names of the intimate group at the wedding. Then I crossed out Leanne and Colton. No way the bride and groom were involved. Then I also put a line through Nova and Turner; they'd had the presence of parentals to prevent them from attacking Miles. "Which leaves Easton, Haley, and Jada."

Kelvin traced the names with his index finger. "No eyewitnesses for any of the three."

"Although Easton and Haley have the ear cuff connection."

"And Jada had a sound witness, who heard her music playing in the tent."

"Miles dead," I said. "Then Colton poisoned. What's the connection between the two?"

"They're family, aren't they?" he asked. "Someone must have a lot of hatred for the Wus. Unless it was a case of mistaken identity, like I'd suggested before."

"Miles and Colton don't really look alike," I said.

"I don't know then, and it's almost time," Kelvin mumbled, moving to the front door and flipping the sign to read OPEN.

A ding chimed from his pocket, and he pulled his phone out. "Update from Leanne," he said. "Colton's doing better. Unhooked from machines and getting PT now. He wants to let things go, insists the poison was an accident."

I let out a sharp laugh. "Not likely. Poisoned drink *and* a tampered wheelchair." I wondered if Colton was letting things go because he thought it was Nova, his friend with a hot temper.

Kelvin scrolled on his phone. "There's a postscript. Leanne's been cleared by the cops."

"Yeah, I remember. The hot plate she borrowed."

"Not only that." Kelvin lifted his screen up. "The police got an anonymous tip a little while ago. About the fake email, telling them to research the creation date of the account."

Huh. Someone had tipped off the cops about the account not being genuine. Why?

Kelvin strolled back to my side and unpinned the

boutonniere from his shirt. He laid the white rose down on the table on top of the kraft paper.

I picked it up. It was a beautiful bloom, a tightly coiled rosebud.

"Stopping to smell the roses?" Kelvin asked.

That tickled something in my brain. I turned the rose in my hand, examining its soft petals. Understanding hit me.

We'd been talking about the Wus and relatives. Look-alikes. I'd been pursuing the wrong angle. Maybe it wasn't hate that had spurred on the crimes, but love.

I rushed out of the flower shop, almost crashing into the customer meandering in. I knew where I had to go next.

When I arrived, the shop was open and the door unlocked. I walked in, but no customers were in sight at Peace and Hairmony. Strange.

Haley came darting out a side door and stopped short upon seeing me. "What are you doing here, Felicity? You're not due for a trim yet."

"I'm here to talk to you," I said, "and it looks like it's the perfect time to do so. Quiet in here."

"That's because I cancelled my appointments and sent the staff home." She shifted the purse on her shoulder and pulled out what looked like a hex key. Ignoring me, she inserted it in the bar handle, locking the front door, and flipped the shop sign to CLOSED. "I'm taking a break."

"Where are you off to?" I asked.

"Gonna check on Colton."

Grabbing her arm, I said, "I can't let you do that."

She flung my hand off and stepped back into the middle of the store. "Are you feeling okay, Felicity?"

I didn't have all the pieces of the mystery puzzle in place, but I had enough to try to appeal to Haley. She'd listen to reason, right? She was so young, she could change course even now.

"The flower behind your ear at the wedding, you replaced it. It was in full bloom when I first saw it, but later"—I pulled out the white rose boutonniere—"it turned into a rosebud. How? Only if you'd replaced it with a look-alike."

She shrugged. "So what? I lost it while running around. That's why I stopped by the rosebushes."

Running around trying to kill Miles? I thought; but I said, "That was your alibi. When you retraced your steps. But you had a *second* alibi."

She gave me a confused look.

"On the day of the wedding, you told me you had to leave the ceremony tent to get your makeup done with Jada. But according to Jada, and our simulation, she was all alone."

Haley made to speak, but I cut her off. "I think, instead, you were confronting Miles. With pruners. I mean, you clearly had to cut the second rosebud with a tool."

Wait a minute. That couldn't be right. How did Haley have time to stop by the roses and then circle back to kill Miles before the ceremony? And he'd definitely been stuck in the neck with shears—I shuddered at the image.

Haley smirked. "Not so sure of the facts, are you? I think you're reaching. Because you didn't like that the man you love got accused of murder. But he's clear now, so you should just let things be."

The man I love? My body temperature rose higher,

but the word "love" also reminded me of the central basis behind my murder theory.

That's the angle I would take to appeal to Haley's humanity. I stood in front of the door and took a wide stance to block her from leaving. "It *was* all about love for you, too. Everyone was thinking it was about hate—for Miles or for Colton. But it wasn't. It was about love for Leanne. The two of them weren't good enough for her."

Her face scrunched up. "Miles? He was a fling, never a real threat. But I thought he might prove useful with his speech and passionate declaration at the bachelorette party."

"Useful how?"

"To stop the wedding. But the doc got erased, and his words didn't matter," Haley said, her eyes glittering. "So I thought his body would."

I'd gotten the timeline with the rosebush backward. "I met you in the cake tent—probably right before you killed Miles."

"I figured a killing would stop the wedding," she said matter-of-factly.

"Except it didn't."

"It might have, only it was so dark in that tent. Nobody realized. I thought the caterers would—or you, when you went to light the votive candles."

I hadn't, and then Leanne and Colton were formally wed. So if Haley couldn't stop the wedding, maybe she'd wanted to pause the honeymoon. "The drink," I said. "You poisoned Colton."

"Whether he decided on another martini or water, I figured I'd help him out."

"The clear liquid you had at the send-off must not have been water."

"It was hydrogen peroxide, industrial strength." She

pulled on one of her blond strands. "The perks of working in a salon. He was so far gone, he probably didn't even notice the off taste."

"What about Colton's wheelchair?" I asked. "Did you also tamper with that?"

"Ding, ding, ding. I figured he might crash into something, hurt himself. Nope. So I'll have to finish the job myself, but you're in my way."

She seemed casual talking about hurting and killing others. Was I wrong in thinking I could appeal to her reason? What about emotion? "If you love Leanne so much, don't you want her to be happy? With Colton?"

Haley's eyes narrowed. "It's just a phase. Like when she attended UC Merced. She came right back to me once I got her a job."

I could think of a dozen other reasons why Leanne had returned home. But if Haley had gotten Leanne a job . . . "You connected Leanne with Turner? Wasn't he the one who introduced her to Colton?"

"That was unexpected," Haley admitted. "But it'll turn out fine. I can still make my own happy ending." She rummaged through her purse.

What did she intend to do? If I bonded with her, I could talk her down. "I know what it's like," I said. "To be left behind. Kelvin did the same. But he came back of his own volition, like Leanne."

She paused rummaging. "Kelvin, Kelvin, Kelvin. Can you even hear yourself? If you think he's such a great catch, why aren't you two *really* together?"

I remembered our ruse and started to protest.

"Please. I know you're faking it. So Kelvin could blow me off. Don't worry, I was faking it, too. Just needed to get close to him to see where he would leave the pruners."

She hadn't brought a weapon to the wedding. "If it wasn't premeditated," I said, "the police will probably be more lenient—"

She giggled. "Why, of course it was planned out. I sent that fake email to Miles, knowing he'd fall for it."

"He didn't notice it wasn't from Leanne?"

"Miles was a sucker, probably got distracted by the profile pic. Only I didn't realize the cops would get ahold of it and think Leanne was to blame for the murder."

"Especially when you wanted to use Kelvin as the scapegoat." I shook my head in disgust.

She stepped up close to me. Her pupils were dilated. "You want to truly know the grisly details? I met Miles in the main tent and lied that Leanne was on her way. Then I damsel-in-distressed him, saying I'd dropped something below the cake table. In retrospect, maybe I placed it too far under the cake table."

"I'm not following you . . ."

Haley continued musing out loud. "At first, I was going to use the ear cuff. But the rose was better—didn't have to put makeup on my jewelry that way."

"What makeup?" I asked, confused.

"The scarlet lip tint I pretended was blood. Put it on the rose, and he fainted like I'd predicted."

I remembered the lipstick Sally and her crew had found while beautifying the park.

Haley continued, "A quick jab, and it was done."

I cringed and touched my throat.

"Anatomy for the win. You've got to know your stuff for cosmetology." She smiled at me. "Then all I had to do was pluck a fresh rose and act clueless."

Haley wasn't as naive or innocent as I'd imagined. I backed toward the door, while she put her purse on the side counter. Opening the bag wide, she pulled out a straight razor. "This was my first choice for a weapon. Before Kelvin conveniently brought his pruners to the wedding."

I stared at the razor's handle, thankful it was snapped shut at the moment. But I bet the edge was wicked sharp.

She flicked open the razor, and I gulped. The blade looked vicious. Could I dodge it if I was fast enough? I reached behind me and felt the door. It was a push bar handle. But she'd locked it. Did that mean it would or wouldn't open if I pushed?

If I connected heart-to-heart with her, would Haley change her mind? I thought about the lesson I'd learned from interactions with my father. "Sometimes wishes are one way," I said to Haley, "and we're meant to let go of relationships. It's actually better for us—and for them." As I said it, I knew I believed in the truth of my statement.

Haley paused before me, tilted her head, and said, "No, I don't think so. Leanne went away briefly for college, and it left me gutted. If she moves away with Colton to the Bay Area *forever*, I won't survive."

She raised her hand, and I still didn't see any viable weapons around me to fend off her attack.

Although her eyes were misting, making it hard for her to see, she came at me. *Hard to see.* Perhaps a déjà vu moment could help here.

CHAPTER 53

I reached up and to the side, hitting the light bank. Darkness descended.

At the same time, I pushed at the door handle, hoping it'd work. The door whooshed open, and I let Haley's forward motion propel her along. I shoved her to push her out through the doorframe, and pulled it shut tight.

There. With her purse on the counter, Haley wouldn't have the keys to get back in. She'd unknowingly allowed herself to get locked out.

Whew. I dialed the authorities even as Haley banged on the shop door and glared at me. Then she seemed to think better of it and tried bolting. Hard to do in her stiletto sandals. She'd only taken a few mincing steps when the Fresno police arrived. Patrol cars zoomed into view, and I saw Detective Sun also stepping out of an unmarked vehicle. The detective approached Haley, calling out her name.

Haley didn't want to willingly go with her, and Detective Sun attempted to take away the razor gripped in Haley's hand. With a furious cry, Haley brandished the blade at the detective.

Only when guns were pointed at Haley did she back down. She dropped the blade, crumpling to the ground.

She tried to make excuses, but since she'd just threatened Detective Sun, she was led away by police officers.

After I saw Haley locked securely in the back of a cop car, I opened the shop door to the officers.

"I'm sure you've got quite the story for me," Detective Sun said, already reaching for her phone to record my statement.

"Do I ever."

I took my time relaying the details I'd discovered from my recent conversation with Haley, along with the reenactment at Pixie Park and any relevant info I thought the detective would find helpful. She murmured as I spilled everything, and I wasn't sure if she was appreciative or not of my investigative exploits. In the end, she just said, "Let's make sure you aren't injured. After that, you're free to go."

Thankfully, I was soon cleared to leave by the paramedics who'd been called in. I didn't want to go home to an empty apartment or off to the bakery to disturb my mom as she catered to customers.

I decided to circle back and spend time at Pixie Park. It was soothing to be in the wide-open space without needing to think about catering a wedding—or worse, uncovering a murderer in our midst.

Wandering over to the east side of the park, I stopped by the heirloom rosebushes. The pink blooms beckoned to me, and I touched the silky petals.

These roses had meant different things to various people over the last weeks. Kelvin had given one to Haley out of new friendship. My dad had removed pink petals from the cake table (and, unfortunately, floral clues) as a reminder of fatherhood. Haley had used a replica pink rose to falsify her movements. And, finally, Easton, who hadn't taken any of the roses from the bush but left them growing there, had stopped by to refocus himself after arguing with Miles.

Kelvin was right; flowers did bring meaning with them. I took out the white rose boutonniere that he'd made and walked up the hill. At the top, I breathed in the city. Pixie was beautiful from this aerial view, and I knew why Leanne and Colton had picked the park to have their somewhat cursed wedding.

I remembered the elaborate flower arch Kelvin had crafted with his skilled hands in this very spot. Closing my eyes, I savored the feel of sunshine on my face, the gentle breeze blowing against my skin. I swear I could even detect the scent of fresh flowers. Could it be from the boutonniere?

"Hey, Lissa," a voice said. "Got your message."

I opened my eyes to find Kelvin approaching with a single rose in his hand.

"You didn't have to come," I said. "I told you I was going to meet up with you after closing time."

He frowned. "You've just come from a near-death experience. Of course I showed up."

I didn't know if it'd been *that* dire, but I was happy to see Kelvin, dressed in his usual Henley shirt and jeans combo, and accessorizing with his sturdy Doc Martens. A word popped to mind: "loyalty." No, that wasn't it . . .

"You've been in danger two times already," Kelvin said, the words almost getting stuck in his throat.

I waved off his concern. "Everything worked out. Haley got taken away for attempted assault of a police officer, and I'm hoping Detective Sun can wrap up the case soon. And Colton's on the mend."

Kelvin nodded. "He is, and the honeymoon is back on. Imagine a love so strong that it thrives after trauma."

"Yeah, a dead body and a coma are tough things for a couple to navigate."

"We've been through a fair amount of stuff ourselves," Kelvin said.

"We have." Both bad and good. Kelvin's mom passing, the opening of our shops, my bio father returning, and a murder (or two).

"Could we do it all together, as a couple?" He spun the rose in his hand, and I noticed the deep red color. Even I could understand the symbolism of the flower he held.

I thought about Haley's observation about my relationship with Kelvin. Did I want to fake-date or real-date him? "Loyal" hadn't been the only word to come to mind when I'd seen him walking toward me. My heart stirred, and I realized I'd been grasping for a different L-word: "love."

Kelvin continued staring at me with his deep brown eyes, all patience. He'd been waiting a long time. Ever since high school when—

"I know your promposal didn't work our senior year, when I said we should go as friends, but now? I'm older and wiser." I plucked the flower from his fingers. "Let's say, I *rose* to the occasion."

Floral puns for the win because Kelvin laughed, a glorious sound that wrapped me in happiness. Then he pulled me into his arms, and I lost myself in the amazing (dare I say, magical?), wondrous moment.

CHAPTER 54

In celebration of Kelvin and me moving forward in our relationship, I invited him over. After all, Mom was still finishing up at the bakery. We'd have the place all to ourselves—particularly the kitchen area.

"You're in for a treat," I told Kelvin as I gathered the necessary ingredients. Our home kitchen didn't have the extensive equipment of Jin Bakery, but we had everything in stock we needed.

I combined the ingredients and tended to the batter, while Kelvin watched from the sidelines. Whiskers also hopped into the room, peering at me from a corner as I prepped the almond cookies.

The preheated oven dinged, and I watched Kelvin hook his thumbs into his jeans pockets and shuffle from side to side.

"Bored already?" I asked. "Why don't you go put the rose in water?"

He nodded, zooming over to where we kept the flower vases. Our apartment was like a second home to him. Everything felt right that he was here and getting even closer to us—to me, especially.

I rolled the dough into balls. Then I peeked over at Kelvin, who was placing the vase with the red rose on the counter. That inspired me. Instead of the single almond slice, I would use a pair of almonds to create a heart in the center of each cookie.

Searching my kitchen cabinets, I found a bottle of food coloring. Perfect. I took a little bowl and poured some dye in it. Then I dipped the almond slices into the red liquid.

Only one problem. My hands had turned red. "Kelvin," I said, "can you use your thumb to flatten the balls? Then I'll place the almonds in the middle."

"Sure thing." He proceeded to make an indentation in every ball.

Then I swooped in to make the heart out of the red almond slivers. "Cute, right?"

He nodded, grinning at me and barely sparing a glance at the adorable cookies.

I opened the oven door and put the batch in.

"I'm hot," he said as he sat down in a nearby chair. I checked if he was making a punny joke, but he was fanning himself.

I shrugged. He didn't know the half of it. A small kitchen oven was nothing compared to our triple-decker.

Kelvin sniffed the air. "What's that scent? It's so familiar . . ."

I took a whiff. "Almond extract?"

"No, it's more floral." He concentrated for a moment, then snapped his fingers. "A type of rose."

I nodded to the flower he'd gotten me. "That red kind?" I was never good with flower names.

"But it's not scented," he said. "What I'm smelling is the Honey Perfume rose, a kind of spicy, clove fragrance."

I sniffed again. Nothing except the aroma of baked goods and a touch of romance.

"Never mind. I must be imagining it," he said.

Whiskers hopped over to me and nudged my leg. "Hey there, want some love?" I asked.

As I petted her, a blurred image of my mom and my father came to me. They'd baked together. And then he'd had those headaches. I glanced over at Kelvin, who was rubbing his nose. He was fine, right?

I stared at my bunny, who looked at me with her knowing brown eyes. She twitched her whiskers three times and hopped away.

The oven timer going off pulled me away from my reflections. After letting the cookies cool, Kelvin and I dove in. We had just eaten two freshly baked cookies each when we heard the rattle of keys at the door.

Mom entered with bouncing steps. When she noticed us in the kitchen, sharing a plate of cookies, her eyes shone with delight.

"Am I interrupting something?" she asked, looking excited at the possibility of there being something to interrupt. "Were you baking, Felicity?"

I pointed to the tray of cookies on the kitchen counter. She must have noticed the heart-shaped almond slivers right away because she tried to unsuccessfully wipe a smile off her face.

Mom seemed happy, but not only about Kelvin and me. She'd been practically skipping when she'd returned home. And she didn't seem worried at all, which meant that news from Fresno and the showdown at the salon hadn't gotten to her.

"Did something happen today?" I asked.

"Sweet Tooth Sally came in, and guess what? She officially announced that she's running for mayor"—Mom rubbed her hands together—"and wants us to supply baked goods to her campaign staff and all her supporters."

"That's great news."

"Sally's got a grand vision to improve the city, to diversify our population. I mean, she's already lured a certain someone to join our local police department."

I swallowed hard. "Not Detective Sun?"

"That's right. Not only will we be neighbors, she'll be on the streets protecting us. Isn't that wonderful?"

"Yeah . . ." I licked my lips and looked to Kelvin for help.

Although he eyed another cookie, he jumped into the conversation. "You make a great point, Mrs. Jin. There *has* been an uptick in crime, which can put loved ones in danger." He gave me a hard stare, which I chose to ignore.

"I'm sure it'll pass," I said with deliberate nonchalance.

"Well," my mom said, "if it doesn't, I'm happy knowing that Rylan will be around."

I still couldn't get over the fact that Mom was calling Detective Sun by her first name but politely said, "Send her my congrats."

"Why don't you tell her in person? She'll be by the bakery tomorrow to pick up some pastries for Sally."

Okay then, I would. And I'd pump her about how things had concluded with Haley.

CHAPTER 55

Detective Sun arrived in the early afternoon to pick up the large order of pineapple buns, egg tarts, fortune cookies, and almond cookies.

My mom "just happened" to be standing at the counter with me when the detective came by. She nudged my shoulder.

I handed the detective the baked goods and said, "I hear congratulations are in order."

Detective Sun raised her eyebrows.

Mom blurted out, "You're coming to work in Pixie!"

Her excitement was so evident that the detective blushed a little. "Yes, Mama Jin."

"When do you start?"

I began pricing the pastries at the cash register, and my mom whispered to me, "Don't forget to add the friends discount for Sally."

Sure. I keyed in the items and added the percentage off. Meanwhile, Detective Sun was saying, "I'll be part of the Pixie Police very soon. I've pretty much wrapped up my latest case."

"The wedding murder?" Mom asked. That was what Pixians had started dubbing it, and the nickname had even appeared in a news article in the *Pixie Courier*. "How did you catch the killer?"

Detective Sun cleared her throat. "We were narrowing down the suspects and homing in on one. The timeline was clouded by a fake email, which we discovered was the handiwork of the real killer." Hmm, maybe Haley's call hadn't been so anonymous. They might've traced it.

The detective continued, trying her hardest not to turn her head my way. "Certain recent events sped up our investigation."

I busied myself with double-checking the discounted price for the goodies and gave Detective Sun the total.

As she handed me the cash, my mom murmured, "That poor bride and groom. What a disastrous wedding day, and beyond. I heard about the coma . . ."

"You'll be glad to know that Colton's doing well. He should be released in a few days and ready to finally go on their much-delayed honeymoon. In fact, his full recovery and confirmation of the renewed trip led to Miles' killer confessing."

"Huh?" I said while my mom also appeared confused.

"After that bit of news, the murderer broke down and confessed to everything."

My mom looked bewildered but accepted the resolution with grace. "There you are again, Rylan, doing your job so well."

"We just put out a press release," Detective Sun said, "minus the extra confession details."

I thought about Haley. All that misdirected love. She'd wanted to keep Leanne for herself and ended up ruining almost three lives—Miles, Colton, and Leanne. And now she'd permanently separated herself from the object of her affection.

However, I was happy Leanne and Colton could get away from this fiasco and heal in more ways than one. I wished them the very best and hoped they'd get a redo of their newly wedded days.

I glanced at the pastries in the clear display case before me. Maybe I could help them start afresh in my own way.

At the bakery on the appointed day, I took care to perch the last egg tart into place on top of the edible mini pyramid I'd created. This might provide a better wedding cake experience than the traumatic one Leanne and Colton had gone through.

I'd boxed the egg tart pyramid and tied it with white tulle ribbon when Kelvin walked through the door.

"Great minds think alike," he said, as he snuck a white peony under the bow I'd constructed. "We go well together."

Was he talking about flowers and food? Or our relationship? Either way, I simply replied, "Yes."

"Checkout time is right around now, so let's get walking."

He offered me his arm, and I accepted. A quick stroll later, and we'd arrived at Pixie Inn.

Leanne and Colton were hard to miss as they exited the residence with loud promises to return to our beautiful town. They turned their attention away from Mrs. Robson, who I glimpsed behind the reception desk, over to us on the sidewalk.

"Felicity and Kelvin," Leanne said. "Wonderful to see you."

"We heard the honeymoon's on and wanted to give you a parting gift," I said, handing her the decorated pastry box.

"Have a great trip," Kelvin said, "and warm wishes on your marriage."

They thanked us, and I noticed their car was festooned with a JUST MARRIED banner.

The couple took their time ambling to the vehicle. Colton still had trouble maneuvering, and I watched as Leanne opened the passenger door for him.

She leaned in and gave him a kiss. Then she went around the car to the driver's side and started the engine.

From beside me, Kelvin sniffed the air. "Do you smell that?"

"Gasoline?"

"No, it's the fragrance of daffodils."

"Even I know that wasn't what you tucked under the bow," I said.

"Odd, isn't it?"

"What does the daffodil symbolize?"

"New beginnings," he said. "Daffodils signal spring-time."

"Interesting." I liked the idea of new beginnings. As I watched Leanne and Colton drive down the road, I slipped my hand into Kelvin's.

What future path lay before Kelvin and me? I squeezed his hand, and he responded in turn. Wherever life led us, I was looking forward to the enchanting adventures we'd enjoy together.

RECIPE FROM JIN BAKERY

~Auspicious Almond Cookies~

Makes about 24 (2 dozen) cookies

Ingredients:
- 1⅓ cups sifted all-purpose flour
- ⅝ cup white sugar
- ¼ tsp baking soda
- ¼ tsp salt
- ½ cup butter
- 1½ tsp almond extract (1 tsp if less almond flavor is desired)
- 1 egg
- 24 almond slices

Directions:
1. Preheat oven to 325 degrees F. Put parchment paper on a cookie sheet.
2. Combine flour, sugar, baking soda, and salt together into a bowl. Cut in the butter (*very* important, don't skip this) until mixture resembles cornmeal. Add the almond extract. Combine white and yolk of egg; add half of it to the bowl. Mix well. The dough will appear too crumbly in the beginning, but when you mix it long enough, it will get the right consistency (that's why you only need half an egg).

3. Roll dough into 1-inch balls. Set them 2 inches apart on the cookie sheet. Press down with your thumb to flatten each cookie slightly. Place an almond slice in the middle of each cookie.

4. Combine the other half of the egg and ½ tbsp water to make a light egg wash glaze. Using a basting brush, cover the tops of the cookies with the glaze. You can adjust the amount of glaze on each cookie depending on how much almond cookie shine you want.

5. Bake in oven until the edges of the cookies are golden brown, about 15 to 18 minutes.

Note: They taste even better the second day when the almond flavor has set in.

FLORAL TIPS FROM LOVE BLOOMS

Flower of the Day: Honey Perfume rose

Genus: *Rosa*

Family: Rosaceae

Alternate name: JACarque rose; floribunda rose

Common presentation: Apricot-colored blooms that fade to white over time; has a spicy fragrance

Symbolism: Love and beauty

Legend: Supposedly, Cleopatra filled a room with a foot-deep bed of rose petals to weaken Mark Antony's resistance to her charms

Gardening tips: grows best in full sun; water deeply and regularly, but avoid overhead watering

Fun facts:

Named an All-America Rose Selections winner in 2004.

Fossil evidence indicates that roses flourished at least 32 million years ago.

~SIMPLE ROSEBUD BOUTONNIERE~

Materials:
   White rose
   Floral scissors
   Myrtle leaves
   Baby's breath
   Floral tape
   One pin

Steps:
1. Trim off the leaves from the rose.
2. Cut the stem down to 2½ inches below the flower.
3. Add two stems of myrtle leaf; make sure the leaves will lie flat when pinned on the lapel.
4. Combine the baby's breath with the rose, positioning the flower at the bottom center of the boutonniere.
5. Tape the leaves, baby's breath, and rose together with floral tape.
6. Snip away any uneven stems below the taped portion with floral scissors. The entire stem should be about two inches long.
7. Use a pin to secure to your clothing.

~EASY WRIST CORSAGE~

Materials:
- Three different flower buds (spray roses; can be same or different colors)
- Floral wire
- Floral tape
- Elastic corsage bracelet
- Hot glue gun

Steps:
1. Trim the flowers to just below the bud.
2. Poke the floral wire straight through the calyx at the base of each bud. Half of the wire should be on one side of the flower, and half on the other side.
3. Bend down each wire to create a new metal "stem." Repeat for each flower.
4. Cover the metal stem of each flower with tape.
5. Combine the flowers, and tape them all together. Tape from the top (base of buds) to the bottom (end of stems).
6. Use the glue gun to glue the flowers to the elastic bracelet.
7. Wear the finished corsage bracelet on your wrist.

Tips:
When taping the flower, you can hold the tape with one hand and twist the flower with the other to efficiently cover the stem.

The metal piece in the center of the elastic bracelet can have overlapping metal edges that might not be covered by the blooms; fold down the flaps if that bothers you.

LACE VOTIVE HOLDERS FROM PAZ ILLUMINATIONS

Special wise saying from an actual fortune cookie message:

"That special someone loves to see the light in your eyes."

~Lace Votive Candle Holder~

Supplies:
  Balloon
  Sponge brush
  Mod Podge
  Lace doily (6-inch diameter)
  Double-sided tape
  Needle or pin

Directions:
1. Partially inflate the balloon to the size of a small bowl (about 4 inches in diameter).
2. Brush on the Mod Podge over top of balloon.
3. Cover the top of balloon with the doily.
4. Brush a generous layer of Mod Podge over the doily.

5. Hang the balloon upside down by attaching it to the ceiling using double-sided tape.
6. Let it dry overnight.
7. Once it's dry, pop the balloon with a needle or pin. The lace doily should retain the shape of the bowl and can be used to surround the votive candle in a glass holder.

Tips:

After placing the doily on the balloon, you can also use fabric stiffener spray to help the doily hold a more rigid shape.

If hanging the balloon from the ceiling doesn't work, you can also use the double-sided tape to attach the balloon to a hanger and then hang it from a shower rod.